Katy Evans's *USA Today* and *New York Times* bestselling series strips away everything you've ever believed about passion—and asks the dangerously enticing question, "How REAL is what you feel?"

Praise for Katy Evans and

REAL

Remington Tate, the unstoppable bad boy of the Underground fighting circuit, has finally met his match . . . in Brooke Dumas.

"I have a new book crush, and his name is Remington Tate."
—*Martini Times*

"Remy is the king of the alpha-males."
—*Romance Addiction*

"I loved this book. As in, I couldn't stop talking about it."
—*Dear Author*

"Sweet, scary, unfulfilling, fulfilling, smexy, heartbreaking, crazy, intense, beautiful—oh, did I mention hot?! Evans [takes] writing to a whole new level. She makes you FEEL every single word you read."
—*Reality Bites*

"Remy's story broke my heart . . . made me cry! Katy Evans had me on the edge of my seat. . . . Without a doubt I absolutely fell in total LOVE with Remy."
—*Totally Booked*

"Edgy, angsty, and saturated with palpable tension and incendiary sex, this tale packs an emotional wallop. . . . Intriguing."
—*Library Journal*

"Remy and Brooke's love story is one that has to be experienced because until you do, you just won't get it . . . one roller-coaster ride that you'll never forget!"
—*Books Over Boys*

"What a rare gift for an author to be able to actually wrap your arms around your readers and hold them. Katy Evans does just that."
—*SubClub Books*

MINE

"Seductive, wild, and visceral."

—Christina Lauren,
New York Times bestselling author of *Sweet Filthy Boy*

"Steamy, sexy, intense, and erotic, *MINE* is one that will have you hanging off the ropes. And begging for more."
—Alice Clayton, *USA Today* bestselling author of *Rusty Nailed*

REMY

"*REMY* gives us Remington's perspective on the events of *REAL* and *MINE*. . . . Katy Evans could teach classes on the art of the companion novel. THIS is how it's done, y'all."
—*Scandalicious Book Reviews*

"Getting inside Remy's mind is one hell of a ride. . . . You may love Remy now, but after you read his side of the story he is going to consume your heart."
—*Book Angel Booktopia*

"Reading this book is like the best foreplay ever. The sexual tension was incredible. . . . I'll follow Remington Tate to the ends of the earth."
—*Emme Rollins*

ROGUE

"Whoa. Why was I not told I'd need one of those walk-in freezers while reading this book? Apart from being one of my most scorching reads of the year, the 'realness' of the love story took me totally off guard, and held me captive until the very last word."
—*Natasha is a Book Junkie*

"[An] amazing, beautiful story that pulls at your emotions and makes time disappear. . . . I have a whole new level of awe and amazement for the talent that is Katy Evans."
—*The Blushing Reader*

"Completely mind-blowing . . ."
—*RT Book Reviews*

ALSO BY KATY EVANS

REAL

MINE

REMY

ROGUE

ALSO BY KATY EVANS

REAL

MINE

REMY

ROGUE

RIPPED

katy evans

G

Gallery Books

New York   London   Toronto   Sydney   New Delhi

G

Gallery Books
A Division of Simon & Schuster, Inc.
1230 Avenue of the Americas
New York, NY 10020

First Gallery Books trade paperback edition December 2014

GALLERY BOOKS and colophon are registered trademarks of Simon & Schuster, Inc.

For information about special discounts for bulk purchases, please contact Simon & Schuster Special Sales at 1-866-506-1949 or business@simonandschuster.com.

The Simon & Schuster Speakers Bureau can bring authors to your live event. For more information or to book an event contact the Simon & Schuster Speakers Bureau at 1-866-248-3049 or visit our website at www.simonspeakers.com.

Designed by Davina Mock-Maniscalco

Manufactured in the United States of America

10 9 8 7 6 5 4 3 2 1

Library of Congress Cataloging-in-Publication Data is available.

ISBN 978-1-4767-5562-5
ISBN 978-1-4767-5565-6 (ebook)

To second chances,
especially the chance to do it right

RIPPED PLAYLIST

"MAGIC" by Coldplay

"WILD HEART" by Bleachers

"ANIMAL" by Neon Trees

"CARRY ON WAYWARD SON" by Kansas

"ALONE TOGETHER" by Fall Out Boy

"IF YOU SAY SO" by Lea Michele

"THE LAST SONG EVER" by Secondhand Serenade

"HEY BROTHER" by Avicii

"SPECTRUM" by Zedd

P&M'S MASHUP

"LIKE A VIRGIN" by Madonna

"SWEET CHERRY PIE" by Warrant

"MISS INDEPENDENT" by Ne-Yo

"I BELIEVE IN YOU" by Kylie Minogue

"BEAUTIFUL" by Akon

"YOU FOUND ME" by The Fray

"SWEET CHILD O' MINE" by Guns N' Roses

"TAKE A BOW" by Rihanna

"YOUR SONG" by Elton John

"BROKEN" by Lifehouse

"FUCKIN' PERFECT" by Pink

❤ ❤ ❤

Have you ever had a secret?

One that tears at the deepest part of your soul, that's
so overwhelmingly painful you cannot speak of it for
fear it'll break you apart, limb by limb, cell by cell . . .
becoming real, and frightening, and saddening . . .

Or have you had a secret that makes your chest swell
like you've just been pumped with helium, and
you want to shout your secret to the world,
but shouting it would mean the world would
take your precious secret away from you?

I've had both. The secret you love, and the one you hate.

And for the last six years, I've carried both . . .

❤ ❤ ❤

ONE

SECRETS

I'm the only person in my apartment building that still gets a newspaper. It sits on my doorstep this morning, and I love the way it smells. I love the crackling noise when I drop into my dining room chair and slap the sucker open. This sound, this smell . . . they remind me of lazy Saturday mornings reading the paper with my dad, his cologne scent engulfing me. By the time I was seventeen, he was gone. As was his morning rumple of my hair and his cologne—but not the smell of the paper. It's been almost a decade and I *still* find an incomparable little joy in the smell of this freshly printed newspaper. Until now . . .

Now . . . when the headline of the entertainment section stares back at me, mocking me.

Mackenna Jones Is Back in Town! the headline says, and just reading that feels like a punch in the gut.

I squeeze my eyes shut and open them, my stomach trembling uncontrollably.

Mackenna Jones is back in town!

Fuck, I really need to stop reading that.

Mackenna Jones is back in town!

God. Still reads the same.

Mackenna.

The name curls around me like smoke in my insides, and but-terflies I didn't even know I still carried crash into the walls of my belly. I thought it impossible that a single one of these butterflies had survived Mackenna Jones.

He's coming to town, Pandora. What are you going to do about it?

The thought of him being in the same state makes me scowl bleakly. "Seriously, asshole? You had to come here?"

I begin reading the article about Crack Bikini, how the band has revolutionized music. How even Obama has openly said this band is responsible for turning young kids back to the music of the masters—Mozart, Beethoven. But it doesn't end there. It's just getting started turning up the schmooze. The reporter keeps going on and on about how this tour has sold out Madison Square Gar-den faster than Justin Bieber's first show, and how it will be the concert of the year, if not the decade.

Briefly, the band's breakout song flits through my head. For a time, this song played on every radio station in the country, and it made me loathe music with a passion—hell, the mere thought of it angers me all over again.

My hands shake as I set down the newspaper, fold it, and try to move on to another section. I live with my mother and my cousin, and I've always had an appreciation for my quiet time on Saturdays, when Magnolia has ballet and my mother has er-rands. But now, my precious Saturday—time I get our apartment to myself—has officially been ruined. Not only my Saturday, this just ruins my entire fucking year.

Mackenna. In Seattle.

My hands tremble as I go back to the entertainment section and slowly scan for the date of the concert. I find myself clicking open Internet Explorer on my phone and navigating straight to

Ticketmaster. Yep, the show is already sold out. So I head to eBay, where I discover the staggering prices the best tickets command.

I don't know why, but for a moment, I imagine myself in one of those pricey seats, calling him the world's greatest *asshole* from up close so he can hear through all the noise he and his band members make.

I don't know what I'm doing. Or maybe I do know. A cold chill is settling in my body. The show is sold out. The tickets cost a fortune. But no. I won't miss this opportunity. It's been almost six years since I last saw him. Almost six years since seeing that hard, perfect man-butt as he jumped into his jeans.

The first time he took me, I could almost see my V card nicely tucked into his back pocket. He told me he loved me and asked me to tell him that I loved him. He was still inside me when he asked if I wanted him to be with me. I cried instead—because something is wrong with me, and I couldn't. I couldn't say it back. But I *know* that he *knew*.

He kissed me harder than ever when I started to cry, and our kiss tasted of my tears. At the time, I thought it all so painful and raw, the way he kissed me. So beautiful. I trembled as he held me. I couldn't seem to piece myself back together after breaking for him the way I did during my orgasms. I could hear his breath mingle with my breath as he soothed a hand down my spine, telling me over and over that he loved me.

And that wasn't the only time he took me. For days and weeks and months, we made hot, fevered love. I was seventeen and he was my everything, and when he took me, I thought he wanted everything I had to give. He left anyway. Bastard.

Mackenna was a secret, you see. He was the closest I've ever been to a person in my life—but he was a secret nobody could find out about. Especially not my mother. He knew it. I knew it. But we always managed to see each other anyway. We lied, hid, stole out of our homes and into the night, meeting at the docks and hijacking some unsuspecting family's yacht until sunrise. We didn't care who our families were, or what was "best" for us.

As far as I was concerned, he was *it* for me, and I for him.

He was my best friend too.

My world broke when I heard he left Seattle.

He didn't even say goodbye.

The last thing he'd said to me was that he loved me.

Now. I. Hate. Love.

I thought that with his absence, the wound would heal. But the wound is still there. It's festered and bubbled up and grown.

I gave the motherfucker everything that was in my young, stupid heart to give, and he ruined me.

Well, fuck him.

Next week he's in Seattle. He and his mashers are in town and everyone is going. I call them mashers because there's no other group like them. They mash their songs to someone else's—to real music. Bach, Chopin, the masters. The result is a rock band symphony that runs through your body and curls your toes. And if you add in his vocals . . .

Hell, I don't even want to talk about his vocals.

People choose to fall in love because it makes them feel good. Love makes them feel protected, safe. Not me. I choose hate. It makes me feel good. Protected and safe. Hating him is all that keeps me sane. Hating him means what he did to me doesn't matter. I can still feel something. I am not yet dead, because I can feel this hate *corroding* me. He's ruined me for other men. Stopped me from being the woman I could have been. He's broken every dream of a future with him I had. He was my first love and my first everything, including my first heartbreak.

Even after he left, all I've been aware of is him, and what he left me with, and what he took from me.

The tickets are expensive. I spend most of what I make helping my mom care for Magnolia. But three little clicks on eBay is all it would take. Three little clicks and I can go up that last notch of debt on my credit card and see this asshole again, in the flesh.

Totally worth it, I decide, and go online and buy two of the most expensive tickets eBay has to offer.

Opening my calendar, I find the day and mark it with an X.

Get ready, asshole. Your Seattle concert won't be considered a success. Not if I can help it.

❤ ❤ ❤

I DIDN'T USED to like black so much. I liked red, and I liked blue, and somehow *really* liked yellow. Hot pink and purple were good too. But then colors began making fun of me. They felt too happy. Too sweet. Black was safe and neutral. It didn't remind me of things that made me sad. It didn't try to be anything other than black. Right after Dad died, I stopped trying to be anything other than what I really was. I stopped trying to fit in. Trying wore me out, and it only made me more aware that I didn't belong.

I became black and black embraced me. Tonight I blend with all things sinful and dark. It's a dark day, and mine is a dark life. Even the sky is cloudy because Mackenna is in town. In fact, there's a thunderstorm. The stands are wet. The fans are wet. Everyone except the band, who's ensconced backstage until the rain stops, will be solidly on NyQuil soon.

When the rain finally stops, Melanie and I hear the announcement that the SHOW IS ABOUT TO START. And there will be NO OPENING ACTS DUE TO THE DELAY. Just like that, the shot of vodka I had drunk in a toast to my courage leaves my system, and knees that had felt like they were made of steel minutes ago start feeling like jellyfish.

"Stop looking like you have a gun in your bag. You're going to get us searched, you dodo!" Melanie tells me.

"Shh! I got this, be quiet," I scold her as we head back to our seats.

Reaching nervously around my neck, I pull the hood of my poncho over my wet head and tug Melanie behind me as we wind through the crowd to our seats at the front of the stadium. She looks even fatter than I do. Turns out this rain was a blessing— Melanie and I don't appear nearly as voluminous as we really are, loaded with goods under our ponchos. Goods for the band members. One in particular.

Even when my hair is hanging wet down the sides of my face, I think I look good. Intimidating. Black nails, black lipstick, black poncho, black hair—well, my hair is mostly black except for a stupid pink streak Melanie dared me to dye one drunken night, and I can never refuse a dare. Still, I'm going for my usual Angelina Jolie look, and my black high-heeled boots scream, "Men, come near me only if you want to end up without nuts!"

Melanie, on the other hand, looks as happy as a Barbie.

Her boyfriend probably just fucked her brains out.

Lord, why do my friends get the horniest boyfriends?

"I can't believe we haven't reached our seats yet! We're way up front, we'll be like *breathing* them," she tells me with a big grin.

Um, yeah, breathing Mackenna is the last thing I want or need. But the stage keeps getting closer and closer, looming larger as we approach. It almost feels like every step closer to our seats, a year of my life drops away. Until I can clearly remember the way my stomach flipped inside my body as he looked directly at me with those icy gray eyes and watched me take his cock inside me. Motherfucker.

"I still can't decide," Melanie says as we finally sit down, "if I want to get married in a traditional white gown with a big red flower attached to the train, or a simpler pink dress. I've got both on hold until Monday. Maybe I should let Greyson see . . ."

She trails off when an awed silence falls over the crowd. One bright light from above narrows and fixes straight at the center of the stage. My heartbeat starts racing against my will. Furious, I breathe in through my nose for five seconds, hold it for five, and let it go for five—some shit I learned in Anger Management.

The light remains focused on the empty center of the stage, and violins start playing in the background. Just when the violins seem to take control of the rhythm of your breathing, the drums start joining in to take over your heart. Ugh, *bastards.* It's like the music is overtaking me. The music builds, builds, and builds to a crescendo until the lights shut down.

Gasps erupt from the crowd as complete darkness descends.

In the shadows, he walks out.

I know it's Mackenna Jones.

His swagger. His shoulders swinging, his hips rolling, and his long, thick, muscled legs. Hands at his sides, a microphone strapped to his ear and discreetly curled around his rocklike jaw, he approaches the public, and us. His chest is bare. He's wearing black leather pants. And his hair is bright fuchsia today, spiky and standing high. It's a shock to see that color against his tan skin. The smooth muscles of his torso glisten, as do the dark little bricks of his abs.

Through the light of the moon, I can see every bit of the six feet of him, and he's so hot I think my clothes just dried. I try to find something to hate in the way he looks, but there's nothing. I can't even say I hate that little gleam in his eye, which screams, *Bad boy, bad boy, I'm a fucking bad boy and I'm going to fuck with your life.*

I liked it.

I used to like it so much.

Until he did what bad boys actually do, and it turned out that his being a bad boy has been the least fun I've ever experienced in my life.

A dim light flickers over him. The orchestra in the background begins playing. The light intensifies as he grabs the pink wig on his head and throws it into the stands, yelling, "Hel-fucking-lo, Seattle!"

Seattle screams in return, and he laughs this outrageously sexy chuckle as a group of girls try to leap out of the pit onto the stage, fighting like hellcats for the wig he just threw.

I'm not looking at the catfight; I'm looking at him. The fucking asshole who shouldn't even deserve to live, much less look like he does. I can't help but notice the dark, sexy buzz cut curving around the beautiful shape of his head. This only makes his lips stand out more and his nose stand out more and his eyes stand out more . . . the guy is not hot—he's supernova. He's got full, beautiful lips and a sleek nose that flares naturally with each breath—then there's his smile, which makes me angry enough to boil a *horse*. Hurt and betrayal coil and churn inside me as he flashes that smile at everyone.

"Looks like we have a feisty crowd tonight. Excellent. Excellent," he rumbles as he walks from side to side on the stage, scanning the crowd. Mel and I are so close, he'd need only look down to see me. But he's too almighty to look down—and I can do nothing but keep looking up, even if I can no longer see his face because of the big bulge of his cock.

I swear I haven't had sex in so long, I've been revirginized. I can't even remember what feeling good feels like. I haven't wanted to. I like feeling fucking *bad*. So I look up now, and I see him, and the memory of that big, thick cock slides and ripples through me.

I dislike the tingly insecurity it gives me. I dislike it a lot.

He sweeps the crowd with one long, long stare. "You all want some music tonight, huh?!" he asks in a low voice, the question as intimate as if he'd whispered it to each of us.

"KENNA!!" Women are sobbing beside us.

"Then let's hit it!" He lifts one fist in the air, and a drum beats in the background. He starts pumping his fist high, the drum following an identical answering sound. He rolls his hips and lifts his head to the cloudy sky, making a slow humming noise from deep in his throat that sounds like . . . sex.

While the orchestra noise begins building again, the symphony gathers momentum. From slow and melodic, it heads toward something noisier and crazier. My pulse is somewhere in the stratosphere by the time the rhythm feels absolutely wild, when suddenly two men pop up on a platform from under the stage, striking their electric guitars to an explosion of lights that simulate fireworks. They're the other two lead members—Jax and Lexington. Daddy's boys, and identical twins. They got the funding for their first performance from their own Daddy Warbucks, and now the three leads need nothing from anybody.

Mackenna starts singing in a voice that is low and raspy and sexy as fuck. I hate him. How fluid his muscular body is. How it oozes testosterone. How dancers join the three men onstage, dressed in formal black-and-white men's suits. I even hate the way they tear off their suits to reveal their black-painted skin that makes them look sleek as panthers.

Melanie is so enraptured; her lips are parted and she's gaping. I swear, the electric, primal, and animal way these three men move up onstage is something to behold; the three are being irreverent with their bodies but reverent to their music.

My body is in an uproar. I have purposely not been a music girl for years. Mainly to avoid listening to any song of his by mistake. But now his voice is on every fucking speaker. It reverberates in my bones, awakening some strange pain inside me along with an extra truckload of anger.

The concert continues like some form of exquisite torture. The band prolonging not only my torment but the torment of every spectator waiting anxiously to hear their most recognized song. And then . . . it happens.

Finally, Mackenna starts singing "Pandora's Kiss," the breakout song that topped the Billboard charts and hit #1 on iTunes for weeks:

Those harlot's lips
To taste and torment me
Those little tricks
That tease and torture me,
Ooooooooh, oh, oh, OH
I shouldn't have opened you up, Pandora
Ooooooooh, OH, OH, OOOH
You should've remained in my closet, Pandora
A secret I will forever deny
A love that would one day die
Ooooh, OH, OH, OH
I should've never kissed . . . those harlot's lips . . . Pandora

Rage bubbles up inside me full force.

"Now?" Melanie keeps asking me.

I. Loathe. Him.

"Now?" she asks again.

I *loathe* him. He's the only boy I've ever kissed. He took kisses that meant everything to me and turned them into a joke of a fucking song. A song that turns me into some sort of Eve, torturing and teasing him to sin. *He* is the sin. He is the penitence, the hell, and the devil, all in one.

I reach into my bag, nicely tucked under my poncho, and grab the first thing I find.

"Now," I whisper.

Before Mackenna knows what hit him, Melanie and I have sent three tomatoes and a couple of eggs flying through the air.

The orchestra music isn't enough to drown out his muttered "fuck," audible through the microphone.

His jaw clamps and he yanks the mic down over his chin as he jerks his eyes around to find the source of the attack. I feel delirious when I see the genuine anger on his face. I squeal, "The rest!" and grab the remaining things we brought and just keep throwing. Not only at him, but at anyone who tries to get in the way—like the stupid dancers who rush to protect him. One of them makes a whimpering noise as an egg hits her face, and Mackenna jerks her back by the arm so he can take the hits himself, his furious eyes trying to find us in the crowd.

Then I hear Melanie shout, "Hey! LET GO, asshole!"

My arms are yanked behind me, and I'm suddenly shoved and pulled out of my place and down the aisle.

"Let go of us!" Melanie cries, struggling as two burly guards drag us away. "If you don't let go of me right now, my boyfriend's going to find your home and kill you in your sleep!"

The guard yanks me back harder, and I catch my breath as pain rushes up my arm.

"Asshole," I hiss, but I don't even bother to struggle. Melanie's getting nowhere and I know it.

"She knows them! She knows the band! Who do you think he was singing about just now, asshole?" Melanie kicks into the air. "She's *Pandora*! Let us fucking go."

"You know Mr. Jones?" one guard asks me.

"Mr. Jones!" I scoff. "Seriously! If Mackenna's a mister, I'm a unicorn!"

They seem to chuckle among themselves as they lead us past more security, around the stage, and to a small room in the back. One guy starts speaking into a radio as he unlocks the door.

Melanie struggles and tries to kick out, but the enormity of what could happen starts settling on me, and I grow quiet.

Holy. Shit. What have I done?

"You don't have to look so happy, dickface. My boyfriend will find your home too and kill you next!" she tells the other guard.

They yank a door open and shove us inside. I stumble as I take a step, fighting for some dignity as I wiggle free of his grip. "Let go," I grit, and he finally releases me.

The radio transmitter on his hip emits a sound. A voice says something I can't make out, but it sounds a lot like cursing.

"Remove these," one of the guards commands, pointing at our ponchos.

I pry the plastic off my body and Melanie does the same, then we watch helplessly as they strip us of the bags we'd hidden underneath the ponchos.

Melanie groans when they set our things on a table to the side. Cell phones. Two more tomatoes. Car keys.

"Wow. You guys can't take a little joke now, can you?" Melanie asks them with a haughty little scowl.

I close my eyes and try to quell the panic rising in me.

Fuuuuck. What was I thinking?

I haven't done anything this reckless in years.

And it felt good.

Also *wrong*. Very, very *wrong*.

But good. Great, in fact.

Hell, I can still picture the pissed, disbelieving look on Mackenna's face. It gave me intense pleasure. Orgasmic pleasure. But now the intense feeling I'm experiencing is more along the lines of paralyzing fear.

What if the guards call him into the room to ask if he does, indeed, know me?

What if I have to stand here in this small stuffy room and look at him from *thisclose*!

I feel sick to my stomach. Later, Melanie's going to want explanations. Big-time explanations, more than what I've told her so far. She's going to have to tell Greyson what happened, and he's going to want to know everything, because these stupid security guards messed with his girl. I don't even know if I can explain to her the kind of past Mackenna and I share. January 22: the day I unfailingly get drunk and don't bother to even see the light of day—I'd sworn to myself I'd never discuss that day. But Melanie and Greyson? They will want me to open my box of secrets. Of me and Mackenna Jones.

Hot, wet mouths melding . . .

Him, pushing into me, stretching me, taking me, loving me . . .

Promises.

Lies.

Loss.

Hatred.

The kind of hatred that's only born of an intense, out-of-this-world love that went woefully wrong.

What am I going to say to him if I see him?

What am I going to *do*?

Please god, don't punish me by making me look at him thisclose.

I pace and pray, pace and pray while Melanie studies her nails, the wall, and me, sighing with the bored confidence of someone who knows she's getting out of here intact. If I see Mackenna, I really doubt it'll be so easy. My stomach's already in knots, and I'm having the most awful urge to vomit right now.

The concert seems to last forever. One of the guards comes and goes while the other opts to stand a few feet behind Melanie, standing all military-like, as if waiting for something.

Oh god, please let that something not be Mackenna.

I'm wearing off a layer of my boots' soles when, a century later, the door swings open and a chubby man in a suit and tie steps in. My blood pools in my feet from my nervousness. Lionel "Leo" Palmer, the band manager. I saw his face and interview in this morning's paper, but I have to say he looked much happier in that picture.

He glares at us—Melanie glaring back, me standing motionless—and his hands make meaty fists at his sides.

"Have you any idea what you just did?" he grits out, chubby cheeks blazing red. "How long we could keep you two cozy in a fucking lady prison? What kind of fucking fans *are* you?"

"We're not fans," Melanie says.

The door swings open and the twins, in all their male glory, join the melee. They look intimidating all the time, but now—with their blond hair, odd-color eyes, and perfectly pissed-off scowls—they're a force to be reckoned with.

I can't breathe.

"Who the fuck are these bitches?" the one with the snake tattoo demands.

"I'm getting to that, Jax," Lionel says.

So the other one must be Lexington. He charges forward and looks at me, eyebrow piercing and all, then he looks at Melanie. He points his index finger, swinging it from her to me. "I hope you two have a lot of money, because one of our dancers is injured. If she's screwed up for Madison Square Garden—"

"Don't worry, Pandora, Greyson will take care of this," Melanie says easily.

"Pandora," Lionel repeats suddenly. He grows still, his eyes sliding back to me. "Your friend called you Pandora. Why?"

"Because it's my name? Duh."

I'm in the middle of rolling my eyes when the door swings open and a figure fills the space. I don't think my heart is beating anymore. I feel like someone is strangling me and punching me on the inside.

Mackenna.

A few feet away.

In the same room as me.

Bigger and manlier than ever.

He kicks the door shut behind him. He's wearing aviators, so I can't see his eyes, and ohmigod, I hate him with a passion. I came here to hurt him, but I'm so overcome by my anger, I can't seem to do anything but stand here with my breath getting trapped in my lungs, my heart squeezing in my chest, my body trembling as all my suppressed anger bubbles up inside me.

He is tall and dark, and the remains of a red gooey liquid trickle down his chest.

But what a perfect chest, and then that thin trail of hair that leads the way from his navel to his dick. Tight leather pants mold to his bulging thighs. A bulging cock too. I swear girls might think he sticks a loaf of bread down his pants, but I can assure you that fucker is real. As huge as his fucking ego, and I remember it used to get as hard as his fucking head.

Not everyone can pull off a buzz cut, or a diamond stud earring, but he has a perfectly shaped head that makes you want to curl your hands around it and trace the curves with your lips. The diamond glints almost menacingly in his right ear, and when he takes off the sunglasses with an angry jerk, I see his brilliant, furious silver eyes, and I swear that it feels like coming home.

To a home that was wrecked, and burned, and there's nothing left, but it's still your home.

How fucked up is that?

God, please let him not be real. Let this be a nightmare. Let him be on the other corner of the world while I hate him safely from my corner in Seattle.

"She's fucking *Pandora*?" Lionel asks Mackenna.

When Mackenna's hard jaw only tightens, Lionel turns slowly around to study me. My brain is a tangle of confusion because Mackenna is staring straight at me like he can't believe I'm standing here.

I can barely take his steely gaze. I thought this night would give me closure. That I could make him feel in front of his fans like I felt when he left: humiliated. Instead he stands there, every inch the rock god, even with tomato puree on his chest. He owns the room, carrying that unnamable X factor that nobody can pinpoint but that he has in spades, that tells you he owns this room and everyone in it.

And that fact only serves to piss me off further.

"Lionel," he says in a low, warning tone.

Just one word makes Lionel ease back. Now nothing stops Mackenna from staring straight at me.

My face burns as I remember how I loved him. Deep, hard, completely.

Don't think about that. You hate him now!

"Nice hair." He shoves his glasses into the belt loops of his pants.

His voice, oh god.

His eyes run down the length of my hair, and Melanie offers,

"I suggested she add a little spirit to her hair, so at least she *looks* happy."

He doesn't even look at Melanie. He looks at me in the most intense way, specifically the pink strand in my hair, waiting for me to answer. I loathe that pink strand, but not as much as I loathe him.

"Nice tights," I return, and gesture to his leather pants. "How'd you get into them? From the top of a building and with a pound of butter?"

I refuse to let his chuckle move me, but I feel it run down my legs as he starts approaching. "No need to use butter anymore. These pants are a part of me." He holds my gaze helplessly trapped. "Like you were a part of me once."

He's coming closer, and every step affects me. My cheeks burn. The gall of him to remind me. I'm so angry. Years of hurt simmer in me. Of loneliness and betrayal.

"Fuck you, Mackenna."

"Already done, Pandora." His eyes burn with equal fury as he takes a tomato from the table and surveys it with glinting gray eyes. "Is this for me too?"

"That's right. All. Yours."

His lips curl in derision as he tosses it up like a ball and easily catches it, all the while watching me.

"Your show is so bad, Melanie and I felt we had to give your fans some real entertainment."

He runs his eyes across my face, studying me. "Yeah, by humiliating the fuck out of me."

I can't stand the way he looks at me, his eyes tracing the same path. My eyebrows, my nose, my lips, my chin, my cheekbones. He makes me wonder if I looked at the wrong mirror today, as if there's something even remotely interesting to see. I swear nothing prepared me for having his eyes on me again. Nothing. I want to get out of here so fast, he won't even see my butt as I go.

"Let me go, Mackenna."

"All right, Dora. But first a parting gift." Saying my least favorite nickname, he crushes the tomato in one fist, then lifts his hand, dropping little pieces of it over my head, watching me as I gasp and the juice spreads down my face and the side of my neck.

"There you go," he croons, his smile wolfish as he works his fingers into my hair to make the juice seep deeper. When I struggle to pull free, he grips the back of my head and presses his nose to my ear, making me tense to stifle a shudder. "You just pissed off my entire fucking band. Do you realize the kind of charges we're going to press?"

Yes, I do. My mother is a lawyer, so I have a pretty good idea.

So why did I think the fact that he deserved it gave me a free pass to be reckless tonight?

Fuck me.

He's got me fucked.

And he's so close. I'm strangely paralyzed as his lips move by my ear, causing an unwanted quiver down my legs. My nipples hurt all of a sudden and my body is in some strange contracting mode.

"Are you suicidal, or just looking to leave home? Because trust me, jail won't be much of an improvement."

"And your fucking face isn't much improved with the egg facial I gave you."

His friends, the twins, explode in laughter, but Mackenna doesn't.

He surveys me with ill-concealed anger, and somehow I have an acute memory of the last time I looked into those slate gray eyes. His heavy stare and the touch of his tongue on mine zipping like white-hot lightning through my body. Him moving, his hands on my hips, holding me beneath him while I thrash. His groans telling me how much he likes being inside me.

It hurts. The sight of him hurts.

I didn't expect it to.

As if my proximity has just triggered the same memories in his mind, he blatantly studies my body, his gaze lingering on my breasts, my mouth—a gaze hot and tactile and making me squirm—before he focuses back on my face as he speaks to the others.

"I'll take care of the damages," I hear him say, those eyes still on me, ruthless and calculating as if he's just come to a decision. "And I'll settle accounts with her directly."

"Ha! You're settling nothing with anybody here," Melanie scoffs.

He lets out a cold male chuckle and pins his attention on her. "What's your name, Barbie?"

"Melanie Meyers, asshole."

"Leave her alone—" I start, but he cuts me off with a hand and tells the guards, "Escort Barbie to her car."

"Dream on, pink wig. I won't leave without Pandora!"

"This *goth* is seriously Pandora?" one of the twins finally asks. "*Our* Pandora? She was supposed to be a myth, dude."

There's a tense silence as every one of his team members looks at Mackenna. And I can't help but notice with a prick in my chest that Mackenna looks none too pleased in a manner suggesting he'd hoped some eighteen-wheeler had run me over at some point, burying his secret.

He's handed a towel, which he drags over his built chest as he shakes his head, raking his fingers through the beautiful buzz of hair on his scalp as he tries to get all the shit off his head. His silence and the thoughtful lines on his face render me beyond nervous and edgy.

Fuck, I don't like that he's taking control of things now.

I don't like the effect he has on me.

The ways he could torture me.

The power he has over me, knowing how I'm privately afraid of my own mother—he'll fucking know I will do anything to keep her from finding out.

As he's about to speak again, Lionel says, "Kenna, a word."

Mackenna heads over to him, the twins joining the little circle. The twins look like Vikings, and Mackenna a pirate who steals and deflowers girls like me. I can feel them watching us as they speak. Mackenna trails his eyes over my body as he listens. He doesn't even seem to realize how blatantly he's checking me out. Checking me from the top of my pink-streaked hair down to my badass boots.

Finally, he looks into my eyes, narrows his own, and shakes his head angrily. "No fucking way."

"Yes fucking way," Lionel counters.

Sighing over his front man's stubbornness—which is a palpable thing, as big as an elephant in the room—Lionel ushers out the Vikings and the pirate, the door slamming shut behind a cursing Mackenna.

Melanie and I remain there for what feels like forever, exchanging a what-the-fuck glance.

The two guards stay in the room, watching us—watching me, especially—while little pieces of tomato slide down my face.

I want to punch something.

Something with gray eyes and a buzz cut.

Mackenna returns and grabs the towel again, the rest of the guys shuffling in behind him. "Just let her apologize to us and clean up her mess, then she can go." He lifts the towel in the air and signals at me to come over, curling his finger in a mocking way.

"Fuck. You," I breathe, suddenly seething.

"Mackenna," one of the guys groans, laughing in an *Are you fucking kidding me? She's got you this worked up?* way.

"You two look like nice girls. Well, at least one of you does." Lionel smiles benignly at Melanie, then takes in my Angelina Jolie attire before scowling and adding, "Look, we can put you both in jail. Even a day can haunt you. Is that what you want?"

"Pan, don't even listen. Grey will make sure—"

"No, Melanie, this is my problem." I shake my head stubbornly. It's not like her boyfriend and I get along that well anyway. Hell, I'm not on good terms with any man, so fuck that. I don't need rescuing. I'd rather stew in jail for a couple of nights. At least before my mother officially kills me.

"Let's cut to the chase," the twin with the tattoo says—Jax, I think. "Just tell her the deets, Leo."

"No, thanks," I interrupt before they can even say what they want. "I'd rather do jail time than do him."

A muscle works angrily in the back of Mackenna's jaw as he slowly crosses his arms over his chest. "That's assuming you could turn me on."

"Kenna, shut up," Lionel growls, then he turns to me again. "We're currently filming for the Crack Bikini movie. Did you know?"

"The whole world knows. I'm just glad you're not filming now."

"We were filming during your little shenanigan." He gestures at Mackenna's ripped chest. "We're wrapping up at Madison Square Garden, and now that your existence has been revealed . . ." He looks accusingly at Mackenna, then at me. "Now that we know that there is, in fact, a human Pandora whom our lead may have based his lyrics on, we want you in the movie."

"She's not going within an inch of those cameras," Mackenna grits out as he charges toward the door.

"Jones, listen to me. This is brilliant. People will eat this up with a fucking spoon!"

Mackenna angrily swings the door open. "I'm not interested, so you might as well *leave her out of this*."

"Like you left *me* out of your stupid song, huh, jackass?" I suddenly explode. "And I'm not interested either!"

"I'll pay you enough to interest you," Lionel calmly tells me.

Mackenna stops at the threshold, and that glittering serial-killer look in his eyes makes me want to agree just to spite him. God, I hate him. So much so that I feel spikes in my stomach from my rage. But it doesn't feel like his glower is for me. It almost feels as if it's for his manager.

Who continues on with building his case. "Look, you two can fight or not, I don't care. All I care about is that at the final concert, when Crack Bikini performs, you two will be up there and you'll kiss in tribute to our number one hit—'Pandora's Kiss.'"

Mackenna laughs, the sound making me feel like someone just crawled over my fucking grave. All the little hairs on my arms are standing on end.

"Lionel, we've got this. We don't need her. The fans want *us*, not her." He points at me, then runs his hand all the way through his head to the back of his neck in sheer frustration. Then he storms out through the door, calling with deadly authority, "Leave her out of this or I promise someone will have hell to pay, Leo!"

I don't know why, but I don't like him having the last word.

I don't like feeling as if he's protecting me from the cameras.

I don't like any of it, and before I know it, my voice stops him. "Ha! Like your promises ever mean anything, dickhead!" As I speak, I tear free the ring hanging from my necklace and chuck it at the open door.

Time stands utterly still.

Deathly slow, Mackenna steps back into the room to where the ring lies on the floor.

He looks at the small white-gold band with the sparkly diamond resting at his feet, and his expression changes from surprise to anger, then to something I don't comprehend. He lifts it and looks at it for the longest moment of my life, then he lifts his head and stares at me with an expression that wrecks me on the inside. He clenches his jaw, turns around, and slams the door shut.

I'm trembling.

Battling with the urge to run after him and . . . and what?

I hate that I can still feel the warmth from his hand when he used to hold mine. I hate that the memory of his mouth on mine still wakes me in the middle of the night. I feel a dull ache at the loss of the ring I've been hiding under my tops, and I ache at the sound of his voice and the sight of his face, and I hate that I don't know how to stop it.

When I press my lips to my talisman bracelet as I try to hold myself together, fighting for those in the room not to notice how easily Mackenna gets to me, Lionel steps forward and takes my arm. "Dear, you wanted his attention?" he asks me, both amused and confused.

"I don't *want* his attention. I don't want anything from him!"

"You're getting a lot of him, whether you two want it or not."

I yank my arm free. "I'm not for sale. There's nothing you can say or do to convince me to do this."

"How about . . ." He leans over and whispers a very long, very big number into my ear.

TWO

THE WITCH FORGOT THE BROOM BUT NOT THE FUCKING TOMATO BAG

Mackenna

"She's doing it, Kenna. You'll be surprised to know it didn't take all that much. I tell you, these new college grads will work for shit these days."

As I step out of the shower, grabbing the plush terry robe and sticking my body inside it, I find Lionel in my room, beaming at the news.

"You can't be fucking serious?" I demand, rubbing my head with a hand towel. He looks deadly serious, and I shake my head as I grab some clothes. "Lionel! I snorted fucking egg yolk up my nose. I think I've still got some in my ear." I hold the towel against my ear and jump up and down, shaking the water out.

"You little shit. You said she didn't exist," he growls.

I toss my scattered wigs into their trunk and slam the lid shut. "She doesn't," I grit out. So what if I had to tell myself she didn't exist? For six years, it worked. But now she's here. Like some demon—some *poltergeist*—reminding me of what I wanted as a teen and could never have. Reminding me what I lost. What I'd do to get it back.

Pandora.

My nightmare, my dreams, my walking, talking fantasy.

Here.

Flinging my ring.

My own fucking ring right in my face. My mother's ring.

What an irreverent little minx!

And what's with those fucking boots? Jesus, all she needs is an axe and blood dripping from her fingernails. Or a broom and a cauldron.

God, that woman . . .

Something kicked me on the inside when I heard her. Her smooth voice, flat but not quite. Her voice, unique in the world. It's like a song that makes you feel like shit. Makes me feel . . . like that worthless teen who craved her like a drug.

The teen who loved lyrics, songs, drums, pianos, melodies, whatever made me feel my life didn't suck. Songs make friends irrelevant. Songs made me remember her, but also forget her. I love songs. Music saved my life and now it's become my life. But no song's ever been as good as hearing her. And no song's ever been as bad as seeing her there, taunting me, challenging me with that endless black gaze.

"I thought you were singing about a *fictional* woman," Leo continues, and when I settle on a T-shirt with a skull on it—to fit the mood that bitch has put me in—I turn to see Lionel's eyes. They're glassy and deranged, like they are when we get a record deal, a movie deal . . .

Or when he thinks we've just struck gold.

But Pandora is an endless dark mine with no diamonds for me. I want to forget I've just stared into her face, but it's branded into my retinas and she's all I see. That angry little shrew frown, those dark black lips, that ridiculous pink streak, the boots. I can perfectly picture her straddling a man and hooking those boots around his hips. Yeah, I want them around *mine*.

Fisting my hand around my mother's ring, I lift my head in the direction of the door, my voice low. "Where the fuck is she?"

"Waiting. I've summoned the lawyers, and I've already texted Trenton."

"The fucking *producer*? You get her in the movie, she'll be the target of a million angry fans, don't you get it? They'll know her face. They'll know she was *mine*, and she'll never be safe again in her life!"

"Ahh, protective, are we? I like this side of you, Kenna. Never seen it before. Hell! All the more reason we want her in! We want whatever it was that happened just there." Lionel signals to the door that leads to the Meet and Greet hallway. "We want *that*. And we want a kiss-and-make-up scene at the Madison Square Garden concert. For the public, and for the camera. Next, we want her at the premiere, on your arm, before we make up a fine breakup story that leaves you home free."

"Whoa, whoa, whoa, Lionel!"

"Whoa, my ass! I saw how she rattled your cage. I saw drama. I saw more than what we have for this fucking movie, which is mostly you boys drinking and getting laid. I saw an opportunity, and as your manager, you pay me to cash in on such opportunities."

"No," I say.

"Listen, Kenna, all I need from you is a couple of good scenes, a make-up scene near the end of the movie, and her on your arm at the premiere. Give me this, and I'll give you what you asked for."

"You're finally caving?"

"Yep."

I start pacing, considering his offer. I get what I want, what I have long been asking for. And I also get to have her close. Talk to her. Maybe I can't tell her the truth, but I can win her back if I want to.

And fuck, I not only want to, my pride demands I do.

Once, her mother told me I wasn't good enough for her. I vowed to her that in a few years I was going to be good enough for any woman's daughter . . . especially hers.

"You're the best singer, and the prime attraction, but let's face it, Kenna, you're the shittiest actor among you three. But with this . . . it's brilliant. With her, you won't even have to *act*." He grins. "Now go out there and finish the Meet and Greet. I'll take care of your girlfriend."

"My *girlfriend*," I sneer, "is a pervy, tomato-throwing man-eater who seems only too delighted with the opportunity to hang around to give me hell!"

"Yep. That's good stuff."

THREE

LOOKS LIKE I'M GOING TO HAVE TO KISS THE FROG

Pandora

"It's a lot of fucking money," Melanie says as we ride back home.

"Melanie, I fucking robbed them. I would've caved for half. Hell, I'd kiss a hippo's ass for half!"

What just happened?

I'm still trying to grasp the fact that I just signed my life away. Or more exactly, three weeks, a kiss, and a movie premiere appearance away.

I'm on my way back from the most surreal couple of hours of my life. In the space of ninety minutes, I met Trenton the movie producer, a bunch of lawyers, and a big, fat check.

Now we're riding in the back of a limo provided for Princess Melanie by none other than her very own Mr. King. The driver is apparently her boyfriend's driver. I tell you, being with her lately is giving me a fucking complex. Especially after your ex just looked at you the way Mackenna looked at me. Like he wants to murder me, slowly, and then chop off my body parts and hide them in a box. So the legend goes—Pandora in a box, not Pandora's box.

Melanie raps manicured nails against a crystal glass she's lifted from the minibar inside the car. The letters on the nails spell G-R-E-Y with a heart on her thumb.

Ridiculous.

Both my friends are in committed relationships with men who've proven themselves true by doing the unthinkable—leaving their lives for them. I loathed Melanie's playboy because I thought he wasn't right for her, but it turned out he was exactly what she'd dreamed of and more. Hot, protective, dangerous, and alpha *to the max*, he'd do anything for Melanie. And Brooke? Brooke is already married to her guy—no, he's not just a guy, he's like a beast. A tall, lean, muscled, dark-haired, blue-eyed, sexy beast—who looks at her like he *lives* for her.

I don't tell Melanie how it hurts when Greyson shows up at the office to steal her away for the day, or how it hurts to see Brooke and her husband instinctively nuzzle each other when they talk. Maybe it's because I feel uncomfortable letting anyone see that I notice that shit. But I do. I notice it like I'd notice that I'm missing a limb, or like I'd notice slamming into a tree branch and having it stick out of my torso.

Yeah, I notice how Greyson looks at Melanie, and how Remy looks at Brooke. Only a few months ago Brooke and her husband were in town with their baby, and I saw the way he smiled at her across the room. How they each sought out the space in the room where the other was. How, when they were close, he put his hand on her hip, a huge hand, and ducked his head to her, so near that his lips moved against her ear, his lips curled, his eyes twinkling down at her. I noticed Brooke's smile, almost shy, and the way she turned her body to his and cupped his jaw. You could feel the love in the air, and I almost felt like I was intruding on something intimate and special. Seeing them, I scowled down at my lap, because I couldn't take it.

And Melanie? She was probably wishing on some stupid star, hoping that one day that would be her. And now, guess what? It is her. Her fucking boyfriend dotes on her. She's found genuine love. Love that I won't ever let myself wish for because I will *never* have that with anyone. I will never duck my head shyly or be the kind of girl who inspires a man to protect her the way my friends' men protect them. I will never inspire a man to want to change for the better because of me. Because I'm not inspiring. I'm the bitter one nobody likes to hang around with for too long.

All because Mackenna wrecked me.

He fucked my brains out and then he fucked with my heart and what was left of my brains, and I was too young to get over it. Now, after looking into those eyes I absolutely *cannot stand*, I would rather die than back out on a challenge from him. He doesn't want to see me? Well then, I'm going to plant myself in front of him so that he has to. I'm going to make his life a living hell, like he did mine. And best of all? I'm getting paid for it. I think I might just be enjoying my first stroke of luck since . . . my birth date.

"Yes, Trillion, it went amazing!" Melanie cries excitedly into the phone, checking her nails to make sure they're perfect. She calls her boyfriend Trillion sometimes, saying it's because it was the highest number she could think of. I don't get it, but she told me not to worry, because he does.

Whatever. Melanie's just . . . Melanie.

Now she's dropping her voice even more for him. "Yes, I thought of you . . . I need you more. I'll tell Ulysses to step on it. No, it won't be a risk if he steps on it. I need you." She's blushing like her boyfriend has just whispered something filthy he plans to do to her. She bites her lower lip like a young girl and cups the receiver and whispers something, then laughs and hangs up.

"You look like a simpering virgin, Melanie," I say bitterly.

Her eyes twinkle, almost as if her guy just made love to her on the phone. "So what? He makes me feel shy when he describes in detail what he's going to do to me."

"Dude, you have his name on your fingers and hearts on your thumbs. Men like your man like challenges. Careful, or he'll think you're a sure thing and dump you."

"I *am* a sure thing, and he's my sure thing. We love each other, we're getting married, you dodo."

Fuck, I'll be the only singleton of the three. Even our closest guy friend, Kyle, has a girlfriend now.

Fuck me standing and with my boots on. Ugh.

We fall quiet the rest of the way home. Melanie is now texting, maybe with her guy or maybe with Brooke. Melanie always keeps her up to date.

"Will you tell me how you two met?" she demands, looking up from her phone. I've been reluctant to talk about Mackenna for ages.

"Long time ago. In high school, before I switched schools and met you."

"But you don't think he was worth mentioning before yesterday? He broke your damn heart and he sings about it on the radio!"

I stare out the window, pulling up my walls tight around me.

"What happened?"

"Stupid girl attracted to bad boy, V card handed over, heart broken, end of story. I'm not even worried about him. Currently, I'm worried about what I'll say to my mother. I'll probably just say I have work, and I'll talk to Susan to see if she'll let me work from afar the next few weeks. I'll tell Mother the truth once it's all over."

I'll be lying, but who gives a shit. I've lied before. Like when

I used to steal out in the middle of the night, my heart racing, to meet Mackenna.

"Let's talk about the guy, shall we?"

"No, we shall not."

"Then let's talk about this—I can't believe you're going to be in a fucking *movie*!"

I snort. "It's not a real movie. It's like the Katy Perry and Justin Bieber ones, which is sort of lame."

"It's a movie, Pandora. Played in movie theaters. And I loved both Katy and Justin in them! You kept asking how could Brooke just leave town for a guy she loves? Now you're leaving town for one you hate! That's a karmic lesson for you. Stop judging people in love for what they do. You're doing worse shit for someone you don't even love," she says with a smirk.

"Judge all you want. I got this big fat check, and what did you get? Not even a picture with them."

"I have Greyson, duh! He's all I want. And I *finally* discovered the name of your asshole ex. Kenna is the hottest of the three and you know it, dude. Tell me what happened. We're supposed to be friends. Who do you even talk to about this shit? You get sick when you hold it in. You need to let it out."

"I just let it all out, in the form of tomatoes." I grin when I remember, and for a moment, I feel happy when Melanie laughs.

"Will that part be in the movie? Please say yes!" she begs, taking my shirt in her hands and shaking me.

I laugh. "I hope so," I admit, jerking my shirt free. "Hell, I hope I can do it again at Madison Square, just before I kiss him. That'll show him."

"Just so he can take off his shirt. God!"

I hit her. "Mel! He wears *wigs* and grabs his cock when he's dancing. He's *disgusting*."

"Dude, watching him work it up there got half the people around us pregnant, I swear!" She laughs, but I stare out the window and glare, my anger resurfacing as I remember what it felt like to stare into those odd, eerie silver eyes again.

It did not feel good at all.

It felt uncomfortable, messy, complicated, and definitely not nice.

I remember him squishing tomato into my scalp, and my stomach feels like a hot little pot, bubbling with toxicity.

"Pandora, you both looked a little too murderous with each other. Maybe you should talk to your therapist first? So she can give you some pointers on how to stay cool?"

My pride prickles. "I don't need tips. I've got this. She's been giving me tips for *six* years."

"Fine. Just get back here in one piece and in time to get measured for your bridesmaid dress. Pan, it's my wedding, so suck it, bitch."

I groan, and she laughs and slaps my butt as I get out of the car. Mel is always excited. Always upbeat. She's not like me. And I'm happy for her. I am. But I also hate that I feel mad because she's so happy. Sometimes I feel like I can't stand happy people.

I just don't fucking understand them.

I head into the apartment, trying not to make noise. In case you haven't guessed it by my name alone, my mother didn't want me, and she never lets me forget it. The words "So you don't make the same mistake I did" have been ingrained in my head since I got my first period, and I've never quite forgotten that the *mistake* was me.

I should probably live alone. But my cousin Magnolia saved my mother and me. She lost her mom, my mother's sister, to leukemia, and came to us as a baby a few years after my dad's death. She pulled both my mom and me from a deep sadness. If it weren't for seeing her perceptive little gaze every morning, I'd be on drugs. Or booze. Or both. I don't know why I'm drawn to drugs or booze or both, but when my dad died and Mackenna left, and my mom slapped me every time I cried and told me to get a grip, be strong . . . I just didn't feel like life had a lot to offer at the time. Until little Magnolia came to us. My mom focused her efforts on her, and so did I.

I ease into the bathroom we share, turn on the shower, and pull free of my clothes. The water rushes over my head and I see his eyes, glittering silver and angry, and my stomach knots because I thought I'd feel better after hurting him. I felt that little rush at first, when we attacked him during his concert, but then I saw him, and all I know right now is that I don't feel good.

After my shower, I can't sleep, so I sit on the living room couch, listening to the patter of soft rain and the whoosh of wind outside. I tiptoe into Magnolia's room and look at the way she's twisted on the bed, all innocent, her dark hair fanned out on the pillow. She, like Melanie, really likes the pink streak in my hair.

"PanPan, read this for me," she said only two nights ago.

She pulled out a princess story, and I cleared my throat and began reading. Magnolia remained quiet and in rapt attention, until I lowered the book. "Mag, look, I don't think these books give you the right expectations of what a man is really like," I said. She has no father figure, no brother, no male influence in her life, and it worries me. "You'll fall in love with this prince and never find him."

"Eww!" She jumped on the bed, yelling, "I don't read these for the princes! I read them for the magic!"

"But soon you'll be lured by a prince—"

"No prince! I want the dragon to eat the prince. Helena says that the boys with crowns in these stories don't even like girls anymore. They like boys!"

Shit, I laughed my ass off at that.

And then I worried a little.

She has a friend with two dads, and fortunately, Magnolia's completely not jealous of her friend's bounty of fathers. "Why would anyone want two dads? I have none and am super all right—right, PanPan?"

She sounded confident when she asked, but I have such fond memories of my dad, I just don't know. Still, I said she was right, because I didn't have a dad anymore either. But is she truly all right?

As the sun rises, I write her a short note in case I leave before she wakes, then I go and get my electronic cigarettes from the nightstand. The key to quitting smoking is to always keep 'em fully charged. I'm on a two-month streak, and I'm not going to start smoking again because of a fucking asshole like Mackenna. I shove the e-cigarettes into my bag and, on impulse, go to the shoebox in my closet where I've hidden some old stuff. Prized among those things is a stupid rock *he* gave me. Why did I save it? I don't know. It's a real rock, not a bling rock. I tripped on it once, when he walked me home.

"Kick that," I said angrily, cupping my bleeding elbow.

"If we kick it, it'll only trip you again next time you come around. The key to never tripping with the same rock is hang on to it," he said with a smirk. "You can make sure you'll never trip with the same rock if you grab on to it and know where it is."

Thank you, Mackenna, for that nugget of wisdom. I'm going to make sure I never trip over you!

There are people who have an effect on your life. And then there are people who become your life.

Like he did.

I was always a solitary, withdrawn girl, my mother a workaholic, my father a workaholic, both of them strict and pretty much expecting me to focus on grades and grades only. They were always wary of me having bad influences, or even friends, really. This, for some reason, and my choice of clothes, made me the cool girls' favorite attraction—or distraction. I was the only goth in our grade, and they loved to snicker about my all-black clothes and call me a cutter. But there was this one boy, the coolest bad boy, who stopped the teasing one day. He approached me with a purple scarf I had seen one of the girls wearing earlier, and he draped it around my neck, pulling me to him almost intimately close. "I'll see you after school," he said and kissed my forehead. The other girls shut up.

Because everyone would have given a limb to get that attention from "Jones"—and he gave it just like that to me.

And that's how I fell, like a ton of bricks, for Mackenna Jones.

It turns out he *did* wait for me after school that day. He drove me home and asked his neighbor to sit in the backseat so "Pandora" could sit up front with him. I didn't even know he knew my name. "Why'd you do that?" I asked when he walked me up the stairs to my building.

"Why'd you let them?" he returned, those eyes of his making me feel vulnerable and naked and strangely pretty. For a goth, this is big.

Really big.

But I also noticed by his frown that he was displeased.

"I don't stop them because I don't give a shit," I said as I hurried up the steps. He followed, grabbed my wrist, and spun me to face him.

"Hey! Go out with me Friday night."

"Excuse me?" I sputtered.

"You heard me."

"Why would you want to go out with someone like me? Your line of fans not long enough?"

"Because the girl I want is right here."

We started going out in secret, finding hiding places where no one would see us. He told me about music, how he wanted to see the world. He worked as a DJ on the weekends. He had hopes and dreams and wishes. I told him I didn't know what I wanted to be, and I didn't have hopes and dreams and wishes. I guess you never feel so hopeless as when you're with someone who's bursting with ideas and knows he's going to take on the world. Even so, he was drawn to me. He teased me, made me laugh, later made me forget about my father's death and the fact that my mother considered it a betrayal if I ever cried at his loss.

He became my life. I began to wait for his eyes, silver like a wolf's, to turn to see me. I began to quake and shiver in anticipation of him walking past my locker even if he wasn't supposed to come over. Sometimes I dropped a pencil, a book, my bag, just so that he could hand it over with that smile of his and brush his thumb over mine. I suppose people wondered about us, but we never gave them proof. Maybe I wondered if he only wanted sex from me, but I also wanted it. I fantasized about it. When it would happen, where it would be, how it would feel, if he'd say nice things to me.

It ended up being amazing. Every time with him. Amazing. Addictive.

I only wanted him.

We fooled around for months before finally going all the way, and things got even more serious after that. I spoke about telling my overprotective mother about us, about taking care of my school grades so she had no excuse to tell me I couldn't have a boyfriend . . . and just when I was about to say something to her . . .

His father got arrested for drug trafficking. That night, when I got home, my mother was being called by the DA's office.

Mackenna's hopes were shattered, and I had none of my own to pull us through. I tried to tell my mother that Mackenna and I had "something," to which she responded by immediately forbidding me to contact "the son." And after Dad died, even as Mackenna and I planned to leave the city, she watched me like a hawk. . . .

In the end, Mackenna did leave. He left me behind.

I went back to being the goth people laughed at, except now I was not sad anymore. I was mad. I punched some of the girls, and my mother sent me to therapy and, later, to a private school, where I ended up meeting the two girls who've been my only friends.

Melanie and Brooke.

I never, ever mentioned his name to them.

I'd thought he'd saved me, but it turns out he'd only just started to ruin my life.

At seventeen, I had needed him.

At eighteen, I still missed him.

At nineteen, I still wanted him.

At twenty, I still thought about him.

But by the time I heard him sing about me on the radio, making light music from nights that had held me together when I'd felt lonely—that's when I wished I'd never laid eyes on him.

AT DAWN, I hear my mom moving around.

"Hey," I say when I join her in the kitchen. She smiles and nudges a cup of coffee in my direction with the back of one finger. I shake my head. "Thanks."

"You came in late last night," she says.

"I was with Melanie."

"Ahh, of course. That explains it all."

I start buttering some toast for myself so I don't have to look her in the eye when I lie. Otherwise, she'll know in an instant. By profession, she's naturally inclined to immediately detect liars. You have to be really good to fool her—which, I guess, I am. "Mother, I have a business opportunity, and I need to travel out of town for a while."

"Travel?" she repeats.

She's a lawyer. She's used to asking a question and staring you down until you either whimper or cave. I stare back at her and don't respond, forcing myself not to twitch under her stare.

"Travel implies flying, Pandora."

The mere word makes my stomach spin as if someone is twirling it with a spoon. "I just flew with Melanie and did all right with the meds I took. By the time I woke up, we'd landed. I'll take those and try to do some stretches by land," I lie. I have no clue how the rock band works, or if they travel by land, air, or heck, even sea. Still, I open my hand and show her the pillbox I just retrieved, three pills resting inside.

She stares directly at me, ignoring the pills. "So what kind of opportunity is this?"

"It's a good one—*great one*," I amend as I frantically set my mind free to imagine a sufficient lie. "I sent in the proposal for several apartments—dark fabrics, you know. What I like. They're for a big, um, family, and I was hired on the spot. They said nobody can do this but me—it has to be me. And I've been decorating long enough to know it's the kind of opportunity I might never see again. Ever."

"All right, so when are you home?"

"I think three weeks."

"Very well."

We continue our breakfast in silence. I try to exhale slowly so my breath doesn't shake on its exit.

"PanPan!" A cannonball lands on my lap, and I laugh as all the warmth that is Magnolia envelops me.

"Hey, Magnificent!" I say, tweaking her nose. I call Magnolia anything with a Mag. She gets a toothy grin when I ask her what she's up to.

"Nuttin'," she says, pulling free and jamming a hand in the cereal box on the counter.

"Magazine, I'm going to be away for a bit, are you going to stay out of trouble?"

"Nope. Trouble's my middle name."

"We agreed it was mine." I go to the cabinet and pull out a bowl and a spoon. "What'll you do if you miss me?"

She blinks.

"You'll make a list of the things you wanted to do with me when I was away and we'll do them all when I get back," I tell her.

She nods and carries her cereal to the table. I'm a big believer in lists. You write your wants down on paper, and it's like putting them out there to the Universe: *Bitch, you gotta make this happen for me.* I got it from my mother, who's married to her lists, and I think I will probably marry mine . . . when I finally get around to writing one.

"Okay, I will," Magnolia says, starting to eat her cereal. I feel my phone buzz and notice Kyle's car out in the street.

"Kyle's here, I better go." Putting away my phone, I squeeze Magnolia to me. When I stand, my mother nods. I grab my duffel bag, and for a moment, I'm uncertain whether to hug her or not. Since she stands there with her coffee in her hand and makes no move toward me, I nod back and leave. She's just not very tactile, but neither am I. We're more comfortable remaining in our little bubbles—little bubbles only Magnolia seems to penetrate. Well, Melanie sometimes gets into mine too.

I spot Kyle behind the wheel and slide into his nerdy automobile.

"What's all this about?" he asks, confused by the duffel I toss into the backseat. "I'm driving you to some hotel parking lot? Did you become a cartel worker overnight?"

"I'm . . . uh, stage setting with Crack Bikini. So . . ."

"For real? You shitting me?"

He looks amazed, which only makes me want to groan.

He doesn't know I know Mackenna. None of my friends know who "the asshole who made me hate men" was—their words, not mine. I only told Melanie last night because the bitch wanted to pass on the concert and stay home—to probably let her *very* healthy male bang her brains out—so I had to fess up to why it was so important that we go.

Because I just spent a fucking fortune on two tickets, and because he's the fucking asshole who broke my heart and made me heartless and bitter.

Who? The one who sold you the tickets?

No! Mackenna suck-a-dick Jones!

"For real, you're working with Crack Bikini?" Kyle asks.

"No, Kyle. I just like bullshitting you for rides to random hotels."

"When are you coming back?" he presses.

"Less than a month."

We head to where I was told to meet everyone, and as we spot about a thousand custom coach buses at the hotel parking lot, I'm so nervous I'm crackling.

Kyle parks in awed silence, then grabs my duffel and helps me carry it as we head toward a group of band members. Before we reach them, he stops and gives me a brotherly peck on the cheek, and—isn't this just perfect?—there's Mackenna, watching it from the door of a nearby coach. I push on my tiptoes and shove my tongue down Kyle's throat, and before he can figure out why the fuck I'm swapping saliva with him, I pull back with a little moan.

"Be good," I say in a lame seductive voice.

He's not looking at me anymore. He's looking at Mackenna.

Mackenna, who's somehow leapt off the coach, is now approaching, all gorgeous rockstar with that sexy buzz cut, the dark sunglasses, the mocking smile.

"Ahh, our guest of honor!" Lionel beams as he starts forward in my direction, but he gets sidetracked by a roadie.

Mackenna has no such welcome. Those arms I dreamed would hold me until my last day cross over his broad chest, and I notice his eyebrows furrow as he plucks off his sunglasses, hooks them in his shirt, and fixes his silver wolf eyes on Kyle. He takes a very brief moment to survey me, then he sure as fuck takes a longer one to survey Kyle. Cool steel slides along my nerves. The fact that he's a rockstar and heart-poundingly sexy does not—and will not—exempt him from my hell.

"Pandora!" someone shouts, and a camera aims in my direction.

At the mention of my name, Mackenna's head swivels toward me—and I'm not prepared for what I see in his deep, dreamy eyes, dark and waiting, or for the deep, intense flare of heat they cause inside my belly. One second it's there, the next, he turns to the cameraman and stretches out one arm, using his palm to tip the camera so that it points elsewhere. Then he comes over and rakes Kyle up and down with an icy stare.

"Mackenna Jones," he says, stretching his arm out.

Kyle sizes him up, but with the warmth of a volcano. "Kyle Ingram. Dude, I'm a huge fan!"

"Good to know," Mackenna says, nodding.

Why does my friend have to fawn all over the man I hate? Huh? I groan and lift my bag, Mackenna watching me struggle with it with that same mocking smile, his eyes now mocking me harder. Does he offer help? Does he do even the remotest gentlemanly thing? The thing even my friend did? Hell no. Do I want him to so much as touch my duffel? *Hell no.*

Fuck him.

I sway my hips and make sure my boots make extra crunching noises on the asphalt as we head over to Lionel. The Viking twins stop me. They both come at me with unexpected delight. Their expressions are curious as they glance at Mackenna, and the impossible happens. They look even more delighted.

"Pandora," one says.

"Pandora," says the other.

"That's right, guys, that's my name, don't wear it out," I say.

"All right, get your shit together. You two"—Lionel points at Mackenna and me—"ride on that coach. It's the one with the most built-in cameras."

"I can't fucking believe this," Mackenna growls, shaking his head.

I gather my girl-balls and march toward the coach. He's going to complain about it all the time? Fine. I'm being paid to give them a couple of shots. Hell, maybe one of them can be of my boot in his nuts. He's right to be fearful.

"Thanks, Lionel," I say with a suddenly warm smile.

Mackenna stares, dumbstruck, like he didn't remember I could smile. "Yeah, thanks, dude. My life is made," Mackenna suddenly says, and he charges over to the coach too. He stands by the door and sweeps an arm out. There's no missing the flex of muscles under his bronzed skin, and I hate that my body actually *tightens.* "Ladies first," he declares with a grin.

It suits him, that smirk, and it's ruining my panties, which

I don't like. "Ladies first? Then maybe you should go," I reply, pointing to the interior of the coach.

That smirk still holds, but now it's challenging, telling me, *If you're playing, I'm game, and I'm winning.*

"Charming, beautiful girl," he says; interpretation: hateful bitch of a witch. "How old are you, darling? Eight?"

"You're so hilarious. Ready for your own comedy show, aren't you?"

I swing up into the coach and greet the driver then, a little faint when I see the way these guys travel. Luxury on wheels. This shit is bigger than my bedroom and living room combined. The living room area has a small kitchen nearby, and at the far end, through the open door, I can see a big bed.

"Think we can get along for"—Mackenna looks at his phone—"six hours without any bloodshed?"

I drop down on a sofa. "I'll be right here, filing and polishing my nails, just in case."

"Claws, you mean," he corrects.

I stretch out my boots and admire how long the heel is, how sleek and classy.

"Why polish your claws, though? Forgot your broom and your cauldron?"

"Forgot your balls?" I shoot back, lifting my head and noticing he's still standing, arms crossed over that broad chest. "Are you threatened because they want me here on your special movie tour? Or because your balls aren't that big?"

He chuckles, soft and low and unfairly sexy as he scans the bus, his gaze settling on a spot on the ceiling.

As the bus starts moving, I signal to the door. "Last chance. If you're looking for an escape, there's the door."

He doesn't smile like I expected him to. "The girls on tour can be vicious, Pandora," he gruffly warns, still scanning the bus interior, "I'm not your enemy—I'm the only guy who's got your back here. Remember that when they try hazing you one of these days. You don't belong here right now. It shouldn't have been like this."

He looks over my shoulder, narrow-eyed. "There have to be six cameras total here, at least," he murmurs.

"And you want to disable them so there's no evidence of you murdering me?"

"Nothing wrong with making sure they see only what we want them to see."

"Who cares? This is all a big show so you can keep filling your pockets with dough."

"Speaking of, whose pockets are full today?" He chews a stick of gum briefly before taking it out of his mouth, lifting his long, lean arms, and covering one of the camera eyes with a little piece. "How much did he give you?"

"Does it matter?"

"What was your price?"

"Who cares? The point is I was completely sellable. That's what you're getting at, isn't it?"

"We all have a price." He swaggers back to me—the kind of swagger that lets a girl know the dude's cock is leading him forward—and sits by me, sits really close. "Why are you doing this?" he asks, surveying my expression.

He's somber and serious, and it makes me nervous. His sunglasses are tucked into his T-shirt—and those gray eyes are on me like . . . something palpable. He's wearing no wig over the buzz cut I find so terribly sexy. A little kohl remains under his eyes, which only makes the shade of his eyes seem even more silver. Two thick leather bracelets cover his wrists. I'm suddenly feeling not as badass as I want.

"Because," I finally answer.

"Because what?" He reaches up and tugs the pink strand of my hair, his lips curling in amusement.

"They met my price. I'm saving this money," I admit, pulling my hair free from his grasp.

"Hmm." He leans back on the seat and continues scrutinizing me. Somehow I want him to say something mean, so I can say something mean back.

Why the fuck doesn't he? God, this man pisses me off.

"What? No mean comeback?" I demand.

"Actually, no. I'm giving Lionel what he wants because I want something in return—and I'm damn well getting it, so long as I put up with you. Don't ruin it for me."

"Me?! I'm not the one who covered the camera!"

"You're right, you just threw the contents of your kitchen cabinets at me."

I open my mouth to cuss, and he stops me.

"Didn't you get the memo? I like oranges best."

"You're starting to irritate me."

He leans over and whispers in my ear. "Next time you give me a tomato bath, I'm going to make you give me a tongue bath and clean up your mess." He strokes the pink in my hair. "Fair warning."

Something is crackling in the air so hard, I can't speak or breathe. My nipples, my sex, even my skin feel hypersensitive. I wait for him to say something. A strange heat makes my jaw start chattering. Really. I haven't seen Mackenna look at me this close in . . . years.

He puts his arm around my waist, and suddenly he starts pressing closer to me.

"Don't touch me," I growl.

He reaches his arm around me, and the touch of his fingers

spreads warmth and pain in me. "You know you're the only girl I've ever met who actually growls? Like a mean old bear," he whispers huskily in my ear.

I especially disapprove of the tender way his thumb grazes my skin, causing delicious little ripples. And I wholeheartedly disapprove of the way he looks at me with a slight curve to one side of his lips because he knows that I do disapprove. I refuse to answer, so his scrutiny continues.

"What happened to you?" he asks me, his expression intent, his eyes concerned.

God, the gall. The way he moves his thumb . . .

"You happened!" When he's close enough, I swing, but he grabs my wrist midair. I swing out again with my other arm but he grabs that too, setting them both over my head. The way he surveys me, like he's dissecting me, makes me fight harder. "Let *go!*"

"So you can pull out a couple more tomatoes?" he asks, his eyes carving into me.

"What can I say? They looked great with your fucking Peter Pan tights!"

I struggle, but it only makes the current between our bodies crackle more, so I force myself to fall deathly still—every inch of my body aware of his hands on my wrists.

"Did you want my attention, Pandora? The rest of the band thinks you do," he says. His low, unexpectedly soft voice rolls through me, inside my body, and I can't think straight. My eyes blur from the force of his effect on me. I drag in a deep breath to calm down, but his hand sliding down the inside of my arm fucks up my thoughts. "Babe . . . if that's what you want," he finally whispers, a warning, "I can oblige."

"I don't want your attention, I don't want anything from you!" I breathe.

"You do want something. Is it me? Am I what you want?"

"Fuck, *no*!" I growl in outrage, swinging out my suddenly free arm.

Again he catches my wrist midair. I remember wanting his head on a platter. I remember vowing to myself that one day I'd make him tell me he loves me, and I'd laugh and leave, like he did. And I whisper, "My god, it's really gone to your head, hasn't it? You think you can get anything you want and always have it your way? I have news for you, asshole. I'm here to make your life a living hell, and it will all be on film. Your complete humiliation. Just watch me!"

He looks at me and says nothing. My entire body is aware of where he grips me, not hard, but . . . firm and hot. "No, baby," he says, his teeth gritted. "You won't ruin this for me. You got it? We give them what they want, and you won't fucking ruin this for me."

I clamp my jaw. "If you don't want me to ruin this, then when we get to Madison Square Garden, you'll say on that stage that your fucking song is a lie."

"That's our number one song."

"If I do like you say . . . you tell all your fandom that it's a lie."

"Why?"

"Because I hate it, I hate hearing it. If they see me kiss you, they'll think I'm Pandora, and you paint me as . . . you paint me as . . . a whore, a liar, and a . . ."

Mistake. Something dirty. Hidden. Something you regret.

Just remembering infuriates me all over again, but Mackenna keeps those silver eyes leveled on me, as though truly considering what to do.

"I can't take that song back," he says at last, dropping down on the seat and crossing his arms behind his head and his feet at the ankles. "But if you want to write a song about me, we'd be happy to add some music to it and play it."

"I'm not a lyricist. Hello?"

"We'll take it slow. You tell me what you think of me, and I'll help you."

"Asshole. Dog. Liar. Cheat. Scum. If you regret our time together, I regret it tenfold."

His eyes flash dangerously, but he remains in that deceptively calm posture. "Go on," he warns.

"Why? Your pride hurting?"

A smoldering look settles in his eyes as he trails them purposely down my body. "Enough to want you to change your mind, maybe."

I grit my teeth, knowing that once there was a girl inside me who believed that one day she'd marry him. But the only girl left now is the angry one, the one he hurt, and she grits out, "You'll never have me again."

"Your lips say one thing but the rest of you screams the opposite."

We stare for another moment, and I hate that I'm breathing hard, and somehow do feel flustered, flushed, my breasts aching, something throbbing between my legs, before I strain out, "Who cares?"

"You do," he says. "And *I* do." He stands again, comes over, and leans forward. "You hate it, but right now—knowing how much you fucking hate the way you want me—it's making me high."

He surveys my chin, lips, cheekbones, forehead, as if thirsty to see something in my face he fails to see. Then he whispers, "You make me hard too, but that's about the only thing you do for me," and loosens his hold.

"Fuck you."

He flashes me a smile. "Oh, it's such a pleasurable experience, I *will*."

I feel strangely bereft of all fight as he puts some distance between us and settles back in the seat, lips still curled as he watches me in silence.

My insides tremble with a combination of anger and lust that I don't want. God, he's a narcissistic pig. So in love with himself he probably even smiles like that for his own sake in the mirror. His smile is one of the things everybody in the world can't stop talking about. It's one of those manly smiles that makes him look even sexier. It softens the silver in his eyes, at the same time melting your insides. Now the fact that he has a beautiful smile makes my insides boil while still attracting me.

GOD!

I want to say something painful that will hurt him. But no. He wants to punish me because I ruined his concert? I'm going to ruin. His fucking. Life.

FOUR

WHEN LIFE WAS GOOD

Pandora

A little over six years ago

"First we will get a small apartment. A loft!"

"That's right," a low voice answers over the top of my head.

"And all we'd need is a bed in it," I add.

"And you," the husky voice murmurs, and I turn into the arms holding me. Silver eyes meet mine—silver like a wolf's, heavy-lidded, both tender and eerily sharp. His lips are curled into this adorable smile, and I know right then and there that my boyfriend loves that I suggested a bed, of course.

"We can even get a dog," I add cheekily.

"And a fish."

He lifts one arm to point at the desiccated swordfish on the wall of the yacht we've stolen into. It's not ours, but this is one of our hiding places. One of the many places where we meet and spend as much time together as we can.

It's almost dawn now, and though we haven't slept and could easily stay here forever, he grudgingly gets up and shoves his long, muscular legs into his jeans.

"Gorgeous," he calls as he shoves a hand into his jeans pocket.

I turn from where I'm slipping into my sweatshirt.

"There's been something I've been wanting you to have . . ." He steps over and holds something small and shiny to the thin streaks of light that steal through the round yacht windows. A sliver of excitement runs through my body when I realize what it is.

"Is this a promise ring?"

When my lashes raise, I find him watching me with somber intensity.

With the intensity of a boy who loves you.

Just like you love him.

"It's beautiful," I whisper, reverently reaching out for it.

"It was my mother's." His voice is textured with emotion, his beautiful face harsh with it as he watches me slip it onto my finger.

"What are you promising me?" I taunt, lifting my face to his.

I will never forget the cocky lift to the corner of his lips when he said, "Me."

Oh, god, I love him. I love him like a storm loves a sky and a smile needs a face. Mackenna is the best of me, the rock that holds me, the only one who understands me. He's all that is left of my life that is tender and happy. I throw myself at him and he catches me, squeezes me, hugs me tighter than anyone else hugs me. "I'll say yes and take all of you, so don't joke about this," I warn.

"No joke," he promises, lifting my hand so he can see. "Looks pretty on you."

I squeeze his fingers with mine as my heart squeezes at the very same time. "But my mother and your father . . . they both need us right now."

Our lives are so imperfect. Cluttered with obstacles between him and me.

After my father died, my mother turned even more strict and bitter.

After Mackenna's mother died, his father turned to drugs. *Dealing* drugs.

And now, my mother is the DA in charge of convicting Mackenna's father, and the case is destroying our every chance at happiness.

I can't wait to get away.

We *need* to get away.

He strokes my face with his long, guitar-playing fingers. "I know they need us, but they won't need us forever. The hearing isn't until a couple of months. Whatever happens with my father, whatever the judge decides . . . we'll meet at the park that night, and we'll run away. Get married. I can get a couple of gigs at a few local bars, I can support you through college."

"Will you really help me pay my college tuition, Kenna? Are you sure you can do it?" I ask hopefully.

"Hell, I'd do anything for you." He's deadly serious as he speaks the words, giving my shoulders a squeeze. "I'm tired of hiding, you know."

"I'm tired too."

"I want to be with you. Out in the open. I'm sick of being your secret. I want to be your guy. I want people to know you're mine."

"But I am." I lift my hand to his line of vision again, wiggling my beautifully adorned finger. "I *am* yours. And our plan's still on, whatever happens. I'll meet you at the park after the trial."

He smiles a sad smile at the mention of the trial, then he kisses the ring on my hand, and then, well . . . then he pulls me by the small of my back against his hard, broad chest and kisses me stupid. "I love you. Always," he husks out.

There are ways people love you.

There are all kinds and types of love, I've found.

The way you love pets. Your friends. The way your parents love you. Your cousins. And there was this whole other way Mackenna and I loved each other.

Our love was like a raging storm and a harbor: unruly and unstoppable, wild and endless, but steady and safe . . .

Or so . . . my fool seventeen-year-old heart thought.

Months later, I sat on a rickety old bench for hours, until the park grew pitch black, empty. I could've been robbed or maybe even kidnapped, it was so dark. I was so stupid and naïve, I still waited, my toenails freshly painted, my shoes new, my dress the one I thought I looked prettiest in—at least one of the few that was not black but a light yellow. And I waited, running my hands down my loose hair. I twirled my promise ring on my finger until the base of my finger grew red and I realized he wasn't coming. And my eyes stung and my lungs closed when the figure that appeared that night was my mother's, my mother who couldn't possibly know I was dating him, extending her hand.

"He's not coming," she whispered.

"He's coming, Mother. I'm leaving. You can't stop me," I said with more conviction than I felt.

"I don't need to stop you. I just convicted his father, Pandora. You won't be leaving with that boy. He's not coming. I saw him with someone else. I'll wait in the car."

With someone else . . .

Just like my dad.

Mackenna lied to me.

And just like that, Mackenna broke me. . . .

FIVE

HAZED

Pandora

Okay, so here's the deal. A fact of life I've just proven. Everyone believes rock bands live in this sick little world, where all the band members get stoned, drunk, and laid, curse and argue, and every day is like this big ol' party?

Well, it's true.

They rehearse, of course. They work—some of the time. But holy shit, do these people know how to party. Even Trombone Guy, Violin Guy, and Piano Guy are hitting the booze tonight.

Party animals.

The whole lot of them.

"You wanna drink?" Violin Guy offers, but when I say no, I watch him simply shrug and leave with his buddies, the Harpist and the Flute Guy, instead.

Really, all I want to do is go to my room and order a burger and French fries, but we're supposed to be "partying," and the cameras are making sure not to miss a single moment of the stupidity happening here.

I even begin to wonder if some of it is purely for marketing purposes.

Hanging close to a cameraman so he won't tape *me*—I'm sure I'm wearing my most sour, tart face—I spot Mackenna by the beer pong. The amount of alcohol around here is mind-boggling. Body shots all over the place. Beer pong, drinks, booze, drugs. Even a *shisha* is going around.

I might try that if I were with my friends. Mel and Brooke, Kyle . . .

As it is, I won't drop my guard for a second, especially with Mackenna Jones nearby and a thousand cameras around us. Imagine me drunk? With Mackenna nearby?

I might kill him.

I might . . . well, he's so disgustingly male, I might *feel him up* while I kill him.

His lean arms are resting on the table as he waits for his opponent to throw the ball into his beer cup. His opponent happens to be one of the twins, and after he fails to make his shot, Mackenna smoothly dumps the ball into his cup, laughing while making the Viking—I think it's Lex—drink.

Yeah, those two are pounding the booze.

I want to stop staring, but I can't. Mackenna laughs out loud a lot, and the sound easily reaches my ears even though I'm across the room.

He's changed in all these years. He's still got that aura of a boy, but he's so much a man now. I can't stop cataloguing the differences. His jaw is squarer and slightly shadowed. Fuller lips. Thicker throat. He's got muscles on his arms like there's no tomorrow. He's just so tan and . . . man. I watch as he waits for Lex to throw the ball into his beer cup again.

Then I notice that a dancer, Letitta, keeps eyeing me maliciously. She cranes her neck out like a mean bird as she comes to me. I'm disappointed to see the cameraman follow.

She hovers by my side and signals in the direction of my gaze.

"He's such a good fuck." Her greedy, beady little eyes slither over Mackenna, and, wow, her smile is just like I imagined Cruella De Vil's right before she skins the fucking puppies.

An evil feeling crawls through me when I realize she, of course, has fucked that body in far more ways than I ever, in my stupid innocence, could have. I force a smile onto my face and twirl my pink strand of hair as I say, "I know, I broke him in." I start to leave, but her voice stops me.

"You think you look cool and badass, but you don't. Not really."

"Thanks. I've been wondering what you thought about me. Now I can go rearrange my whole personality to suit you." I look at the guy behind the camera, who's grinning like he's just struck gold, and I try to keep my cool, even though my anger is simmering under the surface of my skin.

She scrunches her face up until she looks like a little gremlin. "He hates your guts, girl. I swear the lyrics of 'Pandora's Kiss' just needed to add the fact that he wished you dead. Why would he even look at you, if not to break you right now?"

I laugh. This kind of laugh, I'm actually used to. The kind that means I'm the opposite of happy and mirthful. "He already broke me, there's nothing to break anymore, and when I reglued myself, I made it a priority not to put the heart back in. So it's cool. Thanks for worrying about me. Your concern is touching."

She jumps ahead of me and grabs one of my arms. "And yet you keep staring at him like you think he's yours. He's not."

"Let go of me unless you want me to punch you," I warn.

"Wow. You're just like a man, aren't you," she says.

"Hey, Tit," Lex calls, coming over to her and eyeing us both as though sensing we're about to have a real live catfight, right here. I'm surprised he didn't ease back and enjoy the view.

Maybe he isn't such a douche bag after all.

Tit's face switches in an instant from angry-gremlin mode to sweet-coquette mode as he comes over. He wraps his arm around her waist and kisses her on the mouth. God, I can't believe these guys just pass around a woman like that.

Or actually, I can.

But I *can't* believe they call her "Tit."

I turn away when I catch Mackenna surveying me with a strange kind of proprietary gaze. Red plastic cup in hand, he starts walking over, and a ball of nervousness fires up in my belly as he approaches. *Will you puleeze stop making me nervous, asshole?* I want to yell.

"Making friends already?" he says with a smirk.

This smirk is different, though. Almost as if he's displeased with Tit, which is ridiculous.

And suddenly I remember how, on the weekends after Thanksgiving, I'd escape with him. I remember us going to the ice rink, the day snowed in and cold. We'd watch guys making ice sculptures and we'd skate, and I loved to press close to him because he was always so warm and strong and steady on his feet. We'd see the frozen ice, stiff and white. I'd put on my skates, line up my boots, walk unsteadily into the ice. Then I'd slide over it, and he'd circle me like he was born on it. My Ice Man with silver eyes and warm skin and the world's most perfect lips. Muscled and strong, it was always so easy for him to reach out and spin me like a top. And then he'd stop me from spinning with a hug, hold me close, and lift the ears of my cap so he could whisper, "You're so hot you'd thaw this whole ice rink within hours."

My heart melts a little as I remember, and I try to reach for the ice I need to guard myself against him. He's no longer the boy I skated with, hid with, and thought myself in love with. He's a famous rockstar who plays with women. Me being the first of legions and legions of others.

"What? No reply?" he asks me. To be honest, I don't remember what we were even talking about, but his lips quirk and he adds, "Not so sure about yourself when you're not armed with vegetables?" There's a playful challenge in his eyes, that bad boy gleam that still makes my pulse skittish.

"Kenna, do you want a cupcake?" one of the dancers asks as she comes over and nearly decorates his face with it.

"Not now," he tells her, shoving the offering away, his eyes homed in on me. His alluring voice—his chiseled cheekbones, that twinge of charged air—is torture to my girly parts. Tor-ture. I feel a little drunk from having the attention everyone wants.

"More drink?" she presses hopefully, offering her red cup to him.

That catches his attention, and he stares at the red cup. "What you got there?"

I don't intend to stay here and watch this poor girl embarrass our sex in this way, so I head off in search of Lionel. I need my room key.

"Leaving the party early?" Mackenna calls as I leave.

I direct my answer to Lionel, who I've spotted, instead, watching the manager put his whiskey down as I reach him. "I'm tired. If it's okay with you, I already gave a juicy tidbit to one of the photographers." I point at the blond guy.

"Noah? Good. Appreciated." He flips a key out. "We've got the entire floor. There's a communal media room that will be open in the presidential suite. Some food storage closets in the hall."

"Thanks."

It takes me a while to make sense of the rooms. This is an extended-stay hotel, so the rooms are more like apartments. I hear footsteps behind me—shuffling, then giggles. It sounds like Tit and Lex, making out, but I'm not sure. I don't bother to turn around. The urge to get away from whoever is behind me hits and on impulse I grab the next doorknob and it opens, so I peer into pure darkness.

Before I realize it's some sort of closet, the door slams shut behind me and a celebration ensues just outside.

Great.

Fucking perfect.

They've locked me in here. Just like Mackenna predicted, I'm being hazed. Damn, I hate him being right.

I press my ear to the door, straining to hear them outside. They're still out there, and I hear giggles combined with male whispers. Sighing, I look around the closet and wonder if I'm going to sleep in here. It's a four-by-four space and not long enough to take me stretched out on the floor. So, what, I'll sleep sitting? All fucking night? No. When they leave, I'm going to try to unlock this sucker.

Minutes pass until, suddenly, they grow mysteriously quiet. I sense them still out there, waiting for something.

But what?

Then I hear the voice. Even though it's muffled, I know exactly who it belongs to, because all the little hairs on my arms rise to attention.

Fuck *no*. Please. Anyone but *him*.

"What did you fuckers do?" Mackenna growls under his breath. When nobody answers him, he adds, "What? Is she in there, you pricks?"

"Hell, I don't know. Why don't you check and see for yourself, dude?" one of the twins answers.

There's a cackle.

And then I hear the low, sensual, male sound of Mackenna's panty-wetting, heart-melting, toe-curling chuckle coming closer. "Seriously? You're such assholes."

He gets the door to open and there he stands, those eerie

silver eyes fixed on me. And they are *on* me. Like a touch. Doing
things to my heartbeat that I don't like but I can't stop. There's a
tattoo on his forearm, a ring on his thumb, a thousand leather
bracelets on his wrist. His lips curl, and I hate the feeling I get,
like a bell chiming in the pit of my stomach. I especially hate the
little tingle I get when he stretches out his hand.

"Hey," he says as he studies me with amusement. "Told you,
didn't I?"

He talks to me good-naturedly, with one sleek eyebrow up
high, and I feel a flush creep up my body as I stay rooted to my
spot, bravely battling a surge of unwanted lust and old, familiar
anger.

I want to get out of here, but I don't like that *he* gets to play
the hero.

Laughter rings out behind him, and before I can take his offered hand or brush snottily past him—which is what I was actually planning on doing—Lex and Jax shove him and, suddenly, all
six feet three of Mackenna is crashing into the closet.

The door slams shut behind him. "Woo! Remember seven
minutes in heaven, Kenna?" Lex shouts against the door. "How
about seven hours in hell, dude!"

They start humming "Pandora's Kiss," and anger rushes
through me. I fist my hands at my sides and close my eyes, praying for retribution one day.

Sounding bored as could be, Mackenna replies, "Very funny,
douche bags," and turns to grab the knob just as there's a loud
screeching of heavy furniture being dragged across the floor outside.

"Are they seriously blocking the door?" I ask, trying to sound
bored as well, but in actual fact, I'm alarmed. They are seriously
locking me in here?!?!?! With *Mackenna*?!?!?

This is beyond hell. So far beyond I don't even have a term

for it, but the closet already smells of . . . man. Man-wolf, and alcohol, and . . . ugh!

True panic floods me when I hear more screeching. The guys seem to be piling chairs against the door and jamming them against the doorknob. I mean, what the fuck?

After the screeching, there's a bang. "Careful, Kenna, she bites!" one of the twins calls out, laughing again.

Mackenna swears under his breath and jiggles the doorknob. Their laughter intensifies, so he stops trying and turns around. The light that seeps in under the door causes attractive shadows to hit his profile as he looks at me. "All right, I'm not giving the assholes the amusement they want."

I raise one eyebrow in an are-you-serious gesture.

He raises his eyebrows in an I'm-deadly-serious gesture.

I bite the inside of my cheek and slide down to sit on the floor, sighing dramatically.

He drops down too, and suddenly it's so much more cramped in here. He's so near. His thigh is all against mine. Hard as rock, and it's having an unwanted effect on me. This is the nearest I've had him since . . .

Hell, I don't know, my brain can't get past his thigh. Against mine. Being this close to Mackenna, and his fucking X factor, is pure torture. My female parts are as responsive to him as the rest of the world is. My lungs feel leaden as I try to breathe, but every breath smells of him, and his eyes glow in the dark as he studies my profile in the silence.

The air feels charged between us. I feel awkward, like I want to say something. I guess we'd better start fighting. So I open my mouth.

"Don't fucking ruin this," he says in a voice that's low and commanding.

Startled, I snap my mouth shut.

But my anger resurfaces when he leans forward and a strange surge of anticipation runs through me. "Come any closer and you'll find my knee in your balls," I warn.

He stops advancing and laughs softly. "You've been thinking of my balls, haven't you?"

"Only how much I'd like to chop them, slice them, and add salsa to them."

"And have them against a nice juicy taco. Hmm."

"Ohmigod! You're disgusting!"

I try to push him, and he catches my hands in his warm ones, making me gasp when he pins them over my head, against the wall. Outrage bubbles in my veins. I feel so trapped and helpless, and suddenly my heart is going a mile a minute, pumping in my throat. A crazy, wild wave of lust follows my outrage.

God. Seven hours of *this*?!?!

I groan in protest. The sound of my groan seems to do something to him, because he tightens his hold and weighs even more heavily on me. All two hundred pounds of muscled *him*. Our eyes hold each other's in the darkness, and the electricity rushes through me as I warn, *"Let go."*

"You don't mean that."

I struggle futilely, and he tightens his hold. I nod. Yes, yes I do. I do mean it. But he transfers both my wrists to only one hand and leans his head against mine. The thundering of my heart echoes in my brain as his breath bathes my face. Oh god, he's so close, and I've dreamed about being this close, in dreams and nightmares, during the day and during the night . . . I've dreamed of his eyes and how I used to find them always staring at me through those thick lashes of his. I'd dream and think of his lips. The top one shaped like a bow, almost as full as the bottom, the bottom one so plush and curved . . .

And then he kisses me, placing that mouth on me, cupping

my head in his free hand, and parting my lips with the same lips I hadn't realized I'd been staring at in painful hunger. The unexpectedness of his kiss makes me struggle halfheartedly to wrench free. I don't want to want this. I don't want this soul-searing thirst, the dreadful, inescapable feeling that I'll break if he kisses me and I'll break if he doesn't. I whimper, as though it would make him have mercy on me. He doesn't. He groans softly and tries slipping his tongue into my mouth, and when I part my lips and let him taste me because I'm clearly out of my mind, suicidal, and horny, I make a sound I haven't ever made in my life. More than a moan or a whimper, a sound of true, quiet pain. He pulls back when I do, and so do I.

We both stare, in shock.

"Asshole," I hear myself murmur, breathing hard.

"Bitch."

He looks at my lips, and my sex squeezes in reaction as he lowers his head and covers my lips again, more viciously, with his own groan of pleasure.

For a fraction of a second, my body is a trembling mass of contradictions. My hands have not touched any man. Only a boy. Seventeen. Before he got the tattoo that peeks on the inside of his forearm. Before he became larger than life, a star, before he grew up to be this man.

One second, I'm a woman with a thousand walls, who rarely touches anyone or allows a hug. In the next, I'm six years younger, and he's the guy I let in. I don't want that girl to take over, but I live in her. This is *her* skin, and nobody can make it tremble like he does.

I'm not only trembling, I feel like I'm burning from the inside out. A hot, quivering mess of desire under his lips. The same lips that sing crap about me, hurt me, haunt me, somehow remain the most beautiful lips I've ever seen, felt, or tasted. God. Tasted.

In a sudden frenzy I grab his shoulders, my tongue pushing hungrily into his mouth, my hips rolling toward his. God, I hate this fucking asshole.

I hate him for making me feel like this after all these years.

But my hands have a mission. Memorizing the texture of him. The feel of him. How he's changed in six years. He'd been long and lean before and now he's longer and harder. Smoother. Bigger. No more teen limbs, now he's all thickness of a man, and though my arms are now free to roam, my head is trapped under the weight of his kiss. And I can't get enough of his hot, wet, thirsty, mean, dirty, delicious mouth!

Hell, I can't unleash all my anger in just this kiss.

I can't express what he has done to me—how he has ruined my life—with just this incredible, pulse-pounding, life-altering kiss.

I want to bite and claw at him, kick and scream at him, take his cock in me and ride him until he can't walk!

The bastard.

I want to hit him while I kiss him, curse him while I kiss him, push him the hell away from me while I kiss him.

I want to . . .

I just WANT.

As though channeling our frustrations and anger into this one kiss, we keep rubbing tongues almost ferally, rubbing our bodies against each other in as much anger as lust. He leans forward, grabs one of my thighs, and hooks my leg around his hips, still nearly kissing my lips off as he aligns his erection to my cunt, our sexes scraping through our jeans. One big palm cups my breast, and his thumb swipes across the hardened peak, to and fro, shooting angry sparks through me.

His hand slides under my T-shirt and I make a noise in the back of my throat as I slide my fingers under the fabric of his shirt as well, touching the smooth, bare flesh beneath. It's harder than ever, the grooves of muscles hard and defined under my fingers, rippling as our bodies shift to get closer, our mouths remaining fused.

He winds his arms around me and sits back, adjusting me over him so my nipples brush against his chest as he pulls his mouth free and looks first at me, then at my swollen mouth. His face burns with a harsh, animalistic passion.

"You haven't been kissed in a while, have you?"

Oh god, it can't be that obvious. "That's none of your business."

"It *is* my business. And I'm making it priority business."

Need slams into me at the possessiveness in his tone. His grip tightens on me, quieting my denial. "You haven't been fucked in a while either, have you?"

"No, but I don't *want* you," I grit out.

God, he's like a sexually charged nuclear weapon about to detonate me.

"Don't be petulant," he whispers softly, smoothing a hand down my hair. "Do you want me to fuck you?" he asks. I can taste him on my tongue, and my panties are drenched with arousal.

"This won't be for the cameras." His voice is deathly sexy in an I'm-so-ready-to-fuck-you way, his breath a warm gust of air against my throat as he nuzzles me like he's mad about me. Like he's Dracula and I'm Mina, and this little foray into the closet? This will be our undoing. "This is for me—for you *and* me. I need to fuck you out of my system. We'll play whatever game they want, but we'll have our own game. I don't want this on film. Our lives are on film, but this can't be in it. Do you understand me, Pandora?"

Please excuse me, but my brain is in a fog of lust and I can't think straight. "Wha . . . but how are we going to . . . ?"

"Shh. I'll find a way." My muscles start quivering as he reaches between our bodies and I hear the rasp of my zipper.

He eases his hand into my jeans, his eyes glowing. "Have you been thinking about this?"

Fuck, considering that at one point yesterday I wanted to lick the tomatoes off him, YES! But I refuse to say it, refuse for him to know. I swallow back a moan when he slips a finger inside my sopping wet pussy and rasps, "Yes," as if answering himself.

He rubs my insides, and it feels so good, I arch for him.

He's smiling against my temple, because of course he knows—we both know—I'm drenched. And swollen from arousal. And god, it feels so good, but my pride is smarting because I'm so wet. I fight the desire he makes me feel, and I put my hands on his shoulders, battling within myself and gathering the strength I need to push him away. But then I realize . . . he *owes* me this. He fucking should pleasure me until I can't get enough. So I grab the back of his head and start kissing him again, groaning softly when he does the same, his mouth taking control of mine. His skull is round, perfect. His tongue works its magic on me as I feel the knowing strokes of his finger rubbing me inside.

"Part your legs. Lift your shirt so I can suck on those tits."

"If you want it, lift it yourself," I huskily reply, still clinging to my pride.

He laughs darkly. His hips move against my body in a punishing roll that makes me gasp, and he groans at the stimulation as though he could get off just dry humping me.

"Do as I say, damn you."

My head falls back as I pull my shirt up to my neck. He yanks my bra down and hooks it to the underside of my breast, then latches on to one puckered nipple. I am in full-blown arousal and pumping to his finger, moaning as he sucks my nipple. God, what is this? I'd forgotten this. How he consumes me. Delights and moves me.

I'm so aroused I'm in agony when he peels his mouth and his fingers away for a moment. Then he takes my hand and I hear a zipper, and I feel pure, hard, smooth cock in my palm as he shoves my hand into his jeans. "Oh fuck, you want me bad," I cry.

"Work me, honey," he urges softly. I try. Really I do. But he's pumping into me with that magic finger and his mouth is fastened onto my other nipple, and I am so close. I'm moaning mindlessly when the snickering starts outside. Crashing back to reality, I pull my hand out of his jeans as we hear screeching.

"Shit!" I say.

Mackenna groans. *"Fuck them to hell!"*

"Get up!" I cry as I leap to my feet, slip my shirt back on, and try not to look like we were just making out in this closet.

Ohmigod.

That was the most incredible seven minutes of my fucking life!

I stand on wobbly legs and have just finished adjusting my shirt and hair when the doorknob turns. When they fling the door open, the outside light burns my eyes.

"So, Kenna? What the fuck, man? You teach her who's boss?"

I wonder if he's moping on the floor because he didn't get to come, but I don't get to worry for long. He brushes past me, fully composed. "Oh, she knows all right," he says in a husky murmur, his buzz cut hair perfect, his entire demeanor as attractive as every rock god's should be.

The twins snicker, and I tip my chin up as I walk past them down the hall, aware of the girls who are with them staring at me. When I turn, I see both of those girls embracing Mackenna, whining, "You don't really like her, do you?"

He grabs their asses and squeezes. "Nah, I just like pissing her off."

He looks back in my direction, his eyes still so ravenous they're burning holes through me, and I'm so angry at what I just let him do—put his hands on me, his tongue in me . . . god, I was about to jerk him off in the closet!

My whole body tightens in anger as I storm into the room, slam the door, scan for something to throw, then just grab the pillow and scream.

SIX

I KNEW SHE'D
SCRAMBLE MY BRAINS

Mackenna

"So, you fuck her in the closet?"

The twins? Yeah, these fuckers have had too many Jäger-bombs and lemonshots. "You two fucking dickheads are going to get fucked, by me." I shove Lex first, then Jax shoves me, and we push and shove our way into our suite.

I fall down on the couch and the girls soon follow, manicured fingers rubbing up my arms and chest.

"She's such a bitch," one whispers.

"She's not that pretty either," says the other.

My stomach writhes with need. Not that pretty? She's all I fucking see. Right now. In my head. Dark hair, liquid dark eyes, that dark mouth of hers that apparently still makes me hard as a teenager. "Do me a favor, get me something to drink," I whisper to the girls, and I rub the back of my neck as I wait for them to come back.

Whoa, this encounter worked you up, Jones!

Fuck her, she's getting to me again. But I can't let her.

"Come back so we can fuck," I shout after them. Shutting my eyes, it's no use. I can't get rid of the way she looked at me, with those angry dark-as-sin eyes, that ridiculous pink streak in her hair. I'm still throbbing under the zipper of my jeans, aching for her touch.

I need to work it out of my system. I need to work *her* out of my system. I suck on my middle finger, and my cock twitches. She tastes good, smelled good, felt good. She smelled like my teen years. Back then, her skin and hair smelled of coconut—like a damn beach. And now, even though her looks are dark as sin, she smells like anyone's dream vacation. Her tits are fuller than I remember. Still not big, but just right on her. And, here's an odd thought, I want them again. In my mouth. I want to fuck that girl. God fuck me standing. I want to fuck her until she can't walk and neither can I, for that matter.

Jax grabs one of the girls and pulls off his shirt, then his pants.

"No one wants to see you naked, Jax," I cry, tossing him a pillow.

"Only a million people," he returns.

I narrow my eyes as the girls bring me a whiskey, straight up, and I down it in one second as they rub my body like it's made of the most precious material on the planet.

There's a strange modern drawing on the ceiling of the suite, and my eyes trace the swirls as I think of that mouth of hers. That mouth of hers. I could kiss that mouth of hers again. She kisses like her kiss could kill, and I'm suicidal enough to want that fucking kiss again, just as badly as I did when I was younger.

I like bad things—booze, threesomes, orgies, smoking. But the baddest thing I've ever wanted is Pandora, and I want her deep and hard, like wanting to tie myself to a sinking ship and letting it take me under. So when one of the girls tugs on my shirt and presses her mouth to mine, the moment she trails her tongue along my lips, I pull away and laugh at myself.

"You know what? I think I feel like torturing Pandora a little longer," I tell them, easing away and zipping my jeans back up.

"Kenna . . . ," they chorus, pouting.

"Where you going?" Lex calls.

"Obviously back to hell." One of the cameras follows me down the hall. I stop the cameraman, Noah, and tell him, "Not this, dude."

"I can't come into her room. Leo said it was the only way she'd sign a contract."

"*Really* now?" I stare at him as I register the singular truth that Pandora's bedroom is a safe place from cameras. "Excellent. She's smart, that woman. And mad. Stay away from her."

"Like you are?" he snorts.

"Stay away from her," I repeat. "Stay the fuck away from her, and a couple of feet away from me."

I charge back down the hall and knock on the door. There's a flash at the peephole as she seems to peer through. She groans. And holy shit, even that groan I can feel in my dick.

I knock again. "Gonna knock all night if I have to!" The door swings open and she's . . .

Fuck.

Her pupils are dilated, her hair loose, and she's in a short T-shirt. I can't take it. The blood storms hot in my veins. I open my mouth, my tone low. "I'm fucking desperate for you."

She glances at the camera, then at me. She opens her mouth to say something, sees the camera again, and says, "You're such a drama queen."

"Drag prince," I shoot back.

She frowns and makes a move to slam the door in my face, but I stop her with the toe of my boot. "Come on, Pink," I say, my heart pounding as I grab her by the neck so she looks into my eyes. "You want this," I urge. I dare not even consider what it'll be like if she sends me back to my room. Failure is not an option here. My body is tense with the need for me to sink myself inside this woman until she comes for me. "You're desperate for me too," I whisper, massaging her scalp with my fingers. "Aren't you? You're wishing you hadn't kissed me in the closet, but you did. We both did. And now we can't stop here."

Her eyes keep drifting to my mouth, and that act alone makes standing here with a hard-on only one step inside her room nearly the most impossible feat of my entire existence. "What happened to your threesome?" she dares me, and I can hear from the texture in her voice she's caving in.

Go for it. Seduce her stupid, Kenna.

I lean over in the hopes Noah can't hear me, whispering close to her ear, "Obviously I passed on it for something better."

"Really? You had a better offer?"

I reach up and trail my hand down the pink in her hair. "I'm hoping for one."

"I don't even like you." She pushes my chest using the heels of her palms with great effort, and for a second I indulge her by taking a step back.

"But your mouth still likes mine, and I can't even begin to describe how much I like yours—"

She slams the door in my face. I swear out loud and run a frustrated hand over the back of my idiot head. "Motherfucker."

Behind me, muffled laughter. "Crash and burn, Mackenna?" Noah taunts, camera trained on me.

Scowling, I flip him the bird. "Just watch. I'll be practically living in that room right there." I point to her door, then angrily stalk back to my suite, where the guys' private party is raging full blast.

Everyone's fucking or doing blow or drinking, and I'm stone fucking sober. One of the girls is bent over Lex. She signals to me that I'm next. Fuck that noise. I stomp into my bedroom, my entire brain filled with Pandora. Her stony little glare. The solid door in my face. Her pussy felt so goddamn tight in the closet, like she hadn't had anyone in five fucking years and I'm suddenly obsessed.

I should have closed the distance between us and crushed her mouth under mine, until neither of us remembered anything at all. My hands are restless at my sides. I push them through the buzz of my hair, run the water in the sink, and splash some onto my face.

I imagine her crawling up against the headboard, spreading her legs for me. She'd sigh out my name and I'd dip my tongue to taste the sweet honey between her thighs.

Fuck this shit. I'm not settling for less than what I want, and suddenly I want in that room like nobody's business—and I know just how to get in there.

❤ ❤ ❤

MINUTES LATER, I'M pounding on Leo's door.

"What the fuck, Kenna?" He swings the door open and motions at one of the girls to stay put in bed. Obviously entertaining him.

"Key," I growl.

Leo's eyes get glassy with cash signs; clearly I don't need to say to which room.

He grins and nods. "Take her to your room so the cameras can get some of the heavy petting," he instructs.

"Write Santa Claus a letter, see if he listens, Leo."

My manager rolls his eyes, then goes to rummage through his

stuff while the girl comes over, tying a robe around herself. "Hey, Kenna, looking good."

Leo comes back with a key. "Try to throw the cameras a bone soon."

"If I throw anything tonight it'll be the ass of a cameraman out the tenth-floor window."

I march down the hall and pop that fucking door open. The lights are dim and the room is completely silent.

On the bed, Pandora is sprawled, facedown. My chest feels cramped as I take in her long legs, the soft, pale skin peeking out from under the T-shirt she wears. She's out like the dead, her head tossed to the side, all that dark hair made for my fingers. Before I can think twice, I've shucked my clothes and climbed into bed with her. Just like old times. And the demons that have ridden me all night quiet down enough so I can relax against her. I pull her close to me.

She sighs in her sleep, her body seeking my warmth.

She fits me so right; she's always fit me right, this girl.

We were both virgins once. You'd expect it to be awkward that first time, but it wasn't. It felt like being swept up by a storm. Disheveled and destroyed inside on some level I never recovered from. When we were done, she was softly crying in my arms. I felt as unhinged as a building shaken to its foundations. I'd lost control, and so had she. I didn't know what to do, what I'd done wrong, how to make it right.

I feel like that now.

Back then, I waited it out, wanting her to explain how she had all that emotion for me when she was usually a girl who displayed none. When she finally composed herself and wiped her tears, I kissed her and told her I loved her, and I asked her, *"You love me, don't you? Don't you, Pandora?"*

For the two years we dated, she never did say she did.

Yeah, I don't think this girl can love anybody.

I don't know why the memory slaps me now. It doesn't bring the anger it usually does, or the sadness and frustration. I fell for a girl who would never love me back the way I wanted her to. Hell, I'm over wanting declarations of love. I'm over craving it. I'm over feeling the way she made me feel all those years ago.

But will I ever be over *her*?

I exhale.

She'll probably punch my face when she sees me in bed with her in the morning. Blue balls and a purple eye, that's what a guy who messes with this girl gets. But fuck me if I care at all. That's not really my problem.

My problem is I can never seem to find a way to get this girl to let me in.

I whisper in her ear, "I'm just going to hold you, all right? No funny business."

I think she nods and whispers, "Okay."

And though I'm not sure if she really did answer or it's just my imagination, I slide my arm around her waist and hold her tight.

SEVEN

BIG DOSE OF REALITY

Pandora

The big dose of reality hits me when I wake up and he is sprawled, in all his muscular glory, across my hotel bed. It takes a second for me to remember that I, uh . . . I let Mackenna stay over?

I groan and slap my palm against my forehead. *Fuck.* Why, why, why does he weaken my willpower? The mattress squeaks as he shifts in bed, one arm reaching out as he mumbles something in his sleep and seems to search for me. I roll away quickly and watch his hand settle on a pillow.

"Mackenna," I say, toeing his side with my foot. *"Mackenna!"* I hiss.

He rolls around and sits up, and thank god the covers are halfway around his waist because if I see one more inch of bare flesh I might explode from the heat spreading through me. I feel myself blush even deeper when his muscles bulge as he pushes himself up with his arms. His eyes adorably heavy, he blinks to adjust to the light, his mouth as perfect and generous as it was yesterday. And then he looks at me. That gaze is softer silver in the morning, not as sharp or as intimidating, almost . . . intimate when he sees me. Glimmering playfully.

And too late, I realize *why* he's fucking grinning. My T-shirt got caught on the waistband of my panties. And he's taking me in, in one quick sweep. "Well, fuck, someone woke hungry this morning," he says, his voice bedroom sleepy as he looks at me, and I grab the pillow to cover myself.

"I'm not hungry," I say.

"I was talking about me. Come over here."

"No, Mackenna! Come on. Get out of my room already. I told you to leave!"

He grins and gets up, and I toss the pillow and flush as I pull down my T-shirt while he heads to the bathroom. It takes him only a minute to come out. Not enough to comb my fingers through all the tangles in my hair. *If* I were into that and cared what the asshole thought. Which I don't.

His eyes run up the length of my legs, continue from the hem of my T-shirt to my neck, then land on my head. "Leave your hair, it looks all right," he says huskily, stopping to loom before me.

Heat flows through my body as he looks down at me with blatant need. What is wrong with him? With us?

"Nothing's wrong," he murmurs.

"I said that out loud?" I groan.

"You've been . . . vocal, all night. I quite like it."

God. I dreamed. I dreamed . . . I'm not even sure what. I dreamed about the closet again. I dreamed we were in bed. I dreamed he tried to kiss me, and when I turned away, he sent a thousand shivery kisses up and down my neck.

The memory makes me flush cherry red. Did that happen during the night? By the intimate way he looks at me, I think he wanted inside me real bad. I didn't let him, thank god. He fingers the collar of my tee, then watches me as he slowly drags his finger up my neck, his thumb caressing my bottom and top lip. Even though his hold is loose and he's not physically holding me down, I feel trapped. His gaze alone holds me motionless.

He used to look at me with this same proprietary gleam when he was my boyfriend. My *secret* boyfriend, who nobody knew about . . . except me. I guess, in the end, my mom too.

But while it lasted, we hid in the janitor's closet in school and made out until I could hardly walk, my legs unsteady as I headed for class with his taste in my mouth, the scent of his soap clinging to my clothes.

I'm fighting the urge to smell his neck now. It's a war to just stand here motionless, tracing every inch of his masculine face with my eyes when I want my fingers to do the same. The years become nothing.

The hum between us is just like in the old days, when I was the center of his galaxy. When the girls in school would stare longingly at him when he walked past my locker, having eyes only for me. Sometimes, when the halls were vacant enough, he quickly leaned over me and kissed every part of my body, from my toes up to the back of my ear. I'd grow hot, and the place between my legs would start pulsing.

Too easily I remember coming home and squealing.

Me—squealing.

I would play love songs, only to replay the words he said to me and the ways he touched me. I would shower, eat, and sleep Mackenna Jones. . . .

But deep down, my mother's bitterness and my father's infidelity poisoned me. I kept all these feelings to myself—kept them from my mother so she wouldn't take Mackenna from me. But because I didn't want to lose him, because I feared it wasn't real, I also kept my feelings from him, and now I'm used to saying nothing. Keeping it bottled up.

Why do I feel like I'm about to burst now?

"Don't, Kenna," I say when he uses his thumb to open my lips. He stands dangerously close—his height, his breadth, his size, his do-me-now-woman sex appeal intimidating the hell out of me.

He grins wickedly and strokes a hand over my hip.

"Why not?"

"Because it's not going to happen," I say breathlessly.

"Yeah, it will." His smirk says, *It definitely will.*

He pats my butt slowly, and the familiar way he brushes his lips over mine brings my temper to a boil. Who does he think he is? Does he think because we *made out* by mistake he gets to play my *boyfriend*? When I growl and slap his hand away, he chuckles and heads back to the bathroom.

Ohmigod, I cannot believe I let him put his filthy paws on me in that closet—and stay the night over!

Soon I hear the shower, the sound of the water slapping his delicious man-flesh. Then I hear him hum a tune, a tune I've never heard before. My chest moves when I remember he used to do that when we were teens. God, *no*, stop thinking of those moments. It hurts. Truly it does. Think of the bad ones. When he left. When he left me on my own after making me need him and believe I couldn't live without him.

Refusing to get all sappy with memories, I grab my phone and think of Melanie.

She's probably at the office, missing the delightfully bitter morning company that is me.

I quickly text, I kissed him

Every second I wait for her answer, I feel worse and worse, not only about the closet incident but also about falling asleep with him around. When I woke up, the bastard was almost spooning me.

Melanie: What?

Me: I kissed the bastard! He spent the night. Oh god!!!!! This is suicide!

Melanie: Why? Was he into it? You know what they say about where there was once fire . . .

Me: He was into the kissing, into using me for his selfish reasons and I was selfish too.

Melanie: So what's the problem?

Me: The problem is he's going to think he WON!

And he will. He really, really will, because he's so full of himself I'm surprised he fits inside this building. How can I even explain to Melanie, who's happy and carefree and innocent, that when a douche bag breaks your heart, you cannot let him have it again, you cannot let him touch you again. I'm about to try when she writes, Look, Maleficent, if he's being a dick let me tell Greyson to send someone to rearrange his face—stat.

I blink.

Me: Melanie your new bloodthirst scares me

Melanie: Heee! :)

The thought of someone hurting Mackenna makes me sick. Only *I* get to hurt him. Damn it!

I toss my phone aside and breathe in and out, remembering my tricks from anger management. Then I force myself to think of Magnolia and my mother.

Mags.

I left my poor Mags alone with my mother, who's even less

merry than I am because I was determined to find closure and
save all this fucking money to have some freedom in the future,
for me and for Mags. Closure to me equaled Mackenna realizing
that leaving me was the biggest mistake of his life. And how did I
plan to do this? By getting involved again?!

We *can't* get involved. We can't be buddies—*especially* not
fuck buddies.

Can we?

No, we can't, because I'm too wimpy to survive him twice.
Because even if he likes me a little bit once more, he won't like me
for real when he learns what sort of secrets I hide. You get struck
by lightning once and survive, lucky you, but you won't survive
twice. That's for sure.

How can I make it clear that the closet and a sleepover do not
make us friends?

Remembering what he said on the bus about giving me
a chance to redeem myself with a song, I grab a pen and start
writing. I'm growing madder by the second. So mad it's like I'm
not writing words on a piece of paper but chiseling them into a
slate.

Soon he steps out of the shower, strutting like he'll have me
yet. Yeah, he's good. All wet, with droplets of water sliding down
his golden flesh. His silver eyes meet me with quiet assessment—
like he can sense the shift in the air. Well, at least he's smart.

With a fake smile, I walk over and hand him the paper. "Your
song," I say.

His eyebrows fly upward in surprise, then he reads the words
out loud.

Mackenna's mouth
Spits all lies
A sewer tastes better

He looks at me in pure, undisguised amusement. "Seriously?" he prods.

"Go on," I say through my teeth.

I can smell his shampoo. *Hate it.*

He continues reading.

A donkey's ass is sweeter
I hate Mackenna's mouth
And his fucking lies
He can kiss my ass
And it will taste better than his fucking mouth

He lowers the piece of paper, and before I realize it, he's caught me by the back of the neck and kissed me flat on the mouth. Then he yanks back and strokes his knuckles across my wet lips, still grinning.

I wipe my mouth to get rid of the tingle his touch leaves. "I'm still working on it. Just thought you might like to start thinking of a tune," I say, scowling.

"Why let me pick if you're on a roll, baby? Let's just use the background music for *Jaws*."

"Stop kissing me when you feel like it, Kenna."

"Stop opening your mouth and sticking your tongue at me when I do, Pink."

"I didn't . . . ugh." I flip him the bird and feel entirely too warm when he heads for the door, taking my song with him.

"Thanks for this." He grins like it's a love sonnet. "Glad to see you're making lists again."

"It's not a fucking list."

"Well it's not exactly a song either, Pink."

Suppressing the urge to kick the door when he leaves, I decide to go cool down and take a bath.

"I hate you," I mumble, just to get it out of my system as I undress.

But the worst part of it all is that I'm starting to wonder whether I truly mean it.

AFTER A BATH, I'm calmer when I drop on the bed. The covers are rumpled. The room smells a little bit like him. I let him . . . hold me? Why'd I go and do that? I felt him slip in behind me. I felt the mattress give in to his weight and then I felt all his warm muscles surrounding me. I pretended not to notice because *I didn't want him to go.*

I groan and bury my face in my hands.

God. What have I done?

I'm not letting him get through my walls—protective layers it took me years to mend. But I'm wandering right into the most painful moments of my life, and I already feel a little bit too rumpled. Like the bed he slept in with me. The rumpled feelings crawl their way into my chest, and I try to perk up and think of the future Magnolia can have with all the money.

I sit down and check the clock, then mentally go through Magnolia's schedule. Since it's summer, she must be home.

I dial from my cell, and all my pain and confusion ease when I hear her little voice answer.

"I miss you, Panny, I have thirty-eight things we're going to do when you get back!" she proclaims.

"Wow, you're going to keep me busy, huh?"

"Yessss! Guess which is number thirty-three?"

"Hmmm. Let's see now . . ." I pretend to think until I hear her practically panting. "We're going to lay around in pajamas all day and play board games."

"No! We're going to make a lemonade stand and sell orange juice."

"What? Whoa, wait. You can't sell orange juice at a lemonade stand—it needs to be an orange juice stand."

"Yes you can! Why not?"

I'm so exhausted by last night, I can't even think right this morning. So I backpedal. "Okay, you're right. Let's break the rules. Everyone who sells lemonade at a lemonade stand has no creativity like *we* do."

"And we're gonna add water so we get more orange juice to sell."

"What? No, oooh no no. I'm drawing the line there, Mags. We are not watering down the orange juice. That's for complete delinquents."

"Delinquents! I wanna be a delinquent with you!" she squeals, and I grin like a dope and stare at my bracelet as she starts telling me about what she's done. The bracelet has little gem charms, colorful and rugged in texture. They're supposed to protect all my loved ones from wrong. I don't ever wake up in the mornings without rubbing it.

I don't like that Mackenna made me forget until now. So I brush my thumb over the rocks, letting that simple movement ease me like Magnolia does.

Little did I know I'd especially need as much calm as I could muster this morning.

❤ ❤ ❤

SO, THERE'S BAD news. Not surprising. I expected this trip to be a disaster from start to end, so I shouldn't be in full panic mode. I already woke up with Mackenna in my bed, so now? Now, the interstate highway is closed due to construction, and the ever-efficient Lionel has chartered a plane to fly us all to the next location. But then again, that isn't just bad news.

That is a *disaster.*

I am not a tactile person, but I desperately need to hold someone's hand when I fly—desperate as in I'm-afraid-I'm-going-to-yank-off-an-armrest-or-something-now-that-Melanie-Brooke-Kyle-my-mother-or-Magnolia-aren't-here.

But . . . *sigh* . . . I've got meds, right?

And meds make the world go round, so . . .

And at least I wasn't forced to ride alone with Mackenna to the airport. I took the same coach as the dancers, and Lionel didn't have time to protest before we were on our way. True, they all gave me enough evil eyes to give me a lifetime of bad luck—but it's not like I've enjoyed much great luck in the first place, so I might not even notice the difference.

Once we shuffle into the airport, the Viking twins keep staring at me. Their expressions are curious more than antagonistic, and I briefly wonder what Mackenna has told them about me.

This girl not only throws a good tomato, but I popped her cherry when she was seventeen too . . .

"Hey," one finally says.

"Hey," the other follows.

They're both smirking now, big and blond, and worst of all is that, like Mackenna, they reportedly have brains too. From the clothes they wear, to the carefully calculated appearances for the paparazzi, Crack Bikini is a meticulously plotted piece of merchandise. Mackenna's wigs, the Vikings' chains, tats, and nipple rings are all part of "the look," though today, Mackenna wears a black T-shirt and jeans and a cap on his buzz cut, plus aviators. The twins are dressing the part of rockstars to a T. Chains hang around Jax's neck, while Lex wears a spiked choker.

"ID?" Lionel asks, and I hand it over as he checks me in.

Mackenna joins his two boys and the guys stare in my direction. All three of them.

I hate how his energy pulls on mine. He's the only person in this world I can actually feel spiking my adrenaline. He has a way of making me feel supercharged—as if my own body pumps extra hormones when he's near.

Jax surveys me with quirked lips. "Kenna didn't tell us much about you, you know."

My eyes slide to Mackenna, and my tummy dips for some reason when I see he's not smiling but watching me intently.

"Except that I was a witch?" I quip.

Lex laughs. "Not in those words."

"Well, tall, dark, and mean is just part of his charm. Isn't it?"

They grin at me, and I slide a look at Mackenna, my tummy dipping again when I see him looking at me as if there's an intense pondering session going on in his brain. Lionel comes back with my ticket, and suddenly it's real.

This flight is real.

There's no way I will allow myself to be weak and vulnerable in front of Mackenna, but my nerves skyrocket as we head toward our gate.

I'm acutely aware of him silently walking next to me. One thousand percent bad boy rocker, with lazy swagger. With a sidelong glance I check out the tattoo on his forearm, the one thousand leather bracelets on his wrist, and the silver ring on his thumb. The memory of that ring on my skin when we went a little bit too far in the closet skims through me.

And what does that tattoo say?

Several men in suits walk with the group and attempt to keep people away from the main men. The guys have always been an entity—like two balls and a dick.

"You okay there?" Mackenna asks me.

"Dandy."

Relax, Pandora. Just take a pill, take a whiskey, and knock yourself out.

I repeat it as a mantra as we board the plane. The scent of airplane is suddenly choking me.

Mackenna is talking with the guys. Lionel greets me with a huge smile as he lightly guides me into first class. A group of dancers start chatting up the guys. As I put my bag in the overhead compartment, I watch Mackenna. All the guys seem bored with the conversations, but not Mackenna. Ohhhh, no, not player Mackenna. He smiles and teases the girls, stealing little touches on their arms.

God, he's unbelievable.

Scowling, I slide into my seat and pray for a smooth landing, breathing in and out as I check—for the tenth time today—the pillbox in my pocket. If a piece of metal can fly, then I can fly in it, safely, like everyone says.

But as I strap on my seat belt, I remember how my father died. He died this way. I picture that plane lurching and crashing. I picture him going numb. Thinking of Mother, of *me*. I wonder if the others screamed. It's a fear that's grown with me through the years as I've lost my innocence and become more cynical and, at the same time, more vulnerable and therefore more guarded. Fear bubbles and fizzes in my stomach as I try to stop thinking about that flight. How my father's last goodbye was truly a goodbye. How no one survived.

My mother and I saw the crash on the evening news before we even realized my father was on board. "Ohmigod," my mother breathed as we both watched the images of shredded airplane among sirens and stretchers and debris.

She checked her phone. "Your father's flight should be landing soon," she said. "And we are due for a nice family dinner."

I checked my phone because I'd promised Mackenna I'd meet him by the docks.

My mother was pacing. She'd never paced before. A feeling of dread settled on me. Like when you see those dark clouds hover across the sun, blocking it from your view. When the phone rang, and my mother answered, I knew.

She started crying. I started crying too.

"He was on board. He was on board with his assistant. He wasn't flying from Chicago, he was coming back from Hawaii."

"What? Why?"

"Because . . ." My mother wiped her tears, and all the emotion fled from her face. "Because he's been lying to us."

The phone began ringing nonstop when people started to find out that my father had died. I knew that wasn't the only thing they must've been talking about—they were talking about the fact that he was with his assistant too.

I stole out of the house, an hour late, and I ran into the darkness, and then I saw the figure out in the street, watching my house as though making sure I was all right, knowing he couldn't go in there.

"Kenna!" I flung myself at him, trying to hold back my tears. "That flight. He was on it. He was on that flight."

"Shh." He rocked me. My safe haven. I closed my eyes and held on to him. "He lied to us. He's been lying to us all along."

"I'm sorry," he rasped, kissing my eyelids. "I'll always be here for you. I will never lie to you. . . ."

I jerk upright when the flight attendant announces she's going to shut the plane door. The orchestra flies in the back, the singers up front. There are plenty of seats available—hell, they chartered the whole plane. Jax takes one seat and sets his stuff on the empty one beside him, and Lex takes another. And Mackenna is talking with the two flight attendants now. He's twisted his cap around and looks young and delicious while wearing it backward. He looks like he used to look . . . when he was seventeen.

I'm trying to steady my nerves when he startles me by dropping down on the seat beside me, prying off his cap, and jamming it into the seat pocket in front of him, as if there weren't a thousand and one bacteria in there. He leans on the armrest, his weight turned toward me. Is it his inborn fate to torture me?

"You lost? There are a dozen empty seats here," I say.

He looks at me intently. "I want this one."

Shaking my head, I grab a little manual from the seat pocket in front of me and start flipping through it. I will not lose my senses in front of him. No. Way. And yet I'm acutely aware of the alien noises surrounding me. Shuffle of feet. The engines. The shut of the plane door, his breathing.

His *breathing*.

I focus on that and try to match my breaths to his, all the while hoping he won't notice. I could use him to relax. Or distract myself.

Soon we're being offered drinks. I pull out my pillbox and keep it discreetly tucked into my palm as he stretches his long legs.

"Whiskey, sugar. And bring her the same," he says, gesturing at me as he pushes his seat back. The manual says that during takeoff, the seat must be in an upright position, but he clearly doesn't give a shit.

He never coddled me. Even when we were kids. He treated me as an equal. I rarely cried, but when I did, he just waited for me to stop. If I fell, he just pulled me up and acted like I wasn't supposed to cry, so I didn't. He knew I had trouble expressing emotions, and when my father died, I bottled them up completely. I stopped crying at all, and Mackenna was all right with it. I think.

He never pressed me to talk about it. He's staring at me now, and I can see him trying to assess the situation, without pity and clearly without any intention of coddling me, so I blurt out, "I still hate airplanes."

His eyes gain a concerned glimmer. "I have an idea for you. Tell Lionel to fuck off and get off the plane then. We can both forget about this."

He's wearing probably the most serious expression he has, and for a moment I consider it. We kissed in the closet—then I pretended to be asleep so he could spoon me last night. Things are awkward today. I really don't want to have the temptation of him all day, every day, for over three weeks. But the money could get me independence and Magnolia a secure future.

"I won't back out. I signed a paper. Like I told you, I'm poor and purchasable," I grumble.

"Then I'm disappointed. If anyone seems unconcerned with worldly goods and the mundane, it's you."

"Spoken like a douche bag who swims in dollars."

He lifts his whiskey to his lips, and I realize he's holding out another glass for me. I take it from his grip, making sure our fingers don't touch. He lifts one finger, though, as if to purposely make sure we *do.*

I scowl. He smiles. As if he knows that little touch sent a current racing through my bloodstream, vein to capillary.

On the other side of the plane, Lionel stares at me like he's seriously in love with me, and then, unfortunately, the plane starts moving. I have no idea how long it takes the pill to kick in, but I better down it. I'm so nervous, my body feels charged and buzzy.

My dad. I imagine him in a seat like this one. He was flying back home under perfect conditions, and he never arrived. I was staring at my homework when we got the call.

"Want to talk about it?" Mackenna asks.

"Not with you," I mumble, grabbing and skimming through a catalogue before jamming it back into the pocket of the seat in front of me. I wish Mackenna would go away right now, when I'm not at my best. "Please go away," I breathe.

"Please just let me be here for you," he says. There's no mockery in his voice. Nothing but sincerity in his eyes.

The fortress guarding my emotions goes rubbery, and this frightens me so much, I nearly beg, "No, you. Please. Go away."

We engage in a staring contest.

For a moment I think I'm going to lose.

Then he murmurs, "You can count on me, Pandora."

Before I can remind him why I don't anymore, he unlatches his seat belt, and I want to take it back when he stands up and crosses the aisle to another seat.

This is why they say you have to be careful what you wish for.

I mourn the loss of human life next to me the instant he's gone. Not human life—him. The loss of his challenging, exciting, and infuriating presence.

He knows how my father died. How he was on business and the plane just crashed. Like in a movie, and in your worst nightmare. He'd been with his assistant. Not on business. I lost my father the same day my mother realized he'd betrayed her. Betrayed us.

With another woman.

I couldn't mourn, because my mother felt I was betraying her. Because he'd betrayed her. The only emotion she was okay with me feeling was *anger*. If I started to get a trembly chin, my mother would snap, "Don't you dare cry over him! Look at how he left me! Look how he abandoned us!" And so I always made sure I snapped my mouth shut and never did cry. Anger was safe. I was allowed anger. Lots of it. And when Mackenna left me too, it became all I knew.

The nerves have my senses hyperaware as the plane turns to takeoff position. I hear every sound of the engines roaring, the clink of ice in Mackenna's glass several seats away. His smell lingers in the empty seat, strangely comforting me.

I pop the pill into my mouth, grab the whiskey glass, and down it.

One cameraman is up in front, watching me, moving his camera. I swallow and stare out the window, my nails digging into my seat as the plane positions itself on the edge of the runway. I feel the camera on me when I hear a voice murmur, "Give her a fucking break and aim that somewhere else," and then I feel the lean, hard body of Mackenna plopping down next to me.

"Suppose it does fall," he says.

"Excuse me?" I sputter.

"Suppose the plane can't lift and falls." He cocks an eyebrow at me.

I glare at him, and he remains sober, his eyes roaming my face. "I wouldn't mind dying today."

"I would. My father died this way. It's my worst death imaginable."

"Worst death would be alone, with no one to even listen to your last words. Or drowning, that could—"

"SHUT UP!"

He stretches out his hand. "Take my hand, Pink."

"Thanks, but no."

"Fine. Thumb wars?"

"God, you're such a baby."

"You're a coward. Come on, fucking use me for something. Want to fight? Fine. Want to hold my hand? Even better. Not sure? I bet you can't pin my thumb under yours no matter what you do."

Gritting my teeth, I clutch his hand, because I know—and he knows—I desperately need the contact. A frisson runs through my body, and I wish I had the strength to deny him, but I'm shaking. And he looks strong. Like nothing can touch him.

My boyfriend.

My ex.

The only guy I've ever had sex with. Ever wanted. Ever loved.

He holds my wrist and tugs. "Come closer," he urges. The tenderness in his eyes makes the walls around my heart wobble.

"What? We're playing with our thumbs, not our tongues," I say defensively.

"Really now." He smiles again, the smile tender. Even his hold on my arm, his whispered voice, sounds tender. "Come closer, Pink."

I narrow my eyes and move closer.

He presses my thumb underneath his, and I realize he was tricking me. He chuckles wickedly, and I can't even protest, because the plane is taking off. I suck in a breath and glance out the window at the ground speeding beneath us. For a couple of minutes I try to calm down, but it's near impossible. Mackenna's hand is still on mine, but instead of squishing my thumb, he's rubbing it.

And it feels so wrong and right and deep in me and soft over me that I could probably stand the plane falling right now, but I can't stand his hand on mine.

"Let go," I say.

He lets go, and an odd glimmer of pity or sadness passes his face. "Just relax," he says.

I squeeze my eyes shut. His voice does things to me. He groans and says, "Come here, baby."

"The wolf says to the lamb. Don't call me baby," I whisper and refuse to obey, tucking my hand under my thigh. I'm acutely aware of every inch that separates us.

He leans over. "You're anything but a lamb."

Our eyes meet and everything about him, from his voice to his scent to his eyes, unsettles me to the point where I want to cry or scream.

The plane jolts again, and a couple of nasty clouds are coming toward us. My eyes blur, and everything in my body presses into the hollow in my tummy. I'm tense as I grip the seat, praying for the clonazepam to take effect. If it weren't for Magnolia, I might not give a shit about dying. But aside from Mom, I'm all she has. And Mom is . . . *Mom*.

Mackenna's glass is refilled. I watch his hand every time he lifts it, sips, and drops it. His fingers are magical. He once played the piano like the keys were an extension of his fingers, but right now, he's a rocker dude. He's always been bad, but he is a real guy with a real love of music and sound.

The pill starts taking effect and my eyes flutter shut. I make sure to slide my head to the opposite side of where he sits.

He says nothing.

As my head starts getting fuzzy, I cuddle to the window, trying to make sure my shoulder doesn't touch his.

I remember stealing out to see him every afternoon. It didn't matter that my mother worked for the DA. It didn't matter that his father was a criminal. We were both in the courtroom that day, and I was already half crazy in love with him—unbeknownst to me, to my mother, or to him.

I insisted on going to court with my mother that day, telling her simply that I felt like going. She eyed me warily but could not deny me. I sat outside on a long bench, with him close. I had heard that his father was going to be given many, many years for dealing.

Maybe I shouldn't have slid up to sit closer to him the day they set bail. We could've been seen, but I couldn't help it. He was sitting there, looking at his hands, when his father and my mother were at it inside.

"I'm sorry," I said.

"Me too," he said.

He lifted his head, and I could feel him looking at me as intensely as if I was burning. I reached out to take his hand.

And that was all that we needed.

He'd defended me from bullies at school, and now I held his hand whenever we were alone. That day we were alone in an empty hall on a single bench, and the boy I couldn't stop thinking about was ready to hear how much his father would have to pay to remain free until the trial date.

"Meet me at the docks where we met last time," he said to me, squeezing my hand just as the courtroom doors swung open.

With a quick nod, I pried my hand free.

My mother walked out and called me back to her with a clear, crisp, lawyerly command. I felt him watch me—lonely, motherless, and, soon, fatherless—from that bench as they took his father away from him until he made bail. My mother said once the trial took place and his dad was convicted, Mackenna would be taken in by some uncle who was just as bad a gangster as the father and that soon, he'd probably be an outcast in school and would have to move.

It seemed like my mother was a witch. Everything she predicted came true.

But before he left, and between bail and trial, he was *mine*.

For days, weeks, months, he was all mine and I was his.

Sometimes, when I walked home from school, he walked with me. All my bullies mysteriously got purple eyes. When my mother saw him one day, she pulled me aside. "He's up to no good, that boy. Revenge, that's what that boy is up for. You stay away from him, Pandora."

"He's not," I kept telling my mother.

But how could she understand? She didn't see Mackenna and his remote, sad eyes. So sad even the silver turned to gray sometimes.

She didn't know that nobody else had told him they were sorry for him. She didn't know that when I kept going to "study" at other people's houses, I really was going to meet Mackenna. She didn't know how we talked, how we laughed. Sometimes we just sat by each other, doing nothing. Sometimes all I was aware of was the position of my hand and how it was in relation to the position of his hand. Sometimes all I knew was the sound of his voice—despite whatever words it said. Sometimes I caught him staring too. At my mouth. My boobs. Sometimes we went to the marina and stole a boat at night. We'd take a dip in the chilly water, and when we came up to the boat, we'd take off our clothes and warm each other.

He'd saved me in school. Now it felt like I was saving him.

He told me he loved me, and I wanted to say it back. But in all our time together, I never said it. He showed that he loved me in little things he did for me: carrying my stuff when no one noticed, quietly following me after school, sometimes waiting outside my house, in the rain, until I could sneak away for another moment with him. Maybe I was his source of compassion, and he couldn't stand anyone hurting or touching me.

My mother didn't know that long before the trial, I'd begged Mackenna to have sex with me.

He promised it would happen the following weekend. It did, and it was magical. He took me to the wharf, where we stole past the guards and into a hidden nook under the Ferris wheel. We climbed into one of the cabins, he spread out some blankets, and we made love.

He said he loved me. He asked if I loved him. I did. I really did. He made me tear up. I felt so beautiful, treasured, so *perfect*.

We kept meeting. Always in secret. Every time it was even better. Better than perfect. He hummed songs to me in his deep voice. At school, we'd have foreplay with our eyes, and then we'd touch each other at night.

Then the trial happened, and soon he didn't come back to school.

But our plan still stood. After the trial, we'd run away.

Except he never showed up.

I even went to look for him at his uncle's house, but he wasn't there. Two older women were in his bed. "You looking for Kenna?" they asked.

I swallowed, wondering if they'd touched him, and if they hadn't, where he was.

"He's gone. Took a flight to Boston. One way. He said he sent you a message."

"He lied. He didn't send me shit."

I ran, and ran, and when I got home, I locked myself in my room and went to pull out my box and tear up every picture of me with that lying, mean, cruel fucking asshole.

Nothing survived, except for that stupid pebble in that box from the time when he told me not to trip again.

Aren't I tripping with the same pebble now?

I've told myself that it's not like I remember. His hands. His lips. Our first kiss. He used to get so jealous about me.

One day, before Mackenna asked me to be his official girlfriend, we were arguing about Wes Rosberg. "He's taking you out?" Mackenna asked, his eyebrows furrowing over his nose. "Where's he taking you out? Why'd you say yes? I thought you didn't like him?"

"He's just a friend," I said, shrugging.

He shoved to his feet. "Oh, yeah? What if he wants to have a girlfriend?"

I shrugged again. "Well, maybe I would like to have a boyfriend."

"I want to be your boyfriend."

"What?"

"You heard me. I want to be your boyfriend."

"Kenna! Get over here!" a voice yells from somewhere in the background, bringing me to the present. Hearing the rumble of his voice under my ear, I'm momentarily confused.

"I'm a bit busy here."

Jokes, laughter, and bad words are exchanged, and I can hear his chuckle.

Under. My. Ear.

He's eased his seat back and lifted the armrest, and his arm is around my waist. My brain is dazed as I try to understand why my ear is on Mackenna's chest, and why his hand is spread wide and big across the small of my back. Conveniently my top is raised. Or did he raise it? His thumb ring is on my skin, tracing little circles over the dent of my spine.

I feel a pressure between my legs as I struggle with this realization, but I'm so drugged I can't even open my mouth. Am I dreaming?

When the twins come over to engage in a discussion with him, Mackenna shifts his body and stretches beneath me, muscles rippling under my body, then he slides his hand from the small of my back up and up, to my nape, then up, to cup my ear. His husky voice is low, as if he doesn't want to wake me while the guys discuss a party tonight.

"She coming?" I hear the muffled question.

"Obviously," Mackenna rumbles. They laugh. I can still hear him under my ear. Between my legs, I tingle harder.

"Might not be such a good idea. The girls are plotting her murder."

"Bah. This one could chew them up and spit them out," Mackenna says.

I can't figure out if he's insulting me or not. Is he taking my side instead of his floozies'? Something inside me feels warm, but I quell it. It's been too long since we were friends. Sure, we had a closet make-out, but that was crazy. Lunacy. An animal moment. Currently, I'm too weak to fight the pull of his hand. I can't get up, but the fact that I'm right here doesn't mean we're okay.

I drift off again, thinking about his name. His name means "son of the handsome one." I looked it up when I was young because everyone made fun of *my* name.

I'm familiar with Pandora and her mistake—letting all kinds of bad shit into the world when she opened the box. I've always been at war with my name. I'm angry at it because, right away, it makes me think I can never be really good. I'm a jinx. I cause bad shit and represent nothing lucky, I suppose. But him? He's this rock god. *Son of the handsome one.* All my feelings return to my body in a flash when I realize he's brushing his mouth over mine.

What's he doing? Stop him!

My body seizes as my brain shouts the command, and I make an inventory check and hear plane motors. He's tonguing me now. I feel his tongue in my body, a body that was last used by him. And his mouth was last used by me.

I want to get angry, but I'm too busy lying here, absorbing this kiss that's almost like the kiss in all Magnolia's fairy tales. She doesn't believe in fairy tales, she says, but the truth is, I do. Now Mackenna is the villain in my story and the reason I should've become a lesbian. If only my body had gone along with the plot.

But now he's kissing me like he's enjoying me. He probably got horny and decided I was handy. I stiffen at the thought and try to pull away, when a hand cradles the back of my head to prevent me. He whispers, "Shh. I'm just tasting you." Languorously, he fits his lips harder to mine, his mouth moving.

"You need to drug your women to kiss them," I slur as he continues rubbing his tongue to mine.

"Just the wild ones like you," he gruffly teases.

I cannot process. I cannot control myself when he teases me—I've always liked it because it makes me smile, and I never smile. He tastes good, like whiskey and lazy, cocky male. I never thought lazy, cocky male could taste so good, or that being relaxed would make me savor lazy, cocky male even better than when I am on full alert. I can't comprehend what's going on. The things awakening in my body. The hole in my chest suddenly feeling full.

Protests form in my brain, but they don't reach my tongue because his slick, warm, whiskey mouth is caressing it.

He's toxic for me, and I can't pull away. Instead, I'm rubbing my tongue against his slowly, savoring him. When I tell myself, *Enough!* and edge back, he follows me and croons, "Shh, relax your mouth, baby. Let me in."

He shifts so I can feel it—the bulge between his legs. I suddenly want it feverishly, but to my despair, I hear snickering. Then I hear him ask the flight attendant for a blanket. I didn't even realize they still had those, but I feel him cover me. The drug is still heavy in my system and I try to open my eyes, but before I can look into his face, his lips cover mine. "How could I forget for a moment what you tasted like . . . how addictive you are . . . ," he whispers to me. He's devouring me with lazy abandon. He cups one breast under the blanket. I don't know what I'm doing.

Yes I do.

No I don't.

Yes I do.

My mouth is moving faster, and his rhythm matches mine as he thumbs one nipple. Years of repressed longing seem to flood my body and energize my mouth. Nothing has ever tasted as good as him. Nothing.

The way he felt last night crashes over me, and suddenly I'm the one kissing him back with abandon. He groans. The sound reverberates inside me. "God, that's right. Want me, Pink? Want this? Fuck the rest. Let's have fun. Just you and me."

His voice jerks me back to the present.

Fun?

The pain of losing him hits me full force.

Using all the force I can muster, I edge back, wiping my mouth angrily. He looks at me and blinks as if dazed from our kiss, and we both survey each other's mouths. He looks openly ravenous, but I'm still trying to decide how I feel. Trying to find my usual anger.

"The cameras just caught that," I say.

"Yeah, couldn't be helped." He eyes my mouth again, smirking in obvious satisfaction. "You were too tempting, Pink. You smell like fucking coconut, and I haven't smelled that in years."

I scowl. "You're just a pervert posing as a rockstar to hide your love of bras."

We land. I try to reach upward for my carry-on, but he takes care of it for me. His T-shirt lifts as he pulls our shit out of the top compartment, and I can see his abs and the tattoo on the inside of his arm. It says something I don't understand.

"What does that tattoo mean?"

He quirks one eyebrow and says nothing as his eyes move to my mouth. "Says I'm a dickhead. You know, if that mouth doesn't look well kissed, then my name is not Mackenna."

I'm waiting for the indignation to come, but I'm still so relaxed, it doesn't.

"Fuck you. You're lying. What does it say?"

He smiles, because he clearly won't tell me. Then he surprises me by leaning over and tipping my face with his curled thumb, his silver ring cold under my chin. "I may not have been good enough when we were seventeen," he whispers, holding my eyes with a pair of wolfish ones that shine with an arresting intensity, "but trust me, I'm good enough now, Pink. I'm *more* than good enough."

"You're wrong," I whisper angrily. "Money. Fame. That has nothing to do with it. You were good enough before, but you're certainly not good enough now."

"Look at you spitting fire like some angry little crow. How many fucking pills do you need to take to chill?"

"One, actually. You're the antidote."

I brush past him and out of the plane, feeling him amble behind me. I know he's close when camera flashes at the arrival gate start exploding and girls start screaming, "*Crack Bikini!* Kenna! Lex! Jax!"

Lex and Jax were in some private school, and they met Mackenna when he moved. Supposedly the twins liked pissing off their rich dad, and nobody pissed off Dad more than a guy like Mackenna.

Mackenna Jones was rumored to have been on a suicide mission. He smoked whatever he felt like, drank, played loud music, made a mess, didn't study. He also did extreme sports, and he beat people up. After his dad was convicted for drug trafficking, his uncle took him in, but he was no better. Judging by Mackenna's lifestyle, it'll be a miracle if he lives to his fifties.

Crack Bikini was present at a bar fight years ago, and a reporter at the time managed to capture a quote, a quote that has since become famous—or infamous.

"What is this? This a fight?" Mackenna reportedly asked.

"Yeah," someone said. "Don't know whose."

Mackenna grinned, a little mayhem clearly making his heart happy. "Well, it's mine now." He whistled to the Vikings, and they jumped right in, not even caring who or what the fuck they were fighting for.

Now they're older, but I'm not sure they're that much more mature. That is, until a crying woman makes Mackenna stop in his tracks.

"Thank you. Thank you, oh, thank you," she says, reaching out to him as though to touch a vision. I'm stunned when he pauses, confused, and takes her hand. "Nothing in my life has inspired me like your music, hearing your voice turns my day around . . ."

It's almost too intimate to watch. I ease back as I hear him whisper something to her and sign the paper she extends. His eyes shine with sincerity. He's not being an asshole, like he's supposed to be. He looks . . . genuine. His smile is natural, his eyes are on her as he gives her some line that makes her beam and blush.

Again my walls tilt a little. Even the floor seems to tilt.

When he pries himself away from the crowd and heads toward me, he lifts one of his eyebrows.

"What? Nothing prickly to say?"

"No." I walk silently next to him. His actions have touched

places I never expected. I open my mouth and hear myself admitting, "It must be nice to make a difference in someone's life."

He stares straight ahead and keeps his voice low while the camera crew follows the entire band and the bodyguards struggle to keep the fans at bay. "It used to be what fed me . . ."

"But?"

"But it stopped filling me up and started draining me instead. Pretty soon you're walking with a hole in your gut, singing songs you can't hear anymore."

I remain quiet, a strange hurt inside me. I want it to be easy to blame him for leaving me, but he had a dream to chase and I couldn't expect to be his everything. I want to hate him because he hurt me, but he seems so human that I can't do anything but stay quiet and absorb the way he's making me feel right now.

The way his silver eyes look almost warm, an impossibility due to their shade alone, but they do. Warm, liquid, molten silver eyes looking at me as if he wants me to understand. "They all think it's about the sex and the booze. It's not." He drags a hand over the top of his head. "It's about the loneliness of the road. The girls, the sex. The clusterfuck of singing what you feel but having no one to fill the void, and the ache of wanting to feel something."

He stuns me speechless.

I curl my hands at my sides to keep from reaching out as he waits for a reply. I can tell he wants some understanding from me, for he smiles and laughs. "All right. Nice chatting with you."

I want to hug him so bad. If he were a little smaller, I would. If he seemed a little tamer, I swear I would.

But he isn't small, or tame.

The energy around us crackles like a live wire as he waits for me to do—to say—something. Anything. I want to be his friend, to have the sort of relationship where I might high-five my ex-boyfriend. But fat chance that's going to happen. It's like the

Berlin Wall is between us, and even if he wants to let me into his own walls, I'm not dropping my own ever again. So I say nothing and just nod, wryly saying, "Nice chatting with you too."

He laughs to himself, a laugh that actually lacks happiness, and whispers, "You're unbelievable." He winds away, leaving me with a sick feeling in my stomach. I am alone, but maybe I've wanted that. I've been surrounded by people, but I've let no one in, and despite his fame, maybe he's alone too. I judge him because I hate him, but what do I know of what he goes through?

What has he been through in the last six years that I don't know?

Whatever it was, it wasn't what you went through when he left you. . . .

Angry all over again, I stand and try to quell it as Mackenna waves a peace sign out to Lionel. "Be back at the hotel later," he yells.

Lionel nods and turns to offer an explanation to the nearest camera. "Going to see his dad."

"His dad is in jail," I blurt out.

"Not anymore. He's out and living in the vicinity."

At my blank look—I thought he'd gotten almost twenty years?—Lionel walks over to me. "You don't look so good."

"I medicate to fly."

"Oh. Well then, you can ride to the hotel with me."

"Wow, thanks for the respite."

"Miss Stone," he says. "Tomorrow the director and I would like for the choreographer to see you. We'd like you to learn one of the dances—the one where he sings your song. Our plan for the Madison Square Garden concert is for you to wear a mask and dance with Olivia, then remove it at the end of the dance so he realizes it's you—then you'll kiss him."

"You're kidding." I gape. "I don't dance!"

"As of tomorrow, you do. You signed a contract."

"It didn't say I was going to—"

"It said you were to follow our guidance and support the filming in any capacity we saw fit. Trenton and I see fit that you dance, with Olivia, around Jones. Be ready by morning."

EIGHT

THE PAST DOESN'T ALWAYS STAY IN ITS PLACE

Mackenna

Father looks a hundred if he looks a day. He's just ditched the supermarket and now clambers over to where I stand with my hands jammed into the pockets of my jeans. "Hey, Dad. You look beat."

Dad grumbles something under his breath. "Packing vegetables all day. It's killed my soul, it has," he complains as we walk to the corner cafe.

"Hey, it's honest work. *Honest*," I emphasize.

The guy used to give me a good life. Anything I wanted. I can give that life to myself now, and to him. Any guy worth his salt has gotta take care of his folks.

"See, Dad? Good view. We can eat here without you having to lift a finger, not even for the check."

He looks at me, and I pull something from my pocket. "Speaking of checks." I hand it over to him, a check for a hundred thousand. "I'm not sure if I'll be back to visit you until we're done with the movie. But I'm trying. I'm trying to get time out to spend with you."

"Why the fuck you'd want to do that?"

As if on cue, people start whispering and pointing at me, and for the next half hour I'm signing autographs on my table. By the time I'm done, my meal is cold. I push it away and tell him, "Let's get out of here."

We ride to his apartment in the hotel car that brought me here. The apartment is a place a guy who bags groceries could not afford, but he's my dad. He wouldn't let me get him anything near to what we used to live in, but this place was a compromise that both of us were comfortable with. He's been laying off the booze, drugs, everything that used to make him a miniature Wolf of Wall Street back in Seattle.

"How the mighty have fallen," he mumbles as he watches me look at his place.

"You weren't mighty." I laugh and slap his back. "And you fell. But the point is you stood up. That's how a man measures himself, right?"

"I'm standing only because of you, otherwise I'd still be in that . . ." His mind drifts off, and I can only wonder what horrors he saw there, in jail.

"Dad, do you remember the girl . . . the one I used to like?"

"Like?" He snorts. "Mild word for what that was."

"You remember her?"

"The daughter of that fucking DA? Of course I remember."

"She's with the group now. Leo wants her in the movie." I scrape one hand down my face. I don't expect any advice, but I guess I just had to talk to someone about her. Someone who'd take it seriously. Not Jax or Lex, who find it amusing, or Lionel, who finds it financially wise. Dad finds it serious. He scowls and explodes.

"Stay away from her, Kenna! She broke you once."

"She didn't fucking break me," I scoff.

"The day you came to see me in prison telling me you were no good for her . . . I don't ever want to see that hurting boy again. Ever. Joneses don't do that."

My pride rears up in me with the urge to defend myself, but I got nothing. Because she did break me. I flex my jaw.

"You still like her," he gasps.

"Purely sexual. I plan to bang her brains out 'til she can't walk. Hell, you can't blame me for that!"

He looks at me like he can see right through me, and with the worst expression possible in his eyes.

Pity.

"I'm sorry, son. I know you lost her because of me."

"Never lost her. Never had her to lose her, really." I shrug and stare outside, my mind in the past.

Is this a promise ring?

What are you promising me?

Me.

Fuck, we were so stupid.

What did I think I was promising her? My dad was being tried for dozens of counts of drug trafficking. I had nothing to give her but that ring and a promise she ended up flinging back in my face.

I swing around then. "But that's over. We're making changes, you and I. You're becoming a better man. Let the good things in, right?"

With a dreary sigh, he drops down on a couch and signals to his surroundings. "Don't know, son. Not sure this life of honesty is for me. It's so fucking boring."

"Dad, you be honorable. Let the good in. All right? I'm fucking proud of you, Dad, I really am." I go slap his back, and he snorts and continues scowling like I'm asking him to shovel shit for the rest of his life.

"I'll tell you what," he then says, pointing at me. "I will let the good in, embrace this life of honor . . . *if* you work her out of your system, then forget you ever laid eyes on her. You want me to stay clear of dealing? Then you stay clear of toxic girls like her. No fucking DA's daughter bitch is gonna break my son's heart twice. No such thing as love, remember that. The only love I've ever known . . ." He trails off as he looks straight at me. ". . . was my son's love." His eyes go red, and, like a pansy, I can't take it.

"Be good, Dad. I'll try to visit when the tour's over. I'm working on Leo to get some time off. We can hang."

"No such thing as love—remember that! At least, no such thing as a woman's love."

I stand by the door, battling with myself. Battling with the memory of a girl, and an angry woman who wants me inside her like she needs to breathe—even if she hates her body for wanting me.

No such thing as love . . .

"I'm a rockstar, Dad," I say, the words bitter in my mouth. "Clearly, I sing about that shit because I believe in it. I just don't believe in it for me."

Outside, though, I'm morose as shit as I pull my cap over my face, slide on my aviators, and slip into the back of the waiting car.

I drum my fingers on my thigh and stare out at the windows of all the buildings outside.

I used to climb to her bedroom window. It's not as simple as it looks in the movies, but I managed. One particular night, I'd wound through the thorny, spiky bush, up the damn trellis, onto the window ledge, then up to her window—which had the tiniest fucking ledge in the history of ledges—hanging by one arm and knocking until she opened. Then I swept inside, both of us plucking the thorns from my T-shirt.

"Fucking bush," I growled.

"Shhhh," she said as she ran to check the lock on her door. "What are you doing here?"

"Can't sleep. Dad's drinking. Breaking whatever the hell's left. Wanted a look at you." I take her in and holy shit, I never thought she slept in that sort of sleep gear. Tiny shorts. Loose T-shirt hanging over one shoulder.

"And you came to me because . . . you needed a teddy bear?" she asked. "If I were ever to be considered a bear, I'd be more like a grizzly."

"Then, Grizzly, you'll have to do." I kicked off my shoes and slid into her bed, pulling her in with me.

She laughed lightly and tried to stifle the sound. She never laughs, this girl, but she laughs—with me.

"I couldn't sleep either," she whispered suddenly up at me, tracing circles on my forearm. Right where I have my tattoo now. Fuck, she killed me. She's always been a closed little box, Pandora, and not prone to saying much at all about how she feels. She can be bleeding to death and be asked if she's in pain, and this girl? She'd probably shrug even when it's killing her.

I get her. Somehow, I get her. And she gets me. That night, I clutched her tight, and within seconds, she dozed off in my arms. She used to trust me enough to do that. Lie asleep, pressed close to me. I set my phone alarm for 5 a.m. so her mother wouldn't catch us. Then I stared at her ceiling and wondered if she thought of me whenever she stared up at that twirling fan. Or if she thought of me at all the way I thought of her when in bed.

My mother died when I was just three. I remember how she

smelled, and felt, but not her face. I kind of hate that I can't remember her face. Hate even more the fact that my father didn't cope well and got rid of any pictures before I had a say in it.

When my dad was caught dealing, the government was quick to take the cars, the house. We moved in with Uncle Tom until the trial, and he was worse than Dad. Alcohol is all the man knew. My friends? Interesting to see how they scattered once my dad's face was plastered on the evening news.

In a day I went from being the most popular little shit in private school to being the loner at the table. Everything, poof, in the wink of an eye.

It felt surreal. Unreal.

Couldn't sleep, eat, because I somehow knew what would happen next.

I dreaded it, even while I waited for the last shoe to drop. That last drop to spill the glass of water that would drown me. Tighten the last fucking notch of a noose that hanged me. I kept waiting for the one thing I had left—the one I most wanted—to go poof as well.

When your life does a one-eighty on you, you develop fears. And I feared losing her more than I feared anything. Hell, I feared I already had.

At 5:02 a.m. I hadn't had a wink of sleep, but there she was, and all I wanted was to make sure she was there for me. Digging into my pocket, I curled my fingers around my mother's ring. The only thing I could save. Because I'd hid it. Legally, I shouldn't even have had the ring. But it was all I had of my mother, and I wanted my girl to have it. The next day I took her out to the docks and gave it to her before we left the yacht we stole into.

The way she'd kissed me . . .

Guess every time she kissed me back like that, I kidded myself that she loved me too.

One day, months later, the day after Dad was sentenced, it happened.

I found out that the girl I wanted to love me like I wanted to breathe . . . could never be for me.

I had to go. I left, hating every step I took.

No booze, no prostitute, no girl, nothing could numb me enough for me to stop, just fucking stop, needing her.

Not even a song.

Drunk, I poured it out months later, needing to blame someone for my shitty life. So I blamed the source of my pain. And my new friends, the Vikings? Hell, they embraced the anger in it, the irony of mixing it with Mozart. I sing it now, every day it seems, and I could sing it a million times more, but I still won't believe that I wouldn't kill for her to love me.

For a fucking minute.

A second even.

To just give me a fucking kiss and tell me that at least back in those days, she loved me.

NINE

DANCING TO THEIR TUNE

Pandora

I wake up early, and the choreographer waits for me in the hotel ballroom, along with eleven other dancers. Letitta is also there, watching with a smirk as I come in. I'm coffee-less, humorless, and sleepless. I don't even smirk back.

I got no sleep last night. I kept expecting you-know-who to come to my bed. No, not expecting. Almost . . . anticipating. Sad, but true. I kept remembering when we were seventeen, and he used to slip up the trellis into my room, and I'd be waiting— pretending I *wasn't* waiting—my heart leaping when he tapped lightly on the window. I'd let him in in a hurry, and he'd take off his shirt, his shoes, slipping into bed with me with just his jeans on, and I'd smell him and press close, wanting to say that since my dad died he'd been the only one able to make me forget the pain. Wanting to tell him that it hurt to know my mom was, day and night, preparing her case to take his dad away from him too . . .

"It's all right, he did it to himself," he whispered when I told him I was sorry, again. But he sounded sad. How could he *not* be sad?

And then I'd fall asleep, even as I fought not to, too comfortable with his smell, and warmth, and the way he stroked his hand long and lazy down my back. Then I'd wake alone, seeing the dent in his pillow and the slightly open window where he'd slipped out, just in time before my mother came to wake me for school.

"Close the window, it's chilly!" she'd scold.

"You're like a grandma already," I'd grumble.

"That is *so* disrespectful, Pandora."

"I'm sorry," I'd mumble and disappear into the shower, letting the water run over my body, already loathing the day ahead. I knew what would happen, because the same had happened yesterday, and the day before that too.

I'd see Mackenna from afar. He'd look at me too. We'd pretend we hadn't just held hands, or slept with my body twined like a pretzel around his long, ever-growing one. I'd hang out with my tiny circle of friends, feeling him guarding me like a wolf from the table crowded with wannabes, but after the hearing, only the real rebels with troubled families hung out with him. They all waited for his dad's trial and sentence—but Kenna?

Kenna had already been "tried" by everyone in school. Everyone but me. We'd pass each other in the hall, both of us straining to bump shoulders.

We'd go late to class, our methods different every time. Sometimes he'd tie his shoelaces at a tortoise's pace as the halls emptied. Other times, I'd drop my books at the exact moment he passed so he could drop to his haunches close to me and slip my books into my backpack. It was stupid, really, but the day was torture if I didn't exchange at least one word. One word, with him. "Hey," he'd say softly, only one side of his mouth smiling.

"Hey. Thanks," I'd say, when really I meant, *I want to be with you.*

And his silver eyes would say in quiet frustration, "Why can't I fucking be with you?"

Every couple walking down the halls holding hands killed me. I'd never miss the clench of his jaw, the coiled energy as I knew he wondered why we couldn't have that. "My mother," I'd explain. She wouldn't understand. She'd been watching me like a hawk since she'd seen him walk me home. My mother would ruin it all.

"Yeah, I know, I'm just frustrated," he'd whisper in my ear, his breath like a soft wind as he hung my backpack over my shoulder and rubbed his thumb on the skin where my T-shirt pulled, stealing that touch . . . and my heart with it. "Come to me tonight," I blurted out.

"Always," he said.

Always . . .

Six years—a little more, actually—and I still remember that *Always.* How, when he became aroused, his eyes—sometimes without warning: over a look, a smile, a brush, a pair of shorts I wore—looked like dirty silver, and I could never again look at dirty silver without a pang in my chest. Mackenna isn't that boy anymore. And I'm not that girl, waiting in my bed, eagerly watching my window. But last night, I felt very much like her.

I felt exactly like her. Eager, hopeful, scared to be hopeful. Vulnerable.

He's been the most powerful source of pain in my life, and my survival instinct rears up stronger than ever when he's near. Every part of him is a threat—his voice, his kiss, our past, my own heart. I was so sure I'd gotten rid of my heart, but he makes me so aware that it's still here, inside me somewhere. It's alive when he's near, and it screams, *"Danger . . . "*

Now I'm grumpy because he didn't seek me out, like I—even if I hate myself for wishing it—still wished he would.

He's managed to make me restless, to the point where I considered taking my clonazepam at midnight. But I only have two more pills, and what if we need to fly again? I'd die of cardiac arrest, if the stupid plane didn't fall on its own.

Groggily I pour a steaming cup of coffee from a small buffet table on the side, sipping it as I study the two girls at the front of the room. One dark-haired, and one blonde.

Tit and Olivia.

Oh, yes. They're like ringleaders, those two. I can recognize them instantly.

Tit is the blonde, not natural blonde like Melanie is, but a salon blonde with dark eyebrows. Olivia is dark-haired, almost like me, but her face is rounder and her expression, I guess . . . softer. But the look in her eyes? Nothing soft about that.

I meet her gaze square on, because you can't ever look away from bullies. I practiced this to perfection when my father died and my mother intimidated me, and at school, where I was laughed at until Mackenna made sure I wasn't laughed at again.

Now a dozen twenty-year-olds look at me like I'm bound to be their entertainment for the day. The choreographer claps her hands to pull every dancer's eye from me over to her.

"My name is Yolanda," she tells me. "And I'm in charge of getting you to move that body as if you've trained professionally your whole life. Not an easy task, so I warn you, your baths? Should be ice cold after this. You will never in your life be as stiff as a two-by-four and as awkward as a newborn giraffe. You will stretch with us now, and watch, and learn!" She snaps her fingers, and the other dancers start to stretch. Olivia seems impressed I'm even trying to stretch. Can I touch my toes? No. I'm as unbending as a stick, and I almost grunt as I keep trying.

"Gently! Or you pull and break the muscle and it's no use to us!" Yolanda chides.

She's Latin-blooded—I can tell by the passion in her voice and her thick accent. Her body is beautiful, with perfect curves in all the right places. The other dancers' clothes cling to their beautiful bodies. Unlike mine. I'm a bit too flat-chested, and my ass could use a little meat too. I don't have many curves. I do have big nipples that poke out too much, calling way too much attention to themselves, which is why I'm actually glad my boobs are small.

The outfit I'm wearing, sent to my room on behalf of Lionel, doesn't really help my small boobs and small ass.

Trying not to watch myself in the mirror too much—and therefore avoiding a reminder of *just* how flat-chested I am—I make my way to the center. Yolanda calls me over.

"You. You and Olivia are both choreographed differently than the others. Pretend I'm Jones. Now you walk up to me, your moves sensual. Hypnotic. Sexy. Make contact with your inner mermaids . . ."

I feel stupid. Ridiculous. But I try to walk with a little sway of my hips. I hear snorts all around and I stop and scowl, swinging my scowl across the room so every woman here gets the full blast of my displeasure.

"Ignore . . . *girls*!" she chides, clapping, then to me, "Now . . . sensual. Not so stiff. Like making love. You will make love to Jones with your clothes on, onstage. Everybody wants Jones. Imagine his body, moving sinuously against yours. Mackenna Jones has the best moves—Magic Mike has nothing on him. Are you prepared?" She reaches around me and grabs the small of my back, undulating her body against mine.

Our tits are pressing. She's pretending to be Mackenna and looking at me with an expression I believe she believes is Mackenna's. Just thinking about being like this, in front of an audience, makes me want to gag. "I can't—"

"CAN'T! That word does not exist here. We are all doers here. Now circle your hips. Hands on waist. Side to side, front, back, side to side. Just loosen it up!" She goes to turn on the music while all the other dancers stretch and I'm humping the air like a ridiculous little shit. "Good!" she praises. "Very good! Now add your arms . . . circle them to the side . . . up above . . . loosen that stiff little body of yours."

We're dancing to the group's song, and the music starts reverberating in me. The girls swing their heads, and I pull my hair loose and follow suit, going up to Yolanda and rubbing my hands up her sides.

I am suddenly skating, my feet in charge under me, and Mackenna's hands are on my waist, and I know he'll catch me. If I fall, it's not embarrassing but an excuse to get him to touch me and hear his low, rumbling laugh. I like when he laughs. I like his chuckle, how he picks me up, dusts my ass with his gloves, kisses me on the cheek in case anybody recognizes us, and whispers, "Enough?"

And I say, "Never!"

And he spins me like a top with another, deeper laugh, and pulls me down the rink, skating close to him. Suddenly dancing is not that different. I'm swept by the music, following the lead of the girl in front of me, letting my legs repeat the steps I'm shown, my hands moving and tracing my imaginary man. Yolanda silences her instructions as I start rocking, losing myself, picturing the way Mackenna had been up on stage with the two women. Now the one right in front of him will be me.

Reminding him what we had.

This is what you want, remember? Make him lose it. Remind him of the girl he used to skate with. The one he used to twirl around like a top. Remind him that she's gone to him. Gone because . . . HE left HER.

She loved him and he LEFT her.

Make him regret walking. Without a word, or a goodbye, or an "I'm sorry," or a reason . . .

The thought only invigorates me, and I'm still shaking my little ass seconds after the song stops.

"Good job, girls!" Yolanda calls with another clap.

The dancers seem quite composed, while I, on the other hand, am gasping for breath as I follow them to the towel stack and wipe my neck. Yolanda comes over to me, approval shining in her eyes as she pats her cleavage dry. "You have something to prove. I like that." She tips my head up with her free hand and dissects me with her eyes. "You in love with him?"

"Pfft!" I spit accidentally. "Sorry!" I laugh my evil witch laugh. "No way."

She smiles a strangely expressionless smile. "Pandora. Hmm." She walks away.

As if she knows something nobody else does.

THE REST OF the day, I watch the band's rehearsal from backstage, my eyes trained on you-know-who. He laughs out loud. A lot. He curses a lot too. The twins pick on him and he picks back, exchanging endearments such as "fucking jackass," "get to work, douche," and—my favorite—"suck my dick, asshole." At one point, I'm pretty sure they talk about me.

"You get it on with your box of chocolates last night?"

"If I did," says Mackenna smoothly, almost cockily, "that would be none of your goddamn business."

Me? Box of chocolates?

"We're being filmed, asshat. What we do from now until Madison Square Garden is everybody's business," Jax tells him. Is it Jax? I don't know, I mix those two up so much. It helps when they're bare-chested because Jax has a snake tattoo. Lex seems more talkative and is, in fact, grinning at me as I hide between the stage curtains.

I sink a little deeper into the shadows and wait for Mackenna to say more, but he doesn't. Instead he rubs the back of his neck and rolls his shoulders, his body sweaty and moving in complete rhythm to the beat as they start up again.

The twins strike their guitars, the orchestra takes up with a frenzy, and Mackenna adds the vocals while a dozen male dancers dance in perfect synchrony behind him.

Yolanda's right. No man should be so masculine, so muscular, and still be able to dance like that. A thrust of his hips, a swing of his body, and then he's up on his arms, then back on his feet, singing in low tones while Bach and their rock music play in alternate tempos. It's a perfect duet.

Up on the stage, he's a rock god, but I can still remember when he used to give me wildflowers. I remember being so nervous that my mother would find out about us that sometimes I threw them away before I got home. What a coward I was.

He was the one. It's the truest thing I know about me. That he was the *one*.

"I want to be someone one day, you know? Make a difference . . ."

"I don't know who I want to be yet," I said.

"I have an idea." *Kiss.* "Be you."

Relaxed as I listen to him now, I lean against the wall and close my eyes, letting his voice soothe me.

"Making friends already," Lionel says from behind me. I spin around, and he smiles approvingly.

"Heard you did great at rehearsal."

"I made a fool of myself, but at least some of your other dancers had a good time," I say. I find myself smiling when he laughs, a booming laugh.

"Yolanda said you're quite the natural. That you really brought it with you today."

"Huh," I say, disbelieving the compliment.

But it feels really good, actually. I'd forgotten how good. To get praised for something.

When Mackenna walks offstage, Lionel waves at him and proceeds to inform him of the same. "Your girlfriend's apparently a natural dancer," he says.

Mackenna is sweaty and breathing hard, eyebrows rising at the news. "Of course she is. Who'd you think you were dealing with?"

I'm blushing so hard, I can feel my toes grow red.

"She's a great skater too," Mackenna says softly.

When our eyes meet, my heart grows wings. Do you remember, Kenna? How you spun me, caught me, held me?

A long moment passes, and I feel like Lionel gets too uncomfortable with our silence, for he quickly excuses himself.

"So." I tug on the strand Melanie dared me to paint, suddenly feeling shy. "You had a good rehearsal too."

A deep, unexpected laugh leaves him, and we start heading into the back of the stage. "I think I missed you, Pink," he says softly, shaking his head as if that's stunning news. "All this time." He reaches out, and his silver ring rubs over my chin in a soft caress.

Briefly.

One second it's there, the next, gone.

My smile falters as the ghost of his touch lingers on my skin. "I think you're deluded."

"Yeah, I missed you," he says, nodding to himself, his smile sincere. "Such a brave, angry little raven . . . hiding the sweetest, warmest little chick inside."

I roll my eyes, struggling with how genuine he sounds. "Whatever, Kenna," I say. Like I'll ever forget he wrote a song basically telling me how much I suck!

"Hey, Kenna!" One of the backstage roadies passes him a red cup of what I assume is water. He grabs it and starts downing it while the twins come toward us with their guitars slung behind their backs. We watch them head for water too.

"How do you guys do it?" I wonder out loud as Mackenna and I watch the Vikings grin at us. "Perform before all those people." I gesture toward the stage and all the empty seats surrounding it.

He shrugs. "Lex throws up before going up, every time. Jax gets stoned. And me?" He shrugs. "I have a special trick I do."

"Like what?"

"I tell myself no one out there is *you*."

"Really? That's your trick? So, I'm your jinx, and you're just relieved I'm not watching."

He laughs as he heads to his dressing room.

"Hey! Where are you going? We're having a talk here!" I protest.

"I need to shower, Pink. Look me up later, though, and I'll be happy to explain," he says, but something about his gaze tells me he'd like to do more than explain.

For the next hour, movements of all kinds wreak havoc in my stomach.

I tell myself he wanted to get the best of me, or bait me like he baits the Vikings. He's a pirate luring me into his lair, but I won't fall into his trap. Who cares what he meant?

But later at the hotel, I'm wandering out in the hall, unsure of which room he's in, when the delightful Tit and Liv walk by. "You looking for Kenna?" they ask, wearing identical ear-to-ear grins.

Fuck.

"No."

"Oh. Really?" Liv hooks her arm around mine and spins

around, taking me in another direction. "Then want to come to our room? We're going to watch a movie."

"I'm a little sore." I try to pull free.

"Oh, no worries! I've got stuff to help with that."

Since I *am* sore from this morning's dance lesson, I bite back my retort and let her lead me into their shared bedroom. The "stuff" she has is an ice pack, and I squirm as she presses it against the muscle above my knee. "Oh, don't groan and be a boy about it," she shushes. "The guys are the only ones that complain."

I go still and frown.

"We sometimes let the boys borrow our packs when they overdo their workouts. Gym every three days. They dead lift and do all kinds of other things."

"How long have you been dancing for them?" I ask, genuinely curious. They all seem to be friends, but clearly the girls sleep with the men too.

"Me, four years. Tit, two. We love it here."

"I bet." I study them. I'm searching for any traces of guilt in Olivia's eyes, but I can't quite decipher it. I'm so used to the transparency of Melanie and Brooke. The honesty of real friends. But then again, I'm used to my mother. Closed off. These girls are just like her, and there's only one way to deal with this sort of people—from a distance. Failing that, you have to be up front. "Why are you being nice to me right now?"

They laugh in unison, exchanging glances. "Oh, don't be silly. We don't want you as an enemy. We want to be sure you're not messing with Kenna."

"You think you're protecting him from me? That's absurd."

"Is it?"

"Yes!"

"Oh, we don't know." Now it's Tit talking, tapping one man-

icured nail to her lips—painted in the exact same shade as Liv's.
"Since you arrived, Kenna's done nothing but stare at you, walk
next to you, sit next to you, and sniff around you like some dog
with a new bone."

"He'll go find another bone soon."

"Will he?" It's Olivia again. "Because, can I just say, we've
talked to the other girls, ones who've been with the band even longer, and he doesn't do that. Women come to *Kenna*. He doesn't go
to anyone, he's got like legions. So yeah, we're concerned. What's
the deal with you two?"

I shrug. "He's my ex. We have a past. A past which means I
hate him—as you're supposed to hate an ex."

"But you were dancing with Yola like you wanted to make
out. You were imagining she was Kenna." The words weren't a
question so much as an accusation.

"I . . ." Since there's really no point in denying the way I got
lost in that stupid dance, I shut my mouth.

"One of the camera guys said you two shared a room the
other night. That true?" Tit presses.

"Wow, is this high school?"

There's a camera positioned on a stand in the corner of the
room, almost like a live predator, waiting to trap my answer. For
a fraction of a second, I want to leave, but I want the information
I can garner from these girls too.

"We slept together," I whisper, really low, "but . . ."

"You guys did it! We *knew* you had. Those smoldering looks
he gives you must be multiplied times five in the bedroom, huh!"

"Oh, no." I glance back at the stupid camera, suddenly a little
too vulnerable. Admit that he didn't have his way with me? That
he didn't touch me like that? I suddenly don't want them to know
if he did or didn't. Mackenna is *my* secret again and I don't want
to share anything about him with anyone.

I get to my feet.

"Good night, girls. Next time let's get together in my room. I've got a little thing that you don't—it's called privacy."

"Hey, Dora," Liv says as she stops me.

"Pandora. Please. Here's your ice pack back. My guess is, it's about the same temp as you two."

"Tomorrow. Your room. After the concert. We'll bring the skinny martinis. Deal?"

I look at them, and I realize I don't know what to make of these two. Maybe they hate me, but I still need somebody to talk to, or I'll go running back into Mackenna's arms like I was just about to only minutes ago. He's the one—not these girls—who can hurt me. Whatever these girls want to do has nothing on what Mackenna can do to me.

It won't do any harm to remain cautious, though.

I head back to my room and wonder what he'll do when he realizes I'm not showing up. Will he attempt to seduce me tonight in my room? Is he feeling this same strange anticipation I feel? Wondering what his next step will be? What he's going to do?

But by midnight I hear his laughter in the hall. The sound is accompanied by that of women laughing too, and I realize the sudden wave of hate I feel is not even for him.

It's for me.

TEN

CONCERT TIME

Pandora

Concert night is crazy. You need ten eyes when you walk backstage to keep from tripping over anything and crashing into anybody, much less staying in one piece.

I spot Jax in a corner near the curtains, smoking, and I suddenly wish I'd tucked my e-cigarette into my jeans. "Oh, can I get some?" I ask. Jax puffs out a stream of smoke as he hands it over. I give it a hit and cough. "It's pot?"

"What did you think it was?" He grins and lifts his hand to retrieve it from me, but I quickly move away, deciding to take another quick hit.

Jax laughs and pounds my back when I cough. "Easy, Miss Jones," he says.

"Oh, *puleeze*. I'm not *Miss Jones*."

"Well that's what everybody calls you 'round here." He grins at me, and I notice he has the strangest shade of eyes I've ever seen. They're violet. "We feel like we know you, being that Jones sings about you and him and all," he drawls out, acting quite brotherly to me now.

"They're all lies, I tell you. Wait till you hear what I have to say about him." I nod direly, and he lets out a booming laugh.

From out of nowhere, Lionel grabs the cigarette and stubs it out. "Get rid of this, Jax. Jesus F Christ, how many times must I tell you?"

"Umm. Once more?"

Leo scowls at him and turns to me. "Want to watch the concert from the front row?" Clearly noticing my hesitation, he ushers me toward the doors leading out to the stadium. "Come on. It'll be fun for you, and one less thing for me to worry about. I don't want Kenna distracted. He's already obsessing over what wig to wear tonight."

"He looks ridiculous either way, so tell him he might as well go for a Mohawk," I say drolly as I follow him outside.

I guess I knew there could be repercussions to being in the front row: listening to the crowd clamor, "CRACK BIKINI!" as *he* walks in, the Vikings pop out, and the music builds . . . slow at first—like foreplay—then races toward a musical orgasm that grabs you in a choke hold and doesn't let go. I should have known my body would betray me, just like last time. I should have known I'd feel hot and bothered and confused . . .

Just like last time.

But Mackenna? He wears a spiky blue mohawk over his buzz cut, and the things that does to me. Is he teasing me, or indulging me? He's just so good at what he does. The crowd is hyped, and he greets them all with a low chuckle and a vigorous yell.

"Aren't you a noisy crowd tonight!"

The crowd responds by yelling louder, and after a short interlude from the orchestra, he gets into position at the center of the stage and starts to sing.

My body reverberates with the music. With his voice.

He sings with incredible focus—and one of the things I most

marvel at is that he never just stands there. His body is always on the move, rippling muscles and fluid movements that have to be deceptively strong. Those leaps he makes . . . how he leaps from one level of the stage to the other and flips in the air . . . I need to consciously fill my lungs. They've stopped working on automatic.

And, as if the sight of him isn't enough, the sound of his voice bolts through my body and makes my blood pump furiously in my veins. His voice is so deep and masculine, you cannot be both a woman and unaffected. He sings from the heart, and you can see it—*feel* it—in every word. When he sings "Pandora's Kiss," I can hear the anger in the song, even in the mad strike of the twins' guitars . . . and my own anger, frustration, and pain rise up to meet Mackenna's sudden frown.

He looks at me with pained eyes, and my stomach plummets when he keeps singing without looking away from me. Those wolf eyes have hunted me down in the crowd, snagged and captured me. He's stopped dancing too. The dancers dance behind him, but he just sings, and looks at me, and sings, "I shouldn't have opened you up, Pandora . . ."

As he sings his frustration and regrets to me, I know it's for the cameras.

It has to be.

I'm confused. Confused when his anger and mine mix in a powerful combination that brings forth an undeniable, electric spark of lust. People scream, the music vibrating in all of us, but in me it's tangled up like another being. Breathing. Pulsing. Beating.

As the music continues, Liv and Tit come up to his sides and start rubbing up his chest. He's ignoring them, still singing while their fingers trace his nipples and chest. Just like I will in Madison Square Garden. If I don't puke from the nerves first.

Tit looks at me from upstage. It's a brief flick of her eyes that everyone else would miss—even me, if I weren't so engrossed by what they're doing to him—then she leans and licks his nipple. Jealousy flits through me as his voice rumbles through my body, spinning me into a frenzy to the point where I want to go and scream at the bitch, "He was mine first!"

He turns and moves against Tit, looking at her now as he sings, and strangely I feel the absence of his eyes like a punch in the gut. But then the guitars come in for their turn, and when his stare comes back to me, I'm charged with a thousand watts. The night progresses and his attention keeps straying to see that I'm watching him, and I feel . . . sexy, wanted, womanly. I remember how Brooke used to sit when her husband spotted her from the boxing ring. I used to think how ridiculous it was to be so stunned and excited. Yet here I am, trapped in my seat. In trying to show how tough I am, I've repressed the sensual side of me for so long that it feels good to embrace it now. Aware that he's watching, I close my eyes and lose myself to the music, somehow feeling the shift in his voice.

When this last song is done, I open my eyes to see him whispering something to someone. One of the roadies comes out and ushers me backstage.

"What's going on?" I ask, confused.

"Kenna gets a water and costume change. He wants you there."

As the Vikings take over the microphone for a while, I find myself waiting in darkness under the stage until, suddenly, he drops through the same open elevator that lifts the Vikings at the start of the concerts.

I cry out in surprise when he rockets to the ground. He leaps off and grips me to his hard body to steady me, saying against my temple, "Easy."

He holds me, his heart beating wildly under my ear. We're both panting. It's dark, but I feel his eyes looking down at me, gauging me. The silence here is eerie, but I can still hear the roars of the public outside. "I never thought you watching me perform would *get* to me the way it did." His eyes are silver flames. "Did that turn you on as much as it did me?"

Whatever it is I expected, it wasn't this.

And I bite my tongue before I can tell him that it turned me on more. My god, it turned me on more. His desire isn't the only turn-on; it was also the way his stare felt almost intimate on me. I feel it right now, close and heady, and like a heavy anchor in my chest.

"Tell me," he repeats, seizing my chin between his thumb and forefinger. "Why didn't you come to me last night? You're determined to be stubborn about this, when you know I want you?" He tips my head back so I have no choice but to stare into his heartbreakingly handsome face. He wears this beautiful, partly amused, partly regretful smile. "Well, you know what they say, Pandora," he murmurs, stroking his thumb ring over my chin. "If Muhammad won't come to the mountain, then the mountain will come to Muhammad."

"And you're this walking, moving *mountain*?" I scoff, trying to lighten the atmosphere between us. It's too much. It's electric. Magnetic.

He slides his fingers under the fall of my hair and massages my scalp, the movement almost as hypnotizing as hearing his rough rocker's voice so close. "That's right. I heard you were dancing your heart out. You're determined not to embarrass yourself on our final concert night?"

"That's right."

I focus all my attention on his strong jaw and then his mouth.

Anything so he doesn't look into my eyes and see the things I'm suddenly thinking. *I want to impress you. I want you to remember the girl in the ice skates. The one you said you loved . . .*

God, I'm such a bluffer. Black clothes, black nails? I'm a pussy. An innocent little kitty pretending to be Catwoman. This man could kill me, over and over, until my nine lives are done.

"You know," he says. His tone is conversational, but there's a lingering huskiness in his voice, an exertion from his vocal cords roughening it. "When I kiss you in front of the world, I'm going to tongue you. I'm going to fucking ravage your mouth and give Lionel exactly what he wants. A kiss that's going to be plastered on every fucking screen across the country. A kiss you'll never, ever forget, Pandora. It's what you want too, isn't it? To make people see that I'm really into you. That I'm a fucking fool, singing about you as if I don't want you when the truth is, I want you more than my next fucking song?"

These words are so unexpected, my lungs forget to expand and contract. The only things expanding seem to be my throat and my chest, and contractions flutter between my legs. "It doesn't matter. It's an act," I say.

"Is it."

It's a statement, not a question. He keeps his four long fingers cupping the back of my head and uses his thumb to trace the line of my neck. "I'm a singer, Pandora. Not an actor."

One second he's warning me, looking at me, the next he ducks with that strangely sexy mohawk and brushes his lips across mine. A teasing brush, but enough to set me ablaze.

"Urghm, Kenna . . ."

I don't like the sound I make. Like I have longed for this for Lord knows how long, but who cares when he's pushing his tongue through my lips. I'd make that sound again to get him to keep stroking into my mouth.

So I do.

And he rubs in, wet and slick, hot and deeper, lips angling over mine. My world spins and I grab his hard arms and push closer, while his hands settle on my bottom and he pulls me up against his hips. I can feel his big erection against my tummy. But it's at the wrong place. I want it somewhere else.

I'm ready to twine my legs around him and rub myself against him, when he tears free and sets me aside as though it's taking a monumental effort to do so. The mountain unable to stay away from Muhammad. "Stay here, babe. Don't so much as twitch a single of your sweet, long, delectable little muscles. I'll be back in three songs."

He steps onto the elevator platform as a counter lights up in the dressing room, counting from 10 down to 0. Then he seems to remember the costume change. Racing into the room, he swears and jerks off his shirt, grabbing a new one from a hanger before he climbs back up onto the platform again.

I cover my mouth. Wet and hot, it tingles, and tastes of him.

"Stay here," he says again.

His pale eyes glimmer on me, and his feet are braced apart, hands fisted at his sides.

I'm so hot I'm roasting in my skin. I can't answer. *God, what is he doing to me?*

The moment the platform shoots back up, I groan in despair. Then I hear his voice above me. Shit. What am I doing? I start pacing, imagining licking his nipple and rubbing him like those dancers did. I'm feeling a little envious of all those people ogling him right now, but most of all, I feel high. With emotion. Desire.

Lust.

I'm still here waiting. Why am I waiting? I can't think of anything except his nipple under my tongue. Silver eyes. That wig I'm going to yank off him so I can run my fingers over his close-cropped hair.

When there's finally a huge, huge roar—after like a year!—I know the show is over.

My heart is pounding as I wonder where he'll come from. After a few more moments, he charges down some hidden side stairs, his body filling the doorway.

Like two magnets, our eyes lock.

My breathing hitches.

Mackenna yanks off the small microphone taped to his back and the earbud in his ear, then tosses them aside.

He starts walking toward me. There are all kinds of cables and contraptions around us, and I back up until I hit a wall with a metal door. My brain feels as scattered as the butterflies in my stomach.

Oh god, I have to let him.

No. I *can't* let him.

Panicked for what I feel, I turn and run, frantically searching for an exit. Down here, it's a labyrinth. I'm dodging cables and equipment, but there is no exit I can find.

Behind me I hear his footsteps gaining on me and then, low and rough with lust: "Pandora."

He's at my back, hand on my wrist, pulling me back to him. My heart is pounding helplessly in my throat as I feel my muscles sag at his touch. I let him turn me. I face him, full of dread, want, dismay as I let him slowly press me up against the metal door. He eases his hands into the waistband of my skirt as I grab his spiky mohawk and pull on it. He drags his nose against mine as I toss the wig aside, and I kiss the top of his head because . . . I don't even know why. Because he's Mackenna Jones. Infuriating and odious and also . . . an adorable dreamer I once knew, who made his dream come true. The kiss was impulsive, but it makes him groan as though it did something profound to him. I'm shaking with emotion, and he's shaking with something I suppose is adrenaline.

"Are you wet?" he asks through panting breaths.

"Yes," I say. And I am. From watching him, with his chest sweaty, and from the feel of his inked skin, warm under my fingers.

"I'm so fucking turned on," he groans and shoves my panties aside, giving me two fingers. Just like that. They slip in so easily because I'm soaked. I have no control, and I can't stop myself from throwing my head back and riding those fingers with a circle of my hips. *Oh god nothing's ever felt like this. . . .* He bites my lower lip and sucks it into his mouth. It feels hot and wet and good. So good. I bite his lip hungrily, sinking my nails in his scalp.

"Kenna," I moan.

"God, I missed the way you say my name like that."

Except you know this can't happen, Pandora, this is going nowhere but a dark, dangerous dead end.

And because I know this, it's with a strange pain and dread that I stand here, both wanting and not wanting what I can tell by his gaze he's about to do.

He spreads my arms out and pulls my shirt off. The cool air brushes across my skin, and my nipples pucker as he unfastens my bra.

"Don't, Kenna," I suddenly say, stepping back and awkwardly closing my bra.

"Don't fucking cover up, Pink," he gruffly commands.

My hands shake as I try to fasten my bra back up.

He chuckles—the sound sexy, male—and *tsks* as he tugs my bra open again, his fingers brushing my skin as he tosses it aside.

He doesn't know the regrets and memories roiling inside me as he cups me in his hands. He leans down to kiss my lips, and he smells of mint, his hands warm. My breathing quickens and I gasp when he tugs my skirt up to my hips and drops to one knee, spreads my legs, and takes my ankle in his firm grip.

"One leg up around my shoulders," he says.

I lift my leg, and he bends over to set his mouth on my pussy. The heat of his tongue as it flashes over my clit makes me moan.

No, no, no. We shouldn't be doing this.

But he spreads my legs wider by wedging his shoulders in between them, reaching up to let his fingers caress a path up the inside of my thighs. My naked legs tremble as his tongue rushes over my skin.

I reach between my legs and cup the back of his head, arching my back so he can eat me up harder, faster, *deeper*.

His hunger is palpable in every flash of his tongue, every groan he buries inside me. I writhe. I moan. He lifts his head to look at me, and his eyes are molten, his jaw clamped as though he's holding something back with brutal force.

"Look at you," he hisses, taking me in with a sweep of his fevered silver eyes. His lips glisten with my juices. His closely shaven head is still perfect, not rumpled by my hands. I hear a scraping sound as he drags a hand across the back of his head. "Son of a bitch, Pink." He says something that sounds like me being this vulnerable right now undoes him. But there's something odd here. Instead of feeling vulnerable, when he drinks me up with his eyes I feel powerful, like I'm all the air on this earth, and all the water, too.

Back on his feet, he pulls me against his body. Every hot, hard, unyielding muscle against me, his body fevered and damp against my bare skin. And he comes at me like an animal—his mouth, teeth, tongue, lips, working up my body. His groans coming from deep inside him like my own, jerked from the very pit of me.

Our hands are all over, mouths all over.

I can feel his thighs against mine, the line of his cock digging into my pelvis. I'm unstoppable. Rabid. I want him closer, I want him *in me.*

"Hang on tight, babe," he whispers in that low, after-the-concert gruff voice of his, understanding me, understanding what I need.

I wiggle into position, panting hard.

He reaches between our bodies to peel off his tight, black rocker leathers completely down his thick, muscular legs. I hurry to push my undies down my hips, struggling to kick them off as he sheathes his cock with a condom.

He lifts me and my body twitches and quivers as he lowers me down on him, penetrating me, inch by inch. I groan again, shoving my hands under his shirt and pulling it up over his head so that he's naked. He inhales deeply when he can't go any farther. He feels so thick that all of a sudden, I'm ready to burst.

I suck on his nipple as he fondles my breasts in the most delightful ways. His teeth sink into my earlobe and tug as he starts thrusting, the delicious drag of his cock stimulating all my nerve endings.

Our mouths become voracious, and his sudden rhythmical thrusts tell me he means business and I'm open. The way he grabs my hips and moves me on him, setting the exact rhythm he wants, is like I was made just for him to fuck and god, he's so . . .

So much stronger than before. Bigger than before. Thicker than before.

I can't think . . . can't breathe . . . he's hot, hard . . . ooh, god, I need this. I never knew how much until his arms are tight like clamps around me. And he's inside my body. His tongue flashing into my mouth.

Nothing else matters but this—his breathing, my breathing, his grunts and my groans, my body wrapped around his. I'm wrapped to his body, my arms, legs, even my neck, curled into his, my whole body clinging to him. He knows just what to do, with his mouth, his lips dampening the skin on my neck, my jaw, my ear, then meshing with my mouth.

"You feel so . . ." I bite back the word "right" and instead push my lips hard to his. Our teeth gnash, then he pulls free and stares into my face with burning eyes as if he's high on me, plowing me fast and faster, watching me gasp as my breasts bounce.

He rasps, "Come," and comes hard and fast as it starts for me. His cock jerks inside me three times, and the breath hisses out of him as his muscles clench and tighten against me. He grasps me to his body and continues pumping as we shudder together.

It takes us minutes to recover, neither of us moving. I'm still clutching him, but when I realize how clingy I must appear, I lift my head from the crook of his neck and open my mouth to speak. Mackenna presses his finger to my lips. "No, babe," he says, his voice both tender and chastising.

My brain is still buzzing. Feeling lusty and strangely playful, I open my lips again, and I bite down on his finger with a smile. He clenches his jaw and his eyes flash, almost like he's remembering the other times I did that. Then without warning, he leans over and bites down on one of my fingers too. Like old times . . .

Ouch! I playfully protested. *You're going to snack on my finger? Really?*

Oh, stop complaining. Here, take mine . . .

A strange emotion tightens my chest, and it hurts. Gently, he rubs his finger against my tongue, and I do the same.

"You taste like sweat," I say, with a mock grimace.

"You taste like sugar," he husks out, his lids heavy.

I pull my hand free and he continues gazing at me, waiting for me to say something. I'm trying to pull up my walls, but I'm failing miserably. "I . . . ," I begin.

"Don't ruin it," he says, setting his forehead on mine and sighing, "but you'd be surprised to know what I'd give to hear this mouth tell me how it *really* feels about me." He rubs the mouth he's speaking of with his thumb ring and my nipples harden again.

"I expressed it with vegetables, remember?" I say, unable to rein back the lust in my voice.

"Hmm, yes, a memorable experience." He gives one last nibble to the tip of my finger, holding it by the base and kissing the pad before letting me go.

It was such a genuine act of tenderness, I surprise myself when I nuzzle his throat, still feeling oddly playful as I drop one last kiss to his lips, wanting to surprise him by saying something he'd never expect to hear. "I really like the way you come."

He grabs my head and looks at me in shock. "You being serious right now?" He searches my face.

I lick my lip and love that his eyes fall there. I'm feeling the best I've felt in a long time as I peer up at him through my lashes. My body is lax against his and I feel . . . good. Happy. Content with the world. He smells like a man—like the only man I've ever been with. He smells of my memories and my dreams, and my childhood and teens. Of the boy who drew me out enough to make me feel carefree.

He frames my face and searches my expression with complete intensity, his textured voice prickling across my skin. "I don't just *like* the way you come, baby—I get off on it. The way you fight your orgasm but it takes you over and you can't keep your eyes open. The way you can't bite back the sounds you make, and you grip me like you don't want to let go. Do you feel me?" he demands in my ear, clutching me close. "I'm stiffening up inside you and you're still slick and hot, like a fist around me. Do you feel me?"

I close my eyes and shudder as he begins caressing me under my top with one long-fingered hand, relaxing against me as he slides down against the metal door and we stay there for a while.

A flick and the scent of tobacco filters through my daze, and I angle my head to see the tip of a cigarette glowing in the dark as he gives it a hit. He expels the smoke quickly and offers it to me. "What is it?" I ask, narrow-eyed.

"Camel. Just normal tobacco. I'm not into drugs. Guess they ruined my fucking life already through my dad."

The smoke trails out of his lips and I watch it, impulsively bending to inhale it. I cough and laugh, and he laughs and slaps my back. He smokes several cigarettes in a row and I wonder, dazedly, if this is his life. So I ask, "This is what your life is like?"

He looks at the mess around us and smokes lazily. "Yeah."

"Do you like it?"

He shrugs.

Suddenly I realize that even if he still wanted me, even if he hadn't broken my heart, there would be no room in this life for me. And if there were, I wouldn't see Magnolia. He chose this over me. And I choose mine over this.

It makes me sad.

But I don't want him to know that, so I groan and squirm free from the heavy arm he holds around my shoulders, saying, "You're sweaty."

"So are you."

I try to put some distance between us, but he puts the cigarette out on the cement floor and looks at me, dragging his hand through his hair before laughing. "Do I have to be inside you to be touching you? Do you need to be fucked to be touched, babe?"

"I hate displays of affection. They're silly."

"Nobody's here but me. And this is silly." He tugs the pink strand of my hair with a playful smile.

I sigh and yield to the impulse to press against him, acutely aware of our shoulders touching.

"Living with the band gets too noisy almost," he says as he studies the ceiling, absently playing with my hair and making me feel childish and wonderful, just like he used to before. It worries me—a lot—but not as much as I love feeling childish and wonderful.

"Do you get away to be alone sometimes?"

"Not as much as I'd like." He drags his hand over his hair again as he meets my gaze in the dark. "I think about you, Pandora. About us."

We look at each other for a moment.

My lungs—what is *up* with them today? It's an effort to pull in air, and all the while I'm trying to disguise it.

"I guess every time you make a choice, you wonder if you made the right one," he explains to me.

"And . . . ?" I ask, needing to know his thoughts more than my lungs need the oxygen.

"And what?" he prods.

"Was it the right one?"

"You tell me," he shoots back, his eyebrows slanted slightly in assessment.

"No, *you* tell me."

"No. Because it wasn't really my choice."

I stare back with my own frown because, suddenly, it's too

much. This conversation. Him saying he didn't choose to walk away. *Fuck that!*

"Mackenna, I can't do this." I try to rise, but his hand clamps on my wrist to stop me. I'm so hypersensitive, the touch sizzles down my nerve endings. "Kenna," I say, and my voice falters.

Will you come to me tonight?

Always . . .

God, I wish I could get a brain enema and wash my every memory away so that it stops hurting like this, but instead, every memory of our past is with me—with us—as he starts laughing over my quicksilver temper, tugging me back to him. "Come here," he coaxes.

I'm humming with so much feeling it's indecent. Thrumming with life. It's too much, it's not enough. It's torture.

He's torturing me. Prolonging the moment until I finally, *finally*, fall—straight into his lap. Then his hand spreads against the back of my head, his lips on my neck. The gesture is soft. Tender. He follows the arc of my throat and shoulder. Words, thick and sexy, reverberate against my skin. Spilling in my ear. "God, I can't get enough of you. You're such a vixen."

He speaks it reverently, so reverently my heart hardly hears the words. Just the tone. And it is beating somewhere in the sky. But I want it back in me. He broke it and I'm not letting him take it away. I can't let him take it away.

I want to cry but I rarely do—not even when he left. I cried when I lost my virginity because I was happy. I cried when my father died because I was sad.

Your father doesn't deserve a single one of those tears! my mother screamed. *He betrayed us. You won't shed a tear for him, do you hear me?*

When I lost Mackenna, I kept hearing those same words. My

mind replaying them for me, over and over. *He betrayed you. You won't shed a single tear for him.*

I make an angry sound and try to get free, but I can't believe how easy it is for him to stop me, and more so . . . how very much I actually want him to stop me.

Is that why I came? Because I wanted to see if he gave a shit? To see if he'd even try to get a little piece of me back? That thought worries me more than anything right now, and it gives me the strength to pull free and leap to my feet, stepping quickly into my jeans.

"You're going to pretend you don't want this?" he asks me devilishly as he jumps back into his leather.

"It wouldn't be pretending. It's a chemical *animal* attraction, nothing more." I turn around and straighten my clothes before heading to the same stairs he'd appeared through. I hear his footsteps behind me as we head upstage, where roadies and team members are cleaning up.

"I'll prove you wrong tonight," he says, following me to one of the cars meant to take us back to our hotel. A camera catches up with us down the hall, and I know we won't be able to shake it off—at least, until I get back into my room.

"What are you doing?" I ask when Mackenna slips into the car after me. He says nothing as we drive away, the cameraman nicely slipping into the front of the car and aiming back at us, silent. Thankfully, Kenna doesn't press the issue with him here, and neither do I.

Silence surrounds us the entire journey, following the three of us up the elevator, and silence remains even as Mackenna follows me to my room. "Mackenna, what are you doing?" I whisper-hiss.

Alarm, anticipation, burn in me as I open my door.

Always . . .

He flicks his middle finger at the cameraman, then slams the door in his face and turns around to look at me.

"Your room is that way." I point at the door behind him.

"Tonight, my room is here," he says with a cocky smile. He also watches my reaction.

Which is to stutter.

"N-n-no. *No*, it's not."

"Yes, it is."

Suddenly, he scoops me up in his arms and grunts, saying, "You're heavy, babe."

"Put me down or get a fucking hernia! *God!*"

He laughs. "Hernia it is." He carries me to the bed with ease—the fucking clown isn't even struggling to carry *heavy ol' me*. Then he eases me down on the bed, tugs off my heels, and tosses them to the floor. I bolt, alarmed when I realize where this is going again. *Danger!*

"Don't! This isn't happening again, Mackenna."

"It's happening," he contradicts. "I'm spending the night, Pandora."

"But I don't want this!"

He takes my foot in one hand and slides his fingers up my bare leg, a white wolf-smile on his sexy mouth. "Give me ten minutes to prove you wrong. To prove to you how much you *do* want this."

I look at his bare chest, feeling his fingers at the arch of my foot, my voice shaky as I say, "I don't want you here."

He falls silent, and for a moment I think he's going to leave, and it fills me with an unexpected panic that only confuses me more.

He doesn't leave, though.

He shoots me a lopsided grin. "Ten minutes and you'll be singing a different tune."

"I don't sing—you do."

"You'll sing like a fucking canary, baby. Lie down," he says, and the intensity in his gaze goes perfectly with his devil's smile and attitude.

"Okay. I'll give you ten minutes. But with clothes *on*," I say. "And if you can't seduce me in ten, you leave."

He lifts his hands innocently. "I'm not touching your clothes. And consider yourself seduced."

I relax. Somewhat.

My heart is still beating like a drum.

The bed embraces me as I settle back down, and I don't know why I don't protest, except I don't have energy to do anything but breathe. I have never been more aware of my breath.

In, out. In, out.

When his touch returns to one of my arms, starting at the back of my hands, it makes me tense up. I exhale in a rush as he trails his fingers upward, his touch familiar, delicious. Oh, god, it feels delicious. Soft as a feather, but with the voltage of a gazillion kilowatts.

My eyes want to drift shut as I remember the first time Mackenna touched me. I remember his face, how his sexy mouth would form this perfect smile, and I swear his eyes said that he loved me like Romeo loved that stupid Juliet. I felt his gaze in my heart. Now his eyes are dark and hooded and he's not smiling, his expression grave and intent as ever as he runs two fingers up my bare arm. My heart can no longer feel his gaze, but I feel his gaze between my legs. In my nipples. My fucking ovaries. I could get pregnant with this gaze.

He slides his fingertips under the sleeve of my top, then runs them back down my arm. "Relax, Pink," he coos.

His voice has gained a roughness that makes the hairs on my arms prick pleasurably. "My name . . . is *Pandora*."

"I happen to know your name very well and I remember you didn't like it, but you liked it when I called you gorgeous. It made your eyes dark and made you bite your lip, just like you're doing now, because you wanted me to kiss you. Do you remember that, gorgeous girl?"

I scoff, but the sound is feeble. I bite my lip, but now it feels wet, and he's looking intently at it as if expecting me to invite him to kiss me. He keeps touching me with those long musician's fingers.

Never, ever date a musician. Other men will never compare.

Lithe fingers trace my arms and elbows. My wrists and fingers. Then up my legs. Those fingers brush over me and my tummy caves in from the pleasure.

I'm breathing in, out. In, out.

My tense muscles feel bunched up as he strokes his fingers up my throat. Gah, how to resist? Resist the only guy I've ever kissed. Ever loved, ever made love to. I start squirming as his fingers skim over my skin.

"Relax. I wanted ten minutes to change your mind, it's only been two."

"Seriously? Only two?" I whine.

He leans over and kisses my collarbone, his breath warm on my body as he starts kissing up my throat, and I remember it all.

Fingers touching me. *Perfect Pandora . . .*

My fingers curling awkwardly around his cock. *How do I . . . ?*

Babe, I swear, you move that hand and I'm going to go off.

My heart racing, my body trembling with nerves and the excitement of having Mackenna hot, long, and thick in my hand, looking down at me like a hungry sex fiend. *The tip is wet, can I taste . . .*

Fuck, don't move that hand!

The memory creeps up on me, how innocent and hormonal

we were, and before I can stop it, I curl my arms around his neck and I gasp into his ear, "Okay, you can sleep here tonight."

His eyes shoot to my face and he lifts one brow. "Yeah?"

I bite my lip and nod eagerly.

I hear him whisper, "Fuck," and he shoves his hands under my T-shirt and cups me over my bra, looking down at me and licking his lips as if savoring me. I should not want this so bad, I really shouldn't.

"Just tonight," I say. *Always* . . . I hear in my mind.

But he nods intently and says, "Just tonight."

I lift my head and part my lips as he kisses a path up to my mouth, and when our lips brush, he groans and keeps brushing across them. I am so aroused by the thought of kissing him in bed that I have to peel my eyes open.

"What?" I whisper breathlessly, my body squeezing spasmodically with want as he thumbs my nipples. "Don't you want to kiss me?" I wanted to tease him with my kiss, but now I'm the one feeling teased because he won't take it.

His eyes burn with lust as he pulls his hands out of my top and angles my head to his, his hands cradling the back of my skull as he studies me and murmurs, "I want to do more than kiss you."

I lick my lips and stare at his mouth. His mouth, which I really want—no, *need*—right now. I want to ask for what I want, but I've already asked him to stay and asking for more makes me feel open . . . so open . . . so weak . . .

I'm not comfortable expressing my feelings, a trait I inherited from my mom. The relationship she and my dad had was almost businesslike. Since he died, since Mackenna left, my only source of emotion has been Magnolia.

But she's not a danger to me like Mackenna is.

She hasn't broken me like he has.

So I just grab the back of his head, lift my head, and kiss him.

Barely a nanosecond passes before he gets aggressive in return, almost squishing me as he stretches over me with his big body so that his cock is nestled between my thighs. And I feel it. His thick, hard, throbbing shaft. Against my body. Only my jeans and his leather pants separating us.

"This has to come off," he says and tugs my top upward.

I stop him, pulling it back down. "Wait."

His eyes sparkle in challenge and I smile playfully, trying to do it slowly, to make him anticipate it.

Do it, Pandora. He'll get even more excited when you take all this away. Think about the blue balls you can give him, a little devil tells me. The same devil who watched me get hurt.

He watches, rapt.

I pull it over my head.

He reaches for the bra.

"Wait," I again command.

His lids grow even heavier, his jaw tightly clamped as he licks his lips once more. My silver-eyed, hungry wolf . . .

I slowly begin to unlatch and slip off my bra.

His eyes keep darkening and darkening, a muscle working in the back of his jaw as he now watches me unzip.

He follows me and unzips his leather pants.

He looks at one pointed, hard nipple, then the other, leaning over to take one tip between his teeth, tugging as he shoves down his pants and I kick off mine. Moaning, I rub instinctively, skin to skin. This wasn't planned—all this sex—but I haven't had sex in so many years and I just . . . *oh*. His groan. His groan kills me as he engulfs my other breast in his hand and murmurs, "You enjoy that little striptease?"

"Did you?" I shoot back.

He tugs the nipple harder, almost to the point of pain. "How much do you think I want you?"

"Judging by . . ."—I rock my hips—"I'm guessing a lot?"

He laughs against my breast and it makes his laugh that much hotter. "I want you a hell of a lot more than a lot." He lifts his face, then his gaze looks haunted. "Pandora . . . ," he says as if it's the beginning of something else, his thumb ring running up my rib cage. "What happened?" He studies me. "What happened?"

I close my eyes and breathe deep as a thousand words slam into me. *You fucking left! You broke my heart. I weathered my mother alone. I lost my will to live. I lost what we could have had.*

"Hey, hey, look at me," he says, turning my head by the chin. But I can't look at him.

I can't.

Suddenly, there's a noise outside and a knock. "Hey! Dora! DORRRRA! Hey! We've got the alcohol! Open up, bitch!"

I groan.

"That Liv and Tit?" he asks.

"Yeah."

"Dude, you're friends with those two vipers? They want your head on a stake." He sounds annoyed as fuck. And now, with this interruption, actually so am I.

"Any other girls around I can hang with? No. So yes, we're friends."

He sighs and edges back, then quietly stands. *No. No, no, no!* I think, panic rushing through me as my body is rocked with shudders of need.

"You want me to go?" he asks.

No. No, I don't. I don't.

But once again I sit here, watching him, speechless, and he's watching me back. "Nod your head if you want me to stay," he says, softening his voice.

His hands are flexing at his sides as if he's anxious for my answer. I motion my head, and I'm not sure if it's a yes or a no. He sighs, then slips his T-shirt over his head. As he heads to the door, panic grips me. *He's not coming back to bed.*

"Mackenna!" I yell to stop him—at the exact moment he yanks the door open.

"Take the party elsewhere. She's got company," he growls low in his throat.

And slams the door shut in their faces.

I blink, my heart completely motionless in my chest. He turns around to me, his eyes like flames on my skin. "One day, you'll beg for it." He jerks his shirt off again.

My heart pounds as he crosses the room. "In your dreams, Mackenna," I bluff.

He only laughs softly and shakes his head. "You're stubborn, I'll give you that. But you'll wear down."

"Never."

He leans over and, suddenly, all his male weight is hovering over me, his lips pressing to my ear in the most tender kiss I've ever felt.

"No, babe. *Always.*"

ELEVEN

THERE ARE BULLIES AROUND, AND BY "BULLY" I DON'T MEAN ME

Pandora

The band makes it to a rodeo bar in west Texas. Olivia, Tit, and the other female dancers are flirting with a group of cowboys, and they haven't so much as glanced in my direction, which leaves me in the guy section—where the Vikings are treating me like some long-lost sister. The only good thing about this is that my new official, and very first, fuck buddy seems to be a little jealous at my side.

"Hands," he growls when Lex sets his hand on my knee while flexing the length of his arm and showing off his snake tattoo.

"Fuck, you're kidding, right?" he asks, his eyebrows drawing low over his violet eyes.

"It look like I'm kidding?" Mackenna answers with deceptive softness as he slides his hand proprietarily under my hair to lightly caress the back of my neck.

"Don't be ridiculous," I scoff, but I'm secretly delighting in this development as I squirm to get free from his hold.

Nobody has ever—ever—made me feel as wanted, protected, and, well . . . *annoyed* as Mackenna.

But I'm just rolling with it because, well, tonight I feel more of the former than the latter. Maybe because of all the orgasms? He has that ability to relax me with a couple of those . . .

"Hands, Lex," he growls again, gently squeezing my nape, and I don't know what it is about his bossiness today, but does he not remember that all there is between us now is sex? He sounds like he sounds in bed.

But he also sounds jealous. He hasn't got it through that hard skull of his that I don't mind Lex's hand on my thigh. It doesn't give me head-to-toe shivers like Mackenna's hand on the back of my neck. Right now, in fact, the hand on the back of my neck makes me feel so warm, my bloodstream feels like fire through my veins. Every cell in my body, every pore, is buzzing at the touch, awakened by the way his thumb ring runs up to stroke behind my ear. What do I do with myself when he has such an effect?

Do him again tonight?

Do him until you've had so much of him you'll never want him again?

"Dude, I get it." Lex finally pulls his hand away and sets his arm out on the table to allow me a full view of the snake curling around his wrist and up his muscled arm.

"I was born the year of the Chinese snake. Symbol is always with me now," he explains to me.

"Wow," I say, and Jax, who sits across the booth, opens up his palm, and I can see a snake curling around his thumb too. I lean across the table to investigate while Mackenna's hand slides down my spine and rests on my butt, where he gives it a little pat.

"So, you're all into Chinese symbols?" I ask, very much aware of how Mackenna's hand has slid up my butt to my waist, hooking into my waistband to sit me back down.

I shiver when he slips his fingers under my top, skin to skin, and I think now is a good moment to remind him that I don't make out in public—and he's making me want to do just that—but when I turn, the way he's watching me, the way his silver eyes sear me . . . it makes my thoughts scatter.

"Danger," that little voice keeps whispering in my head.

I've been kicking him out of my room every night, but only after we've fucked a couple of times. If he thinks he can use me, and my room, just to get away from the cameras, he's wrong. If he thinks we're cuddling after, he's wrong. But when he leaves, shaking his head at me like it's a mistake to send him away . . . then I lie alone in bed, not liking it one bit.

"Is your symbol Chinese too?" I ask him now, nodding toward his forearm and the inky, runelike symbols on his tan skin.

His tattoo niggles at my curiosity, and I'm determined to find out what it means.

He smirks. "It's Kenna-ish. It's a whole other language. Some say it's a religion."

I roll my eyes and cup his wrist, pulling his arm to my lap for me to examine. "What is it? What does it mean?"

"Hell if anyone knows," Lex says.

I brush my thumb over the symbols, and it's only until about a minute of silence has passed that I realize Kenna is eerily still. When he speaks, his voice has deepened, as if my touch and the light way I brush my thumb over his tattoo are far more than a caress to him.

"Means I'm an unlucky bastard," he leans to whisper in my ear, then, even closer, "Your hair smells of coconut."

When he looks into my eyes as if expecting an explanation for this, I'm having trouble coming up with something saucy. "It's the oil I moisturize my hair with, a little drop to any shampoo I use."

I realize how close we are. One would say we look ready to do each other in public, as if we didn't do each other several times last night. In fact, *every* night . . . for the past week.

He's stroking my nape, and I'm stroking his tattoo, both of us staring, not with animosity, and not with lust. Okay, yes with lust. But also with a lot of curiosity. As though this getting to know each other again is proving far more interesting than either of us imagined.

I feel as though whatever is happening in the bar is secondary. I feel as though the world revolves around the impenetrable bubble of me and *him*. Nothing matters but his hand holding me by the neck, and his strong, muscled forearm under my palm and fingers.

He's noticeably relaxed—I guess that happens when you have ten orgasms in two days—but I feel supermushy, and it's very unlike me. It's like I've been *craving* him, his contact, his affection, for so long, the intimacy of such a simple act is turning me to putty.

Worse is, he seems just as hungry for this. Edging his body closer, he suddenly presses a kiss into my hair, like he's wild for coconut.

Gah. It's one thing to fuck like we do, but this . . . oh god, he just groaned into my hair. He's kissing the top of my ear and groaning like we're doing something intensely sexual, rather than just sitting together. I hold back a sound as I feel his nose nuzzling my hair.

"Do you really want to know what that tattoo means?" he rasps, his breath shooting shivers from my ear to my shoes. He eases back, and his eyes feel like incoming bullets. "What will you tell me in exchange?"

"What do you want?"

"I want you to tell me something that's been bugging me," he says, scraping a hand over his head.

"What?"

Using his thumb, he angles my head up higher so our eyes hold. "Tell me what made you so mad at everyone."

"I'm not mad at everyone, I'm just mad at you," I say. It's part lie and part truth. But he's walking straight into the past, and something frozen has just dropped into the pit of my stomach, leaving my veins as cold as icicles.

"Yet the person you're most mad at is yourself. Isn't it?" He rubs his silver ring along the bottom of my lip, and I hold on to everything I want to say. Holding it tightly, in an airlocked and lidded box, because once it's out, I can never take it back.

I can never take it back.

"Dora, come with us!" Tit calls, just in time to save me.

I expel a breath, then take Mackenna's hand and slowly lower it. "You're going to have to let me out of the booth, Mackenna."

"Why? Little girls' room chat session?" he asks with a cocky lilt. Because I'm so grateful he's scooting out to let me pass, I grin.

"That's right. No boys allowed," I warn.

As I stand, he drops back down. "All right, Pink. Just know I'll be waiting here to pick up right where we left off."

"Don't hold your breath, Wolf. I can find out from the girls what your tattoo means."

"Yeah, good luck with that," he says, laughing his it's-so-sexy-it-should-be-illegal laugh.

"Hey, girls," I greet as I join them.

That's when my phone starts to ring and my heart stops when I see HER flashing on my phone screen.

My eyes widen. Glancing around for the quietest, most private space I can find, I peer into the men's restroom, find it empty, and close the door, leaning against it so no guy can come in while I talk.

"Hello?" I answer.

God. I sound like a chicken shit. Like I'm guilty of something.

I'm guilty of lying and more. So much more.

"Pandora?"

"Mom. What's up?"

"She misses you, she wanted to say hello."

My eyes turn to the tiny window and a slice of moon outside. Hmm, looks high enough. "It's past her bedtime."

"I know, she couldn't sleep because I'd promised she could talk to you today and I was caught up in a call, but we're calling now."

"Right," I say, thinking, *No, actually you're letting her stay up late watching movies as an excuse to check up on me at this hour and make sure I'm not screwing up my life again.*

"How are you?" she finally asks.

"Good, Mom," I mumble, staring at the toes of my boots. They don't look so badass anymore.

"You're keeping busy with work? Staying smart about your choices?"

"Of course," I lie, dragging the tip of my boot down a square tile.

"You know, it's hard for me to give Magnolia the attention you've accustomed her to."

"I'll call more often."

She sighs, clearly displeased but conceding. My stomach hurts. She's the only one who knows exactly what I am and what I can do and how easily I get broken. I "gauge my value by her love," according to Dr. Finley, the therapist who suggested I accept my mistakes, as well as the mistakes of the people in my past, and move forward.

I thought I did.

I thought I had.

Hell, I thought tomatoing Mackenna would be the last "fuck you" I had to say in terms of my past.

I was so, so wrong. Maybe I should consider saying something else instead.

"Are you all right? Where are you?" my mother presses.

"I'm in . . . Kentucky," I lie.

"You're decorating in Kentucky?"

I wonder if she's onto me and worry my lip a little while I worry in my mind. "A bachelor's apartment. I'm using my usual eclectic combination. Steel, dark woods. It kicks ass."

"Language," she chides, but she laughs a little.

We end up talking a little bit. She's not perfect, my mom. But she's the only one who knows how much I've screwed up and hasn't hightailed it out of my life.

She never lets me forget that.

Then I get to talk to Magnolia.

"I miss you, Panny, I have forty-seven things now."

"Wait, let me guess! We're going to dress like gorillas and bang our chests out on the sidewalks?"

"No! But that will be forty-eight!"

I smile with happiness, but the guilt I usually feel when I'm happy slowly creeps in.

I've fucked up. And Mackenna's right, I'm mad mostly at myself.

"You're my hero, Pan," she then says, her voice dreamy as if I really *am* something special.

"You're mine," I whisper. She squeals, sends me kisses, and we hang up.

I stare at my bracelet, then tuck my phone into my back pocket and breathe deep. When I finally get out, the girls are at the guys' booth, Tit exactly in my spot.

I don't like the rush of possessiveness I feel when I see her busy talking with Mackenna. I don't like how possessive I feel of his eyes and his smile and the hand he has spread out casually over the back of the seat . . . where I had been sitting. I have a spectacular urge to go and tell Tit to take her hand off Mackenna's shoulder and park her ass somewhere else. Shit. I'm so over my limits of normal involvement here, I shake my head at myself and head over to the bar. Best to stay away from him.

Dealing with my mother always leaves me raw, and I don't want Mackenna to improve on that.

"See that guy?"

I turn to the low baritone to my right, and a guy—thirty-something-ish, with a black cowboy hat and a huge-ass belt buckle—tips his head in a certain direction. When I follow the aim, my eyes land on you-know-who. You-know-who's silver-laser-beam is staring straight at me from across the room. "You're asking me if I see him? Does anyone *not* see him?" I counter.

"He your man?" the cowboy asks.

"In my nightmares, sometimes."

But Cowboy isn't appeased. "He sure looks like he thinks he is," he drawls.

"Ignore him. He thinks he's many things. God is one of them."

"Bitches with him agree." He points to the girls trying to catch Mackenna's attention at the booth, but nothing seems to make those eyes go away—not even the frown I send his way before I give him a first-class view of my backside as I turn around to order myself a drink.

Why not?

Safer to let the tequila put me to sleep later rather than Mackenna.

"You nervous? Whatcha got there?" the cowboy asks, peering down at my bracelet, which I hadn't realized I'd been playing with.

"Something that always reminds me how human I am when I look at it," I say, brushing his hand off. "Don't touch it, nobody gets to touch it but me."

He rubs a hand down my back and trails it lower. "I think you're hot despite your lips. I like red better. So you're possessive about your accessories, what about the rest of you?"

He squeezes my ass.

Alarm skids through me. "Hey, we were being morose at the bar. What the hell happened to being plain old morose at the damn bar?"

He grins. "See that other guy?" He nods in the direction of Leo as he watches us from next to a big black camera. "He offered compensation if we made the night interesting for your crowd."

"Is that so?" Leo. Ohmigod. What a douche bag.

I remove Cowboy's hand from my ass and consider slapping him and having Leo put that in his precious movie. Cowboy squeezes my ass again. I'm getting ready to knee him in the balls when I hear Lex's voice call out in a friendly way, "Hey, bud, you don't want to lose that hand, trust me."

In the opposite of a friendly way, the cowboy is suddenly pinned back on the bar with a jolt that sends a couple glasses rattling.

"You touch her again, I'm ripping your guts out through your throat." Mackenna pushes him back against the bar even harder.

"Kenna!" Jax grabs his arms and tries to stop him.

"Fucking let go," Kenna growls as he yanks his arms free.

I look at Leo in disbelief. He was *setting up* Mackenna for a show. Their precious manager would let a mass murderer in here if it would get him buzz for his precious movie. Wow. I really don't even know what I'm doing here anymore. What am I doing? Magnolia is alone with my mother, my mother is suspicious, Mackenna is in my head, he's in my fucking *bed*. He's getting into a bar fight because of me, as if he's my . . . boyfriend still. Like all those years. Oh god.

I stalk across the bar, when a familiar hand with bracelets and silver rings catches me by the elbow.

"Hey, come here, look at me," Mackenna says, and he pulls me to his side. As much as I don't want to, I tremble at the instant release of feeling warm and safe with his arm around me as he leads me to some sort of storage room, where we find peace and quiet.

"So," he demands.

I scowl.

"What's going on, baby?"

Seeing him visually checking me to see if I'm all right, I scowl harder.

"You planned to stay at the bar all night?" he asks.

"I was having fun, actually," I bait.

"Oh yeah? That sure looked like fun for that motherfucker." He cracks the knuckles of one hand, then the other, a violence I've never seen before roiling in his eyes. "Where did you run off to before?"

"I was calling home."

He looks incredulous. "You call home in the middle of a bar?"

"Mother called me," I mumble.

"And you can't make her wait?"

"No, 'cause it makes it worse! It makes her suspicious, and she doesn't know I'm here."

"Of course not," he agrees, his entire countenance hard.

"Stop questioning me, asshole, I'm not yours to command!" I push past him, and he stops me. I squirm in his hold, whining, "Let go."

"You still dancing to any tune she sings?" he asks. "Are you?" he commands.

I don't know if I can take the frustrated disappointment in his eyes.

"Do you crave her love so much you'd sacrifice your own dreams and everything you want to please her?" he continues.

I can't answer.

"She's not the only one willing and able to protect you from anything, Pandora. *Anything!*"

A door slams shut nearby, and Lionel walks in. A chill seems to spread. Mackenna's eyebrows crease in contempt. "You've gone too far, Leo," Mackenna whispers, a low threat.

"Kenna, relax. Where's your sense of humor?"

A muscle flexes angrily in Mackenna's jaw. "It'll come back when I have my fist where I want it on your face." Reaching out to me, he hooks a finger into the loops of my jeans and tugs me to his side. "I'm taking her back to the hotel. No cameras."

"One camera. Just one," Leo pleads.

"Fuck you, Leo."

Mackenna pulls me angrily out of there, and I follow. One of the camera guys is stumbling behind us. "And fuck you too, Noah." Mackenna flips the camera. The call with my mother reminds me of why Mackenna and I can never be.

I should tell him right now.

Stop this right now.

But knowing I have to stop it makes me want it all the more.

"I don't need you to give some asshole a purple eye for me anymore," I huff as he guides me outside.

"Great. *Now* you choose to be chatty," he grumbles.

We slide into the hotel limo, and he looks at me as Noah climbs in next to him, camera and all. Silence settles in the car. Mackenna stares at Noah in quiet rage, then at me. I meet his gaze, because backing down is a sign of weakness and I can't stand him to know he makes my knees weak.

His eyes flick to my lips. I can almost taste him. Each of the two hundred kisses he gave me in our teens, and the dozens he's given me since I've been with him again. He kisses so well. I used to name his kisses. The sleepy kiss and the smiling kiss, the seductive kiss and the laughing kiss. Right now he looks like he wants to Kiss Me To Death. He looks concentrated like he's kissing me in his head.

"Tell me something, Pandora," he commands huskily. I know Mackenna, and what he's really saying is "Distract me before I do something I'll regret."

On his thighs, his hands are clenched into fists, and I know he wants to make the car stop and jerk Noah and his camera out of here. He's mad because he was being set up, and I somehow think he's mad because they used me to get to him. He's mad because they can get to him by using me.

"You're a Herculean masterpiece with a penchant for trouble," I say.

He's not appeased. He leans over and grabs my face, then whispers, "Tell me something you mean, Pink. Say it. Nothing silly, nothing angry—something real. Can you do that? Or you only dress like a badass to hide the tenderness within?"

Strangely, my throat is starting to thicken.

He wants to open me up? To open the box in me and let all the bad stuff out?

He reaches out and cradles my face in his palm. I struggle to tame a shiver building at the base of my spine.

"Tender. Right. Pfft!"

"Come on," he presses, leaning forward, elbows to knees, his face as persuasive as his music is.

I can't answer that. I can't even open my mouth while thinking of the answer, so I leap into the first subject that comes to mind. "I'm mad you pulled that guy away when I was so ready to smash my knee between his legs."

"Seriously? You'd kick his nuts?" he asks with obvious delight.

"You think I wouldn't bust his balls? That I only busted yours?"

"You don't only bust mine . . . you lick them too."

"I do not! *Ohmigod*, Noah, erase that!"

Noah grins and shakes his head behind the camera.

We're laughing now. "Mackenna!"

"See the way she says my name right there, Noah? She sounds guilty, doesn't she?"

"Mackenna, shut the hell up!" I reach out with my hand to shut his mouth, but he licks my palm and bites my finger gently and playfully. Then he twists his head and kisses me, hard. We moan as I allow myself this kiss. One second . . . two . . . three . . . then I push him and arch away. "Mackenna!"

"What, Pandora?"

We're laughing, and even Noah is trying to stifle his own laugh.

"I don't want to kiss you. Not here."

"Don't worry, I know where," he says playfully.

My eyes widen when I realize he's implying I want to kiss his cock, not his mouth. "MACKENNA!" I cry again, laughing hysterically.

When we get to the rooms, Noah's still following us as Kenna keeps his arm around me. When I open the door to my room, Kenna tells him, "Night, dude. Bet you really want to be me right now, huh?" and shuts the door on Noah's camera. He spins me around in the middle of the room, saying, "Come here now," and I'm smiling, because his eyes are smiling at me too. But suddenly, his lips aren't.

The atmosphere turns deadly serious, and the air begins to crackle with whatever it is that always—*always*—leaps between us.

I love that Kenna knows it's hard for me to ask for what I need. Sometimes even I don't understand why it's so hard, but he does. I suddenly wonder if maybe he left all those years ago because I could never say I loved him.

What if I still love him?

He takes a breath and reaches up to stroke me, temple to chin. "You all right?" he asks seriously.

I nod. "I am now." His eyes watch me as his fingers trail my skin. My body starts throbbing. Right now, there is no past. There's just now. I want to climb onto him, or want for him to climb into me.

Without warning, he moves his mouth over mine, devouring the softness of my lips, his kiss sending new spirals of need swirling in my tummy. When we embrace and I make a soft whimper, he tears free, takes one ragged breath, and looks at my wet lips with those glimmering wolf eyes. My lips still burning from his kiss, he promptly recaptures my mouth, more demanding this time.

"Yeah," he rasps. The touch holding me against his body is both firm and persuasive, and as his mouth becomes more commanding, my eager response makes him groan.

"Spend the night," I whisper as I clutch his shoulders and sink my teeth into his lower lip, a lower lip I've been watching through the night. Before he can answer, I add, "Spend the night with me, you won't regret it."

"Finally the lady sees the advantages of having a strong,

capable man by her side." His voice is all satisfaction and teasing huskiness. He has no idea who I really am—scared, lonely, vulnerable, and full of regrets—as he lifts me up in his arms and carries me to the bed.

I swear he acts like I'm this big prize . . .

A part of me wants to tell him I'm a big empty prize with nothing inside.

But another part just aches for him to fill it and help me finally heal it.

The thought that I might be hurtling past the point of no return briefly crosses my mind. But only briefly, because his slow, drugging kisses are back on my mouth, my face, my neck, sending the real world spinning on its axis. The bed nearly swallows me as he sets me down and spreads out over me.

His hands work faster as he uses them to strip his beautiful body of his clothes and then strip me of mine, his erection thrilling me as he leans over to scrape his hands over every inch of me. Every hot touch tells me that tonight will be an act of raw possession. *His* possession. I usually take back as much as I give, but right now Kenna seems determined to take—and I am trembling.

He spreads out over me and I slide my arm up the coiled muscles of his back. I move my head to the source of his breath and whimper in the only way I know how to make him come kiss me. He does. He gyrates his hips and presses against my hip bone as though he needs the contact, making a soft, growling noise as he slips the strong, probing hand of his tattooed arm between my legs.

He pushes his finger inside.

I spread my legs wider apart and moan.

He sucks my lower lip into his mouth and releases a low, heady groan as he brushes another finger along my entry. I'm trembling with need as he ducks farther down and sucks first one breast, then the other as he continues fingering me. A fire burns in my tummy, and I squirm as my body begins tightening.

"Don't let me come without you," I moan.

"With or without me, you're coming now." He circles his thumb over my clit, and I remember him promising me, *One day, you'll beg. . . .*

"Please. I like watching you come with me. Mackenna, please."

He stops to look at me, both of us panting harder than ever.

"Say it again."

"Come with me."

"The please part."

"Please, Mackenna," I moan.

He growls, using his teeth to tear open a condom packet. Soon he's armed and ready, and he's pulled my legs around his hips, and with a thrust, a gasp, a groan, we're moving together. His dancer's body, muscles trained for strength and flexibility, moves over mine, cock filling me. Moans of ecstasy slip past my lips as I stroke my fingers up his back to cup the hard, clenching muscles of his ass. We find our tempo and our breaths become ragged—our bodies moving like we're extensions of each other.

As he kisses me again, mouth moving deftly over mine, my emotions whirl and skid, and the fire in my cunt spreads to my heart. My walls are down. I can't stop them from tumbling. *I'll raise them when it's over*, I think to myself, but in this moment the smell, feel, and taste of this man consume me. This isn't just a fuck.

And I know it.

As he pumps rhythmically into me, he seems about as lost in the shape and texture of my body as he does when he sings. The harsh look of ecstasy on his face unravels me, and when the involuntary tremors of orgasm begin, I arch to take more of him, surrendering completely as a hot, powerful climax rages through me, tearing my breath away.

I feel him come, and something just loosens in me as his body flexes in orgasm. A tenderness washes over me as I clutch his body tight to mine and whisper, "That's right, come with me, Kenna."

His groan is deep as he buries it in my mouth, and when we sag, he rolls us to spare me his weight as he kisses me, whispering into my mouth, "On a scale of one to ten, how'd that go for you?"

"A million."

He laughs with me and squeezes me in his arms, and I swear his ego just went Shrek-sized. "You look like a conquering Napoleon, don't you. You feel like you got it all right now," I say, groaning tiredly.

"Nah. Napoleon was a little guy. I, on the other hand, am huge."

"Your *ego* is huge."

"Babe, my dick is just as huge as my ego, and they both enjoy being petted by you."

His husky, cocky way of teasing makes me smile, but I hide my smile against his chest and just lie there, feeling happy and still dazed by our lovemaking. By the new feeling of peace between us. We're still in bed, sweaty and silent, hands somehow still wandering aimlessly over each other, when there's a knock on my door and a familiar voice calls, "Mackenna, open up."

Mackenna groans as he stalks naked to open the door. "Not now, Leo."

"Answer your phone, man." Leo spares a glance toward the bed, where I'm clutching the sheet to my breasts. "You won't be thrilled with it."

He leaves as Mackenna grabs his phone and checks the messages. "My dad's parole officer. Fuck." He punches the number and starts pacing until someone apparently answers. "Hey. What's up? So when was it that you last saw him? No, I haven't heard."

After a brief discussion, he hangs up. *"Son of a bitch!"* He falls to the bed and breathes deeply, dragging his hands down his face, then down the back of his head and all the way to his shoulders. "Dad's skipped his last two parole sessions. They can't find him. He quit his job. Jesus!" He looks at me, shaking his head. "I send him money, you know. But my condition is that he works. Otherwise he'll dick around with drugs again. Well, it seems like he is."

Something's squeezing my chest so hard, I have trouble getting any words past my throat.

"Kenna," I say, reaching out to make contact with his back, his shoulder, anything. But suddenly he seems so tense and unapproachable, I stop before making contact and draw my hand back. "I'm really sorry."

He shakes his head, over and over, lost to his thoughts. "If I'd known it was going to be this way, I would've just let him serve his sentence. I did the equivalent of slitting my wrists to get him out early, and this is what he makes of it. This is what he makes of his chance to do something good with his life."

I'm so bad at this. Torn between the need to console him and the fear of how much I care about the haunted look on his face, I just watch him get dressed.

"He'll be all right. Maybe he found a new girlfriend and lost time in her bed?" I suggest.

"Optimism? From you?" His lips curl softly, and he shakes his head. He leans over. "You really are a softie."

"Am not."

"I'm pudding too. At least, I am with you." He walks to the door and leaves me with that. How can he fucking leave me with that?

Well, he does, and for the next half hour I text Brooke and Melanie in a group chat.

Me: Do you believe in second chances?

Mel: Absolutely.

Brooke: If Rem hadn't given me a second chance I'd be fucked right now.

Mel: If I hadn't given Grey a second chance and I hadn't been spared my life, we'd be fucked now too and NOT in a good way.

Me: Ok. Just asking.

Brooke: Pan, why didn't you tell me you had a thing with Crack Bikini's Kenna Jones? Remington plays their "Used" song all the time before a fight starts!

Me: Cause I hate their songs, that's why.

I'm lying, of course. I just hate one song. The one about me. Although a lot of them do talk about anger, being used, and being betrayed—as if *I* were the one who walked away and left him to pick up the pieces of his heart.

But if any of that hell was true for him too, what's going on right now? Why are we getting tangled up in each other all over again?

He could fuck any of his fans, like Jax and Lex do after concerts. He could fuck any groupie, any one of his dancers. They clearly miss him in their beds.

But, like junkies, one taste of each other and we're obsessed.

"Danger," that little voice whispers.

Oh, shut up, brain! You're too damn late.

I squeeze my eyes shut and find myself adding his father's name to my talisman bracelet.

TWELVE

THERE'S ALWAYS THAT ONE ASSHOLE STONE YOU TRIP ON TWICE

Mackenna

I left ten messages on his cell phone as I waited for my flight. By the time I landed, he'd left a message. Said his parole officer had found him and not to worry myself over it. Yeah, right.

He'd left a hotel name and room number too. I pick up a key at reception and end up having to scribble a couple of autographs, until I'm finally on the twentieth floor, popping the door open to find my father slumped in a chair out on the terrace, staring off into space.

A room service tray holding two glasses of champagne is set up by the window. "What the hell is up with you, Dad?"

The anger on my face gives him pause, and it takes him a hot second to get words out of his open jaw. "Hell I . . . you're here? Son . . . I wouldn't be ditching parole if that bitch hadn't made it such a pain in the ass. I need freedom, Kenna, I'm choking here."

"Look up, Dad. You see that? That's fucking sunlight. You

want to get a good dose of that every day, then you *do* your fucking parole."

"I said I'm choking. Feels like I'm still in jail, only with a wider mile radius."

"Jesus," I curse, then lean over, trying to reason with him. "Dad, I know exactly how you feel. You feel trapped by your circumstances, but don't carve yourself a worse one."

"Do you understand? Do you really?"

"You fucking know I do."

He forces out a smile and looks away, over the traffic and the city. " 'Carry on my wayward son,' " he quotes, his dark eyes framed with the same dark circles he came out of prison with. "Remember that song? You rocked it."

"Yeah, I rock everything I touch with my tongue."

A chuckle. " 'There'll be peace when you are done,' " he continues, raising his eyebrows in question.

"You damn well know I want my freedom too. We've talked about this before. I'll move you back to Seattle when I'm done so I can see you more often. Just don't give anyone reason to put you away—you hear me? Be smart about this, Dad, Jesus. I fucking worry about you. Just think things through."

"Like you're smart about that girl?" he counters.

Fuck, I knew he'd bring her up.

Every part of me is tensing to defend her.

But it's no use arguing with Dad about her. I shrug and say nothing, my jaw tight.

"Son, she's toxic to you. You might want to be sure she's into you before you go and drop a good life for the life of your dreams, only to find out it's all a castle in the air, boy."

"She's real to me" is all I give him, and I growl it out in a thick whisper.

He sighs and drops his face in his hands. "Sorry, just can't forget how her bitch mother put me behind bars."

"Dad, *you* got yourself behind bars. See? We reap what we sow. Nobody made you deal, nobody made you make that choice. Own it. I'm owning the choices I made too, and one of those put me in a tight spot. Nobody made me do it. I had to. We just have to do some things sometimes." I scrape my hand down my jaw, because holy shit, those choices hurt.

"You made a deal with her, didn't you? That's why I'm out. That's why I should still be there. That's why my parole sucks— that controlling bitch probably knows you're traveling with her daughter now and is still trying to meddle with you two!"

"It's crossed my mind."

He stares at me, his eyes widening. "So what are you going to do?"

"She's not fucking up my life twice, she's not taking two people I love twice. Just be good, Dad—tomorrow doesn't have to be today. Mine isn't going to be. I've made mistakes. I hurt people I cared about. I'm fixing it." I pat my dad on the back and lean over. "Fix your life the way you want it. Think of another job, I'll pull some strings. Just give me time to get us back to Seattle. And do your parole."

"Mackenna . . ." He stops me as I pull open the terrace door. "You're the reason I hang on. When we lost your mom . . ."

"You did your best. I know. Come on, let's get you home. I'm taking you out later today."

THIRTEEN

IT PAYS TO BE PATIENT, AND GOOD THINGS COME WITH SILVER EYES

Pandora

Two days he's been gone, but he arrives back just in time for the concert. The cameras were everywhere in his absence. Olivia, Tit, and half a dozen of the other dancers were being nice to me. They even asked if I wanted to hang with them the other night. They were going dancing.

"Pandora?" they prodded.

"Thanks, but I'm staying in tonight," I said.

The cameras are trained on me from the moment I step out of my room. They filmed me in practice with Yolanda, right down to filming me while I asked the twins if they'd heard from Mackenna.

I'm only free in my room, but other than when I'm calling Magnolia and Mother, and trying to answer some client e-mails to keep my work from piling up when I return to Seattle, it's lonely.

Tonight I couldn't watch the concert. My legs are too sore from dancing. I've been taking cold showers and using ice packs, but I can't wear my boots and walk at the same time, so I tell Lionel I don't feel well and will stay in the hotel during the concert.

So here I am, waiting out in the hall, sitting on the floor and leaning against the door of Mackenna's room, staring at the scuffs on my boots, when I hear the elevator ping and the sound of the guys joking around fills the hallway.

It's almost inexplicable, the way my heart turns over in my chest when I catch sight of him. He's wearing a pink wig, much like the one he wore the first day I saw him, and he's dressed in gold leather pants, and sporting little flecks of glitter on his golden chest. He wears his everyday uniform of chains, bracelets, and tattoos.

And I want to lick, kiss, touch, suck, and fuck the living daylights out of him. I also want him to take me in his arms and tell me he's all right. That his father is all right. I want to tell him he's lucky that he even *has* a father. Whether he's fucking up his new life or not, at least his father is alive. Unlike mine. His father has a chance to say he's sorry, make things right. My father was never able to even attempt to explain that the trip was "not what it seemed," or that he wasn't "involved with his assistant." He never got the chance to tell me that, no matter what, he'd always love me.

The laughter fades when the three men spot me. There are two women accompanying them, each draped over one of the twins. Mackenna is alone, and when he looks at me, I know he is alone because of this—of the electricity suddenly sparkling all the way from where he stands, to right here, where I sit.

"Hey, Kenna," I say, trying to stand. The action is a bit awkward on account of my sore muscles.

He's instantly by my side, helping me up by the elbow. "You okay? Leo said you weren't feeling well."

"Headache, but now it's gone. Who knew?" I lie, smiling softly.

He smiles back at me and slips his key into the slot. He tugs me inside with him, and my knees feel weak when he grips my hand in his bigger one as he goes to get his toothbrush.

"Mackenna, he okay?" I ask. I'm so anxious on his behalf. I know firsthand how much, how very much, Mackenna loves his dad. "Your dad."

"Yeah, they found him."

"Do you need something . . . ?" I swallow, because it's so hard to say what comes next. "Do you need me?"

He turns around, and I'm bowled over by the soul-searing, heartrending, raw need I see in his eyes. I suddenly don't need words. My whole body responds to that look. "There are cameras here," he whispers. Then, silently, he takes my hand and leads me down the hall, toward my room. He shuts the door behind us.

"What happened?" I ask him.

"He got drunk. Passed out in some hotel with some whore."

"Oh, god, I'm sorry."

"Yeah. Well. At least he wasn't dealing." He doesn't sound too convinced that all is well, though.

Something's bothering him, and the urge to appease him is stronger than ever.

I quickly say, "Look, my dad fucked up too, Kenna. But he could never . . . *fix* things. Your dad still can."

He pries off his wig, tosses it aside with a sigh, then goes into the restroom and comes out with a damp towel, which he slowly swipes across his muscled, sparkling tan chest. "Do you ever wonder what would've happened if your father had the chance to say he was sorry?" Mackenna asks me.

"He didn't care, he betrayed us." Guess that's all I can do; repeat what my mother's drilled into my head for years.

"Oh, Pink, he *cared*," he contradicts. "Anyone who really knows you can't help but care. That friend who defended you at the concert when you veggie-bombed me? She cares."

"Melanie?" I smile when I think of her. She's my opposite, and I need her. I need her in my life the way any living thing, except for a parasite, needs the sun. "Brooke, Kyle . . . I guess they care too," I admit, then, on impulse, I unlock my phone and show him a picture of Magnolia as he continues wiping the glitter off his arms.

"She cares for me most of all."

"Look at that. Who's that little thing?"

I love his grin so much I ache in a delicious way inside my heart. "My cousin. Her mother battled leukemia but lost. Magnolia saved us—saved my mother and me. I don't know where we'd both be if she hadn't come into our lives."

"We need a little cape for her with a big 'M' so she knows she's a superstar, huh?"

I smile as I set my phone aside. "You're teasing me, but I like the idea. She'd love that. She doesn't want to be a princess, and she seems more inclined to be a cape person."

"Like her Aunt Pink?"

I smile and he chuckles with me, then he turns somber. Oh god, I missed him. I've only been with the band two weeks, but I've felt his absence over the last few days. And I missed him more than ever.

"You know, the band . . . ," he begins but stops to take a breath. "When Dad got arrested—when my life went to shit and I lost everything I loved—" He holds my gaze and nods solemnly. "The band saved me too."

I feel that ever-present pain, acute as ever as it pricks me. "I'm glad it saved you, Mackenna," I whisper.

"I fucked up, Pink."

"How? Because you walked away?" I don't know why I ask this, but the words are out before I know it.

"No." In slow, predatory moves, he approaches me. "Because when I could finally come get you, I didn't. I didn't think you'd want me to, but that shouldn't have mattered. I should've come back for you."

"No, you shouldn't have. Because my kitchen would've had more ammunition than just tomatoes." I fake laugh, trying to lighten the mood.

Unfortunately he doesn't find that funny.

Before he can push me and find all the cracks in my walls—which are becoming weaker and weaker by the second—I pull his head down and start nibbling on his lips.

"You miss me?" he suddenly demands to know. He eases his mouth away until it is less than an inch from mine. He tortures me by holding it still, keeping it from me. "You miss me?" he asks again, sliding his hands under the fall of my hair.

"Please stop trying to make me into some simpering fool over you. Just kiss me."

"You'll never be a simpering fool, just tell me you missed me," he says, looking at me, gaze fierce.

I make a noise of protest, and he laughs softly. "Fine," he whispers, brushing his lips to mine. I think I've gotten away with it, so I move to kiss him. But before I can crush my lips with his, he tells me, "But *I* missed *you*."

FOURTEEN

PLANS

Mackenna

We're in a tangle. No cameras. Nothing. Nothing but me and her. She's sweaty and smells like sex, and that's just the way I want her to smell.

I want her to smell like me.

Hell, this here—her hair with that pink streak spread out on the pillow and her limbs around me—this is so fucking perfect, I don't want to even go take a piss.

I want so much more, I'm a greedy fucking man. Greedy as fuck when it comes to her. I growl softly and nip at her shoulder, murmuring, "I need to go talk to Leo."

She sighs, stretches. "About what?"

I look at her; she's a pistol and a half, and I love having my hands full with her. "I'll tell you later, woman. Cover up so I at least get my mind out of your luscious curves."

"I'm hot and sweaty. I don't want to cover up."

She groans, and I bury my own groan in her neck. "And I don't want to leave this bed." Now I nip at the soft, tender tendon of her throat. "But the sooner I talk to him, the sooner I can come back here."

"Mackenna," she laughs, her arms tight around my neck, "are you seriously going *now*?"

I smack her ass playfully. "Yeah. I've got big plans for your future."

"Come on! Stay here. Tonight I wanted . . ." She looks at me with those pitch-black eyes, then frowns as if she doesn't like what she was about to say. They're heavy-lidded, her eyes. "I want us to be friends," she says at last.

"Friends?" I repeat.

"Yeah. I want . . ." She sits up warily, tugs her hair. "I want to try to move on, Mackenna."

"You want to move on from me?"

Fuck me, but that's just not what I wanted to hear. Still, I sound casual. She'd never guess the size of the blade I feel sticking out of my gut right now.

"No. From the past," she says.

"Really," I say, without inflection.

But I can't let go. I can't let go of the past. How can you let go when all you want is to turn back time and make a different choice? And yet she looks so fucking hopeful, as if this right here is the moment where she can finally live a happier life.

I don't want to tell her that that's not what I want.

"Your hair is fucking crazy." I tug on the cotton candy streak.

She flashes a brief but rare smile. "Tell me about your crazy wigs."

"My wigs are cool, babe. You better watch what you say about them."

"Do you like wearing your wigs, or is it something they make you do?"

"The wigs?"

"No! Idiot! Leo—your contract."

"Nah, I do it myself. Makes it easier. Like stepping into a persona. I dig it."

"Because you're fun. You always did like to have fun. Oooh. And like the technique of pretending no one out there is me. Your jinx."

"You're not a jinx."

"All that pot smoke your bandmates blow out is messing with your head. You don't make any sense. Explain."

"You're not a jinx. It helps when you're the only one I'd want to make proud of me."

An intense but secret expression flickers in her eyes.

My lips curl, an empty smile.

"That's news to you?" I laugh. "You're the only one I've never been good enough for." I'm putting it all out there. "Knowing it's not you out there relieves some of the performance pressure."

"I . . ." She blinks, her face losing some of its color.

"Cat got your tongue?" I lean in and tongue her mouth.

She tongues me back, and I sigh and pull her closer. She sighs back, relaxing into the present. No more past. Fuckups. Mistakes. All those years. All that pain. All that impotence. The frustration. Gone.

She closes her eyes when my fingertips reach her scalp, and her tits rise and fall against my chest, awakening my cock to come play again. But I can't yet. There's something I must do first.

I kiss the top of her head. "Go to sleep."

"Why? For your information, meathead, I wasn't planning on kicking you out tonight."

"Gotta talk to Leo."

❤ ❤ ❤

NO SURPRISE TO find out Lionel has company when I knock on his door. He ushers me into the living room while Tit wraps herself with a bathrobe and pouts from the bed.

Lionel shuts the door between the bedroom and sitting area, blocking her from us. "What happened at that rodeo bar was unacceptable, Leo," I warn.

"Just trying to get a couple good scenes, something organic and natural. Damn, you love jumping into fights."

"Yeah—but not when she's in it," I growl, pacing around like a caged tiger, watched, taunted, pricked. "I need to get her out of here, Leo," I finally tell him, spinning around to face him.

"You don't need to do anything except work her out of your system, Jones."

"I want to drive separately."

His eyes nearly bug out. "Excuse me?"

"You heard me. Pandora and I are heading to New Orleans and Dallas on our own. I want her away from the cameras, the fans, the girls. Everything."

"You can't just up and leave. We have a movie to film, and the producer wants her on the stage of Madison Square Garden. She needs to practice. Plus, your job is to give us some meaty shit for film—that is, if you still want what you asked for?"

"You let me drive separately with her, I'll help her with her dance routine. Hell, I'll practice the kiss until it's perfect. I'll even give you a new song. God knows, it's in my head all the time. Look, she doesn't like flying, and the cameras are driving me nuts."

"You want it all, dude, you want me to give you what you want—"

"Look," I interrupt, narrowing my eyes as I aim my index finger his way, "you're gonna get the kiss and I'll also give you a song. One last song before you release me from my contract. That's more than fair."

Leo looks constipated, but I don't fucking care. With his
eyes narrowed on me as he seems to let everything sink in, I
let him watch me call a rental service and get a car for Pandora
and me.

As soon as the call ends, Lionel is on me with a furious
glare, tightening the sash of the bathrobe that just so happens
to match the one Tit was wearing. "You fucking her? Heard on
camera there was fucking. We want to see some fucking action,
Kenna."

"You're not going to see shit."

"I'll give you what you want," he relents, "but only *if* you
make this movie worth remembering."

"Leo, we had a *deal*," I remind him. "You said you'd release
me if I went along with this bullshit. You wanted the kiss, and all
you're getting is that kiss." Kissing Pink in front of thousands of
fans, her lips on mine—hell, I know she'll be angry. But she gets
her chance to let the world know my song is bullshit. Not that I
care all that much. Every complaint in that song is because I've
been in love with her for *years.*

"Fine. Go drive her around in a car, I don't care. But I get that
kiss and that song or you get nothing, you hear?"

I head for the door. "I hear."

"Make her want it, Kenna!" he calls.

"Oh, she wants it." I slam the door shut after me.

Just not as much as I fucking do.

My father has a second chance, and I realize now that so do I.
Difference is, I'm not screwing mine.

When I slip back into her room, she's lying in bed and quickly
rises up onto her arms when I arrive. *You could never fall asleep
when you knew I was coming, could you, baby?*

"Hey," I say, struggling with the sensation of carrying a grenade inside my chest. Grenade about to go *boom!*

Holy shit, I feel powerful things for her.

I feel everything for her. Anger and protectiveness. Possessiveness and pain. I feel fucking *good* with her. I feel . . .

"Come back to bed," she whispers, lifting the sheets.

God, I'm not fucking it up this time.

FIFTEEN

A ROAD TRIP WITH A ROCK GOD

Pandora

"Mackenna, I'm not getting in that car."

"I see two choices for you, Pink, and two only. It's either the jet or the Lamborghini. Your pick."

"The door doesn't even open right! What's with that, Kenna? You have a big dick—you don't need these gadgets to feel like a man."

"Stone, seriously, get in the fucking car."

"*Jones*, you want the entire highway to look in your direction as we go to the airport? Is your rockstar status not enough to make you feel good about yourself?"

He laughs. "Babe, we'll be passing by so fast no one will get a glimpse of our faces. Come on."

He slams my suitcase and a small duffel into the trunk, then comes around and yanks the door open. "What are you waiting for? *Get in.*"

I edge inside and when he leans over, my insides stir, as if my stomach is in a blender. "Why are you doing this?" His eyes hold mine as he reaches for the belt and slowly starts strapping me in.

"Easy. Because I want to. I want to be away from those bozos . . . and alone with you."

His scent reaches me, and it annoys me that I sound breathless—even if I have been fucked ten ways to Sunday already. "You sure woke up chivalrous today. I never thought you'd grow up to be such a gentleman."

"I can be gentle, just not with this car." He settles down in his seat, then snaps the belt on with a cocky smile. He strokes the wheel almost with the same loving care he strokes me with, then sets the GPS, his arms bulging, the flex of his muscles causing an uncomfortable tickle between my legs. He starts the car with a big roar and presses the pedal, and the engine roars even more.

"So, is there an ulterior motive for us driving to the airport?" I ask.

"We're not heading to the airport."

He smirks and zooms us out of there with a screech of tires only fast, scary cars with expert drivers in movies make. Before I can demand specifics, he drops our windows and the sunroof, and the wind presses his shirt to his chest, every muscle grabbing my attention. I take in the buildings that we pass, then nothing. Every couple of minutes, my eyes drift to him. I can't stop. The wind is the only actual sound, but in my head, there are a thousand.

Why did he leave? What does he want with me now? Does it matter? Do I want to take his love, just so I can fling it back in his face? Or am I trying to prove to myself that I'm loveable? Or am I doing this—this *thing* with him—simply because it's the thing I've wanted most, my whole life?

"So what's the plan?" I ask.

"We road trip to Dallas, spend a night at a hotel, then arrive for practice before the concert. We've got to beware of the fucking paps, but I've got my lucky cap for that." He looks at me, raking his eyes up and down. "Want to stop for a couple of disguises?"

"I can always wear your mohawk."

He smiles and reaches out to take my hand, bringing it over to his thigh, keeping his hand on mine as he hums a Mozart song. I swear it's so fucking sexy when he hums that I almost wish he wouldn't. It's sexy because he likes real music and can play piano and guitar like a devil. All because of the way he listens to the melody, then repeats it, but with his own twist.

The wind doesn't even touch his buzz cut, and it's sexy. How it stays in place. He's holding my hand, and that's sexy too.

And dangerous.

Danger! I pull my hand away. "Let's keep it real, okay? There's no point in pretending shit if we're just fuck buddies."

"Really now?"

"Absolutely."

"So, what am I supposed to do? What's my role?"

He's amusing himself; I scowl.

"Nothing. You be yourself—an asshole—and I'll be me."

"Charming as always?"

"Wow, seriously, what did you have for breakfast today?"

"You'll be my woman."

"The way you say it like I have almost no choice is irritating. But yes, fine. And we just . . . *fuck*. On occasion. And on that day when I have to kiss you, I'll dance, making a complete idiot of myself. Then we finish with whatever terms, and I leave." I stare out the window, but I hear him laugh, like I'm hilarious.

"I happen to hold my fuck buddies' hands." He grins and stubbornly takes my hand back. I groan, and he laughs.

"What have you got to lose? I know you haven't been with

a man since me. I know that guy at the hotel parking lot was a friend."

"How do you know?"

"I just *know*," he dismisses. "What do you have to lose, letting me hold your hand? I've held it tons of times before."

I hesitate. I want to say something snarky, but the way he looks at me, his face uncharacteristically somber, calls for the truth. "Because you'll hold my hand, and I'll get used to the way it feels, and before I know it, you'll let go of it . . . again," I say, my heart hurting as I pull my hand free once more.

His hand comes to rest on the wheel, clenching it tight. I stare out the window, then burst out, "You're . . . it's not like you're normal, or me . . . or this is normal. Dude, we're in the middle of a fucking concert tour, with all your whore dancers licking you up. I'm just the one you're banging."

"You *are* the one I'm banging, and I like my hands on you. Deal with it." He grabs my hand again, giving me a don't-test-me squeeze. I hesitate. His hand is warm in mine, and the air swirls around us. He rubs his thumb into my palm. "I fucking like it, Pink," he growls.

God, he exhausts me. Wears me out. I want to put up my walls, but instead I feel like crashing.

After driving for a while, we stop at a diner. "Everybody's going to recognize you."

Uncaring, he puts on his aviators, pulls out a navy blue cap, and pulls me inside, lacing our fingers together. He tugs me into a booth at the back, then sets his arm around my shoulder. "What do you want?"

I flip open the menu, acutely aware of his thumb absently rubbing my neck as he looks at his menu too.

The waitress takes our order, and when she leaves, Mackenna

pulls off his glasses, turns my head around by the chin, and starts kissing and nibbling my neck in a way that makes my toes curl. I end up leaning into the nook of his arm and cuddling a little as we wait for our food. "I like driving you around in that Lambo," he lazily admits, running a heavy hand down my hair. "Getting that pink strand of hair tangled up with your black."

Delightful little tingles race through my bloodstream. This is how it could have been with us. This is how it could have been if I'd told my mother the truth. If he'd shown up one day. Or we simply hadn't needed to run away.

"Admit it, you like the Lambo." He rubs his silver ring over my bottom lip, the smirk on his face adorable.

"It's so fucking uncomfortable," I hedge.

"Huh. We really should find other uses for that mouth of yours."

He shoves all five fingers of one hand into my tangled hair and I arch my body closer, pressing my breasts to his hard chest to let him know I want him to kiss me again. Reading me perfectly, he kisses my lips—softly, as if I'm fragile. As if he wants to memorize taste and texture and shape.

"Guys with bikes kiss their women harder," he says. "Maybe we should trade the Lambo for a bike? Get something with power rumbling between your thighs?"

Already, there's something rumbling between my thighs.

His voice.

The way it affects me when it gets all husky.

"There's no way I'm riding a motorcycle on a highway."

"No? No bikes?" He chuckles and spares a long, hungry look at me, his eyes laughing too. "I know what you'd enjoy doing. Other than me." There's that smirk again.

"You do, do you?" I think I'm smirking too as I raise an eyebrow in challenge. I'm such a good bluffer, I bet he has no idea I'm squeezing my thighs together under the table, fighting to quell the ripple of need running through me.

He prolongs the moment as though to heighten the suspense, his finger rubbing up and down the length of my neck now. "Well . . . do you want to know? Pink?"

God, I can't stop grinning. I feel . . . young. Carefree. Alive. Sexy. Cherished. "I have a feeling you're going to tell me anyway, Kenna."

He slips his hand under the table and cups one of my thighs as he nods to my plate and whispers, "Finish your meal and I'll show you instead."

Shortly after, on our way to this mysterious place, we pull up in front of a gas station to feed the Lambo's apparently voracious appetite for gasoline. While I get a bottle of water, Mackenna gets some gum, M&M's, and corn nuts, and we head out again.

Mackenna took my hand going in and out of the store, then he takes it in the car again too. I tell myself I'm too tired to fight him, but the truth is, I like it so much, it gives me flutters every time he reaches for me. As we head down the highway, I watch, hypnotized, as he drags his thumb over my knuckles while he drives. The glint of his silver ring in the sunshine is growing deliciously familiar.

"Where are we going?" I ask for about the third time.

His lips hitch up in one corner. "Paradise, Pink."

"Mackenna, if this has anything to do with sex . . ."

"No, babe, but you could say it's damn well close to the next best thing for you and me." He winks. And not far behind the wink is that sexy smirk of his.

I'm so puzzled, I can't think of anything close to sex but . . . sex. Kissing and necking. Making out. What's the next best thing to sex??

It's not yet dusk when we stop at a school parking lot. I've never been in this school, have no idea what he's plotting, but I let him guide me by the hand to a side entry. Mackenna greets a man by the door, then he quietly leads me to an indoor ice rink.

I stare at the cool, smooth ice surface in the quiet school and I can't believe my own eyes. Mackenna grins.

"College hockey team plays here. I pulled a couple of strings."

The strings of my heart? He's playing those so well too. My chest has never felt so full as I take the skates he extends by the laces, and I immediately kick off my shoes and slide them on.

Ohmigod, it's been . . . forever.

And a day.

I line up my skates and slide onto the ice with a floating sensation in my legs. I find my balance within a minute, and I slowly raise my hands and spin, my face turned to the ceiling rafters. "Ohmigod, do you realize how long it's been?"

He ties his own skates and catches up with me fast: as fast as a hockey player. "A thousand and five hundred days," he tells me.

When he slides his arm around my waist and pulls my body to his, aligning us perfectly, my smile fades, but my happiness doesn't. He takes my arm and spins me like a top, for the first time in a long time, and I laugh. I laugh and squeal, "Don't let me fall!"

"Never."

He catches me when I grow dizzy, and then we skate and spin, skate and play, skate and race each other, fool around until we fall. We get tangled in each other's legs and laugh as we go down. He catches me every time, always ready to break my fall, and then we sit there, my body slightly on top of his, catching our breath. Just like old times.

But now, he doesn't need to wear a cap on his head to hide his face, and I don't need an oversized cap on mine to avoid being seen.

His face is right before me, every angle available for my attention.

I give it my all, while he does the same.

I close my eyes when he traces his silver ring along my jawline, up to my temple, around my ear. "I love your face." His voice is thick, sexy. Unique.

I feel it in every cell of me.

My eyes open to find his, and his stare is intent. Unapologetic. Reverent and still very, very busy taking me in.

"And your lips," he murmurs thickly, his ring now rubbing them too. "I love making these lips smile." I find myself smiling and feeling an intense happiness when he smiles back at me.

No bullshit. This is real. And perfect.

"All right, lady, time to go," he says, getting up on his feet.

"Good. My butt's frozen," I lie.

But I never want to leave this place. I never want to forget how I feel when I'm in his arms, spinning and spinning and spinning like a kid.

WE STOP AT a motel, the first we find after sunset. We're both tired. Mackenna pulls me inside, opens the shower, and murmurs, "Come shower with me."

My first instinct is no.

Too intimate . . .

Too risky . . .

Danger.

"No funny business. Promise." He lifts his hands innocently.

My heart seems to lead before my brain can settle on what to do, and before I know it, I'm already peeling off my clothes, aware of the liquid tenderness in his gaze as he watches me.

He keeps his word, but I can tell it's a test of honor. He's very hard. His erection almost gets in the way every time we shift around to help each other soap up. I try to soap up quickly so I can finish quickly and stop feeling jittery and hot, but when he soaps me up with his big hands, I just can't rush the shower anymore. So a quick shower turns into a long shower. He soaps me, and I soap him. We close our eyes. Groan a little. Whisper, "You feel good." That came from me, and he's not far behind as he lathers my hair with shampoo, his wet lips brushing my earlobe. "You smell good. I want to taste you tonight."

The panel steams up.

"I really need to work," I say reluctantly.

"No one's stopping you," he says.

"Okay."

I step out of the shower and wrap myself in a towel, but Mackenna remains, rinsing the rest of the soap from himself. As I towel dry, I notice him in the stall, turning the knob for cold water. He closes his eyes as the water runs down his chest. He groans, and I hadn't realized he was so aroused by our shower; his cock looks like a baseball bat aimed high for a home run swing.

Between my legs, I ache with the want to have that, him, in me. Way to go for saying you need to work, Pandora.

Idiot.

I turn away when he steps out of the shower, and it takes me a moment to have the courage to take a peek. He's got a towel around his hips, a glorious, wet rock god, flashing me a smile. "You okay, babe? Hop on the Wi-Fi and do your thing while I dick about with my guitar."

Did he say "dick"?

"O-okay," I say, flushing like a moron as I pull out my laptop and sit on the bed with it.

Is he still hard?

Did it go soft?

Does he still want to do it?

Hell I want to do it.

We both work quietly, and I peer from my computer to where he sits on the sofa by the window. He looked so fucking hot taking a cold shower I'm still stewing inside. He looks hot stroking those fingers over his guitar. Even when he showers, he can never really get rid of the kohl under his eyes, and Lord, he looks hot with that too. I can't believe how hard he'd been in that shower. Can that possibly be remedied by just cold water? He didn't pressure me when he'd given me his word, and by god, that's superhot too.

Listen to me. This, right here, is all the sex I didn't have for six years demanding to be experienced. Fuck that. I have work to do.

Back to my computer: I have an e-mail from Melanie.

Why aren't you answering your texts?

At least tell me you're alive.

Brooke is worried too.

I'm good I shoot back. Then I peer up at him again, biting down on my smile. *Really, really good.*

I smile. Yes, it's good. But do I really think things will be any different from last time? That he'll stop doing whatever he wants for me? Or I could ever leave Magnolia alone with my mom for him?

I can't. We've hurt each other too much. Our past runs too deep. We can't suddenly just be . . . happy.

Yes, but you can have sex, you silly nymphomaniac.

I set my computer on the bed. I can work when I get back home, to my life, but he won't be here forever.

Quietly, I walk up to him. "What are you writing? Do you need more inspiration? I seem to be good at that."

He smiles and jots down a couple of more things on his iPhone, then sets it aside.

I point at his lap, covered still in a white towel. "I'm going to sit here. You look like an amazing, sexy chair."

"And I'm all yours," he says with a curious glint in his eyes. He sets his guitar aside.

Once I'm settled, I slide my arms around his neck. "So, any crimes planned for the night?" I taunt.

"Aside from ravaging you, flogging you, and making you wake the motel with your yells of pleasure? No, none at all."

I don't understand why he whisked me away, but he saved me an airplane flight. He makes me have fun. Now I want to seduce the sexy fuck, but I'm unsure how to start. I can almost hear Melanie groaning as she'd say something like, "He's a guy. How complicated can it be? Just stroke him and watch him turn to putty . . ."

"I've been thinking about you all day," I whisper, leaning over and licking his earlobe.

"Shit. Fuck. Really?" He grabs me and pulls me back to look at me, searching my face.

"Love taking a shower with you," I whisper, feeling vulnerable to admit it.

He surveys me and his voice thickens. "You're serious, babe?"

I'm so aroused just smelling the soap on his skin, I groan and lean over, licking his ear again. "I didn't realize a man could get so hard just by taking a shower with a girl. Did you like soaping me? Was it on purpose, inviting me to the shower? To make me hot?"

His eyes are starting to smolder.

"It turned me on, Kenna," I moan, rubbing my chest against him. I've never felt so needy, so desperate.

His cock is quickly getting into the game, pulsing thick under my bottom. "Do you want to bring one of those tits over to my mouth so I can give it a good long suck?" His eyes are dirty silver and his words are just as dirty. Just as hot.

"Yes, please," I whisper, pulling off my sleep shirt and lifting one of my breasts to his mouth.

"How about a bite?" He nips my nipple before I can say anything, his teeth sinking lightly around my areola. I arch and rock against his cock.

"Oh, god," I breathe when his cock makes delicious friction between my legs.

My pulse skitters deliciously fast and I bite his earlobe, whimpering, "Yes."

"Hmm. You're so fucking hot for it. How about we do start thinking of whips and floggers for you, hmm?"

"You're into that?"

"Right now, I'm into how fucking hot you are."

Mindlessly, I run my lips over his throat as I moan out, "And I'm into you. And this. And how hard you are under my bum."

His erection is thick and long against my pussy and buttocks. I take my breast and feed it into his mouth again. Dizzy with pleasure, I watch his tongue lave the tip of my nipple. I watch him nibble, then suck me. Watching him do the same to both my breasts arouses me to the point where I'm drenched.

"Put a rubber on my dick and put it in you." When I pull out a condom from the back pocket of his discarded jeans, he catches my face with one hand, holding me in place so I never once stop looking at him as I unravel his towel, slide the condom over his beautiful, straining erection, and then hold his dick up high as I lower myself on him.

"Oh, god," I moan, letting go of the base of his cock so my pussy can slowly slide all the way down.

He groans, "Pandora. Gorgeous. Pink . . . open your legs wider so you can take more of me."

I do.

Another groan, this one from both of us.

"Ahh, Jesus, rock me slowly. Rock my fucking world, Pink."

He sounds so lost in me I end up kissing him, slow and deep as I slowly, deliberately slowly, drag out our pleasures as I ride him on the sofa. He drags his mouth down my neck, nips at my breasts, my chin, rubbing his hands just as slow over my curves.

He grabs my ass and slides one finger down my buttocks, caressing between my ass cheeks. When he uses his middle finger to tease the rosette of my ass, a yelp of pure pleasure leaves me.

"Kenna!" The pleasure as he penetrates my ass twists and pulls my body.

"That's right. I'm gonna rock your world too." He twirls his tongue over my nipples and fingers me deeply to prove it. I'm nearly in torment. My every orifice being fucked by him. I'm being cock fucked, finger fucked, tongue fucked at the same time by the sexiest man I know.

My orgasm hits me, fast and hard, and then for a while, he keeps prolonging his own pleasure by seizing me by the hips and lifting and lowering my body on his.

With my body relaxed and still rocking with the occasional residual shudder, I become his own living fuck doll, aware of his breath, the jerks of his chest, the pulsations in his cock every time he holds me by the hips to lift me and drop me down on him. I enjoy every inch of his ecstasy as he uses me for it . . . my eyes fixed on his face and the way his jaw tightens, his neck arches, and he comes inside me with a growl so sexy, my cunt reflexively clenches around his thickness.

"God, you feel phenomenal," he sighs at last.

He wraps his arms around me and pulls me down on him, catching his breath with deep, jagged pulls of air. He tips my head back for a moment. "How do you feel?"

"Delicious."

"Hmm. Because you are. Delicious. Tasty as fuck."

He drops a kiss on me and then leans his head back. His eyes drift shut and I notice, when I peer up at him, there's this smile of satisfaction on his face. God, he's so beautiful. His body relaxed, his hair so short it's dry, almost instantly. All his muscles are surrounding me, and I'm being held like I haven't been held for years.

I drift off to sleep on his lap with a strange fullness in my chest, my face tucked into the crook of his neck, and I think of how much I wish we could've been if we'd been able to stay together.

SIXTEEN

FEELS LIKE A HONEYMOON EXCEPT WE'RE NOT HONEYS. ARE WE?!?!

Pandora

The lack of paparazzi means that we enjoy our motel stay so much that we book another one in Dallas. Nobody would expect a member of Crack Bikini to stay in such a place—which works for us. When I wake up, the room is bursting with evidence. Evidence of *us*. There's a headset on a table, a guitar, an electric keyboard, and the remains of a bottle of wine and shared pizza.

And there's him too.

I don't even know what to call this feeling, but it's a mix of both pain and pleasure every time I look at him. He smiles when I approach, but he keeps humming, stroking the keyboard with his fingers. The tone is soft, almost like a ballad. "There's this song in my head," he says.

Of course. There's a reason why they've won three Grammy Awards so far and are considered by many to be the modern gods of rock and roll. And as I watch Mackenna—the way he makes music with his eyes closed, murmuring to himself before jotting down words—I feel the walls around me melt. For him. For how easy it is to lose yourself in the limelight. The custom coaches for touring, with their big, flashy lights. Not to mention those blue interior lights that almost make them feel like a damn whorehouse. Hiding your face half the time just to have some privacy. I couldn't ever live with this. Not even for him. But he's coped rather well. He's just like he used to be, except even bolder, and more confident.

And his confidence—his boldness—is sexy.

Quietly, I watch him, for the first time accepting maybe this is how things were meant to be. Maybe this trip won't give me revenge. Maybe it will give me peace.

I study his ears and how they look adorable, just slightly too small for his rounded skull, admiring that he's writing his own material. By the way he hums, I'm now positive it's a ballad.

I remember one article in *Rolling Stone* magazine. He and the twins had been asked about the paparazzi, and they'd said something like, "Half of it is pure lies. Pictures start popping up, and what's worse is you don't remember who took those pictures, when, or even how."

"And the other half?" the interviewer had asked.

They had laughed, and it had been Mackenna who'd said, "True. Every fucking word of it."

They'd talked of how they recorded, taking days to rehearse and do sound checks, singing for hours on end until they got the sounds exactly right. There was talk of eighteen-hour stints at the studio, and topping the Billboard charts. The interview wound down with the guys discussing their relaxed approach to coming up with new material—meeting up to write, scribble, hum. They talked of all that.

But now, it's just him, with a red guitar in his arms that's as scuffed and as badass as the rocker holding it.

He hums the start, then calls me forward with a lift of his jaw.

I didn't cry when he left me. If I'd started, I never would have stopped. But when he sets the guitar aside, pats his knee, and I drop down, he whispers five words of the song in my ear, and the prickling sensation behind my eyes surprises me.

I haven't had to deal with listening to his voice in my ear until this month. I wasn't prepared for how it would shake me every time. How it would hurt so deeply.

"Haven't been able to write in a while," he whispers, an adorable little smile crossing his lips. "Thank you for this song, Pandora."

I nod silently. I can't believe that, in a matter of weeks, I will spend the rest of my days seeing him on TV. Watching from afar.

"I *am* good for inspiration, then," I say, searching his face, delighting in how young it looks in the morning sunlight. "Are you writing about my rotting teeth? And the frogs I eat?"

"Ahh, that's you. How's *your* song going, by the way?"

"It's going," I lie.

At first, I stop my hand from reaching out to touch his hair, then I go ahead and let it touch anyway. "Morning, Mackenna."

He returns my look, a silver color the likes of which I've never seen in his eyes. "Good morning, Pandora."

We're both smiling like idiots when we hear his cell buzz. Lifting a finger, he tells me, "One second, Pink," and lifts the phone to his ear. I get up for the room service menu when I hear him greet someone I assume to be one of the twins.

"No, I'm not shitting you," he says in a tone that says, *I'm shitting all over you.* "The motor just up and died. Gotta get a new car, and they're out of muscle cars. I'm not riding in a pansy car.

Hell, Pink won't ride in anything but a muscle car now. So, I'll just get a bike or some shit."

Ohmigod! Seriously? I wheel around, and he gives me a thumbs-up.

I scowl and plant my hands on my hips.

"Yeah, she wanted another Lambo or a Ferrari, but they can't get them here on time, so I improvised."

Shaking my head, I go take a quick shower. It doesn't take long, and I'm pulling out a change of fresh clothes, when, phone still pressed to his ear, he leaps from the sofa and takes them from me, setting them aside.

Ooooh. He doesn't want me to dress?

He's listening to the other end, saying, "Hmm, yes," and nodding as he peels the towel off me, then turns me to face the window. At first I don't understand—then I spot it. In our parking space. Where the Lamborghini used to be.

A red motorcycle—brand new, as if he's just bought it—is parked outside, two helmets hanging from the handlebars. He hangs up. "I just bought us a couple of more hours away from practice."

"To do what?"

"You."

I glance over my shoulder and into his masculine face as he cups my breast from behind, his hand strong and eager as it pinches and plays with my nipple.

He grins, his diamond earring glinting as he leans over and presses a butterfly kiss to my shoulder. "I had the car towed," he confesses.

"But it was working just fine."

He nibbles my skin, sending a ripple of warmth through me. "Listen, Pink. You don't get to be where I am by not stretching the truth now and again."

He turns me around, and I feel his erection poking deliciously into my stomach. "Mackenna," I protest.

"Exactly what I hoped you'd say, but not the right tone," he murmurs. "Let's remedy that, Pink. I want you moaning it."

He brushes my lips with his. I hold my breath as a rush of hot lightning bolts hit me. He brushes my lips again, and when I mewl, he chuckles at the victory.

"Mackenna," I say, groaning as I grasp the back of his head.

He stops chuckling and slides his open hands around my waist to my ass, settling his lips on mine like he wants to taste every fiber of me. My head falls back and he cups my skull in one hand, scouring every corner of my mouth with his silken, hot, delicious tongue. *That* makes me moan. He groans in return and pulls me up against the wall.

And there, he fucks me.

❥ ❤ ❤

I'M EXCITED ABOUT riding that bike. Bad boy. Bike. I might have fantasized about it once . . . or twice. But I scowl so he doesn't know it. "A helmet? *Really?* In all my dreams of bike riding, I never once wore a helmet."

"We're taking this down to New Orleans after the concert. Hate to break it to you, gorgeous, but you're hardheaded, not immortal, and I want that pretty head intact so I can keep messing with it."

"Oh, well, when you put it that way."

I want to stop the flocks of nervous butterflies inside me. To remind myself that he hurt me, and he will do it again. But apart from Magnolia, he has always been the only one to make me truly happy. To bring out the less grumpy side of me.

"Put it on," he says, strapping the helmet on my head. He

peers into my eyes, smacks a kiss on my lips, then climbs onto the bike. Swinging my leg over, I follow, my whole body aware of where my breasts press his back, where my parted legs rest along his thighs. I tuck my cheek to his back and feel the rumble of the Ducati as he ignites it, all the while telling myself, over and over, that none of this is real.

"You going to hang tight, gorgeous?" he says, reaching behind me and squeezing my butt, pressing me closer.

"I'm fucking tight, Kenna. It's not like I'm going to let go, drop, and die!" I say, my laughter fogging my visor.

"Jesus, that mouth," he says, shaking his helmet. He turns, and under the blue tinted visor, I can feel his eyes take me in as he pulls my arms tighter around his waist. Then he grabs the handle, flicks up the kickstand, and with another delicious rumble, we're off.

I laugh out loud, and I think he hears me, because, through the wind, he turns slightly. Most of his face is hidden, but I can tell his grin is huge. "You like that?" he says, and his voice carries over the noise of the bike.

"Yeah."

"How do you feel?"

Happy, I think to myself.

"I feel great," I call out. "Just please don't crash."

IN DALLAS, THE stage lights crackle as the dancers perform, and as the orchestra blares, Kenna, Jax, and Lex take the stage by storm. Later, when he sings one of their slower songs, Kenna joins the orchestra on the piano while his public waves thousands of lighters in the dark. "Pandora's Kiss" is the last song, and when it starts, the drums kick in with extra vigor, each drumbeat coinciding with the lift of Mackenna's fist.

I watch from below. Lionel told me to observe the female dancers because the producers really want me up there for Madison Square Garden. It's hard, because although I try to keep my eyes on them as they dance all around Kenna—and I really do try—my eyes can't help straying to him. The lights caressing his skin, shining on his purple rock wig, making even his thumb ring glint as he dances in a way only he can. As much as I hate to admit it, I'm beginning to understand why some of the fans cry at the mere mention of Crack Bikini.

SEVENTEEN

BACK WITH THE BAND

Pandora

After the concert, the guys are, once again, determined to party. Mackenna leads me into the bar and hunts down one of the waiters. "What do you want to drink?" he asks me.

"I'll have whatever you're having."

I hear him order for us, and then I'm once again being casually steered toward a booth in the back. "Shame on me for expecting Crack Bikini to party somewhere tamer," I say, glancing at the bar/disco place.

"This *is* tame, babe, but don't worry—we'll get the fun started soon enough."

He's directing me to the darkest booth in the darkest corner of the club when he's stopped by two guys about his age, who both call him "the bomb!" as in, *"You're the fucking bomb, dude!"*

As they high-five, swear, and do generally ridiculous boy handshakes, I watch the Crack Bikini dancers jiggle and dance their way toward a dance floor flickering with lights. The music reverberates everywhere in the room. Under my feet. Under my seat.

Some girls separate from their flocks and fly over to Mackenna and the two men still nearly praying to him, and the moment they reach them, they start dancing around him.

"Dance with us, Kenna!"

He slides an arm around each of their waists and immediately moves his body to theirs, all while still talking to the other guys. He is a great dancer. A great singer. A lover of life. Of fun. Games.

Games.

I drop my gaze to the tabletop. *You're such an idiot*, I swear to myself.

This is just a game to him. A challenge. Like *The Taming of the Shrew*.

"What's up, pussycat?" Lex drops into the booth beside me, jerking my face back up with a fist under my chin.

"Not much. You sound drunk," I say.

"That may be because I am?" He laughs and nods toward Mackenna. "It's because of you he makes good music, you know. Every song."

"Your number one hit is the worst song I've ever heard in my life, FYI."

"No, it's not, and that's not the only song he wrote about you. Maybe it's not a bad thing you broke his goddamn heart."

"Me?" I sputter.

"Oh, *please*! You think you didn't? He's never done more than fuck a passing girl ever since you, and it's all because of the way you burned him."

"Me?" I cry in outrage, completely disbelieving.

"This jerk bothering you, Stone?" Mackenna asks as he sets my drink down and slides in next to me.

I smirk playfully. "He can't help it, I guess."

"Dude, I was just telling her what a great catch you are," Lex tells him. "Trust me, you *want* me to talk to her."

Mackenna slides an arm along the back of the seat behind me and leans in. The gesture is casual in nature, but I'm not deceived. He takes a sip of his drink. "Uh-huh," he says, nodding in a way that says, *"Suck my dick."*

"She doesn't care that you like wearing pink hair during your concerts. She likes that it matches her skunk-look," Lex continues. "She also doesn't care that you talk like hell in the morning. She doesn't care your ten-inch dick can rip her in half. She's all for you, man."

"Tell me something I don't know—like why your ass is parked right next to her?"

"Keeping her warm."

"Get out of here, Lex."

"Dude, I'm tired as fuck, chill." He eases away from the booth, though, and I feel a hand on my thigh. My eyes flick up to meet silver ones, and Mackenna smiles at me.

Danger . . .

My heart starts to pound.

I can't fall for him again. I can't.

But you are. You are. You are!

"Your hand going somewhere?" I ask breathlessly, sounding amused even though I'm more alarmed than amused. And excited. I'm more excited than anything else.

"Yes," he says as he slides his fingers higher, his eyes shining with something. Challenge? Lust? His head ducks, and my stomach dips as I feel his lips, his breath, on my ear. "I can't keep my eyes off you, and I want my hands on you, my lips on you. Really, I'm developing a serious problem with sharing you, even for the night."

I laugh nervously. "Do these lines usually work for you?"

"Remember our first time?" he continues, ignoring me, his

seductive whisper caressing my ear as his fingers stroke up my side, beneath my top, as though . . . as though he really likes to touch my skin.

He snakes his hand around my waist and settles there, on the side of my rib cage, his thumb only a hairsbreadth away from the underside of my breast.

"No, I don't remember," I lie through uneven breaths. "It's all that Diet Coke offing my brain cells."

But my brain contradicts me, and as he presses a less-than-innocent kiss to my temple, I'm transported back seven years, to a booth like this one, hands like these, lips like these. Back to a time when I was confused about who I was, and who I wanted to be, but never confused about this boy.

They'll see us, Kenna . . .

What's wrong if they see? Why, are you fucking ashamed of me?

He's a man now. Hard. His hard thigh against mine. His hand curling tighter around my ribs. He used to be frustrated and pained because I wouldn't allow my mother to know about us. I knew she'd take him away. But in the end it didn't matter. He left all on his own.

"You do remember. I can see in your eyes that you do," he says softly.

I close my eyes as he presses another kiss, this one a soft, seductive flutter, against the corner of my lips. "I don't like to remember either, Pink. It's the worst form of torture, to think of the way you used to look at me. To think you won't ever look at me like that again," he whispers.

I force my eyes open and look at his face, so close my hand itches to curve around his skull. Leaning closer, my teeth tug and play with the diamond earring on his ear, and he holds his breath, as if barely holding himself together.

When I edge back, his gaze is so intense and I feel so drugged by my own effect on him, I start closing my eyes. He stops me. "Don't. Don't fucking close them."

I keep them open and his jaw flexes, his eyes dark as twilight, his pupils dilated, and I'm scared. Scared of everything. Of the heat of his body on mine. Of his gaze holding me. I'm scared of how close he feels, how close we are . . . emotionally.

He smiles, but it's a smile that's not quite the cocky smirk I'm used to. It's tender, so tender. I'm confused as he rubs his silver thumb ring over my jawline, his wolf's eyes staring deep into mine. "I swear you took something from me, but I've never been able to figure out what."

I loved you, you idiot. And you loved me too. And it scared you—like it scared me—and so you left!

The reminder makes me squirm. I try to put some distance between us. To put up my walls. I jerk my head around to stare blindly at the dance floor. "I stole your heart, of course. I chewed it up and spat it out. It's why you don't feel anything now."

"There's my man-eater." The laughter that follows doesn't sound merry, though. He's just following my lead, but I know he doesn't really find the comment funny.

He tugs playfully on the pink strand of my hair. "Okay, Pink," he says, conceding me this one, "so if you won't walk with me down Memory Lane, then at least talk to me."

I don't know what to say, and I find myself using silly words to deflect his attention, like I used to with my mother when I was young. With Mackenna, when we had long, comfortable silences and I felt like breaking it—or when he felt like making me laugh.

"Circumcision," I blurt out.

He bursts out laughing, and this time it's real, and it's a sound I love. "Bad girl."

"Liposuction," I continue, smiling now.

"Ah, babe, you know how to skip the small talk, don't you."

"Tyrotoxism!" I laugh.

He lifts his eyebrows. "Poisoned by cheese?"

"Yup. Sternutation!" I continue, catching my breath when he pulls me to his chest. He squeezes me to him, and emotion squeezes in my heart when he kisses the top of my ear.

"God, I love that laugh," he whispers, smiling down at me. "Dance with me now."

"Nope."

"Come on, dude. Dance with me."

"The answer is no. And I don't answer to '*dude*.' Or 'Pink.' Or 'gorgeous.'"

"How about 'Darth Vader,' hmm?" Smiling, he tips my head back and teases me.

"Why? Do you have a thing for men in masks?" I tease in return.

"I have a thing for *you*." He sighs. "Why is that I can have any girl out there and forget about her the moment I come, but you . . . ? Once just isn't enough. I want to come in you, again and again. I want to watch you come. I'm a selfish prick who fucks girls to feel good. So, why is it with you I want to make *you* feel good? Explain that to me."

"I can't."

"Then dance with me." He stands, and he stretches his large, beautiful hand with the silver ring on his thumb out for me.

Danger . . .

Oh, shut it, brain!

Mackenna offers his lean, corded arm the same way he offered it to me when we were locked in the closet, but this is the first time I get to watch my own hand stretch out and slip into his. The mixture of peace and anxiety I experience at the contact disconcerts me. He leads me to the dance floor.

Danger.

Stop.

All are instructions from my brain to my body, but I cease to hear them when his arms slide around me.

There's sweat everywhere, the music is hot, loud, high. It's okay to have sex. Impersonal sex. But there's nothing impersonal about what we're doing now. Nothing impersonal in the way he presses his lips to the top of my head and drags them to my temple, his hands cupping my ass so he can rock his body to mine, grinding against me. His body is both lean and flexible, and the way he moves means I feel every muscle—including his erection.

"I want to gorge on you, stuff my face with you." He slides his tongue into my ear, then retreats, the passion between us singeing me, shuddering through me. "God, Pandora, the things I want to do to you—"

"Kenna . . ."

"I'm obsessed. I'm fucking mental about you. If you'd only let me in, Pink. Let me in, once and for all . . ."

The stupid internal struggle I'm faced with exhausts me. The constant push and pull between my brain, my heart, and my stupid horny body. I push him away, my voice wavering. "So you can break my every dream? So you can walk away without even a goodbye?"

He blinks as if I just threw a left hook from out of nowhere. "I didn't want to . . . you think I enjoyed . . ." He's stopped moving, and when he finally seems to take command of his baffled thoughts, his voice is edged with frustration. Taking my elbow and pulling me back to him, he growls, "Fuck! *You* were the one—"

"I *what*? I couldn't say I loved you, so you left to punish me. That's what you did!"

"Is that what you think of me?" He may as well have been

slammed by a torpedo—that's how stricken he looks. "You think I'd *punish* you? Pandora, the day I walked away from you was the day I fucking *ripped my own heart out*!"

"Hey, chill, both of you!" Lex and Jax gather around us, and Lex pulls me back against him while Jax sets a hand on Mackenna's shoulder with a look that says he doesn't think now is the right time for us to be discussing this.

Angrily, Mackenna shoulders free and takes one step forward, dragging one angry hand over his sexy round scalp as he studies me. Everyone else is dancing, but we stand here, both of us about a word away from unraveling.

He doesn't like seeing Lex touch me, I realize, for he reaches out and jerks me back to him. "Let's go, Pink," he growls.

"Kenna, we've grown attached to Pink here—" Lex begins.

He pushes him aside. "Stay out of this, both of you."

REALISTICALLY SPEAKING, THE talk was long overdue.

Maybe neither of us wanted to venture there. Maybe we both pretended we hadn't cared. That it hadn't hurt. That we were over it.

Sure.

When we get back into the little cocoon of our hotel—separate from the band's at his insistence—he asks, "Why did you go to the concert that night? Why slap me in the face with the first thing you could find?"

"Because I wanted to. Because I thought it would feel good. I wanted to make you hurt, even if it was just a tenth of the hurt you caused me."

"I'm hurting now," he says gruffly, then he comes close, looking down at me intensely. "Does it give you pleasure? To hurt me?"

"No," I admit meekly, dropping my eyes in a way I rarely do. But, god, looking into his eyes right now is too much to ask. Too much, when my emotions are in a roil, and the emotions he's stirring in me are overtaking everything else.

"Then why stay when Leo asked you to? Why stay and torture me, Pink?"

"I already told you, I wanted the money," I argue.

"What do you want it for?"

"Saving it." I move toward the window, stiff with dignity, staring blindly at the city lights. "For me, and for Magnolia. For independence."

"I would've paid you double to leave me alone."

I stop breathing, then turn around and look at him. He's pacing the length of the room, restless, looking about as unsteady as I feel. My pride prickles as I realize that, of course, he would have paid me. He left. He walked away once before, determined not to see me again. "Why didn't you?" I demand, my hurt and anger rising once again.

"Apparently I'm a fucking masochist. When I saw you . . ." He tugs on his diamond earring and sighs as he lifts his head to me. Our gazes meet. His eyes are darkened with emotion. Dirty silver. Haunted somehow.

By me?

"If you can't stand me, then why did you agree to this too?" I ask in a suffocated whisper, my chest clutching in pain as I anticipate his reply.

"I agreed to it in exchange for a time out—away from the band." He waits for a moment, and then he quirks one mocking eyebrow. "You look surprised."

"Well, what do you mean 'a time out'? You've dreamed about this. You had big dreams, Mackenna, and this . . . this *is* your dream."

"It's not how I dreamed it would be," he says, propping a shoulder negligently against the wall and tapping his fingers restlessly against his thigh. "All I wanted was to make music. I never wanted or imagined everything else. I never really wanted all of this."

"Why create such a big band, then?"

He hikes up one shoulder. "The guys needed a lead, and I needed to get away."

"Because of your dad?"

He pushes away from the wall and starts crossing the room, his laugh soft and bitter. "Because of you, Pandora."

The words stun me.

Cut me.

His continuing approach unsettles me, causing little ripples in my tummy.

"I tried to be good enough for you, Pandora," he says darkly, and with every step he takes, my heart grips harder, more painfully. "I tried to make you happy. I tried to make up for my shitty dad. But I was never good enough to be taken home to meet my girl's family. Nothing I did could ever prove myself to you."

"I never made you prove yourself to me!" I gasp.

But his face is grim now, a frown of remembrance flitting across his features as he stops a good three feet away from me. "You wouldn't walk next to me on the street. By the time I left town, you were determined that nobody know I'd been with you."

"Because my mother would have my head! It had nothing to do with you not being good enough. I thought you were . . ." My words are choked with anxiety. "I thought you were the most amazing human being I'd ever met, Kenna. You had goals, you knew who you were, and who you wanted to be. And what was I? Mourning, confused . . . unwanted."

"You were wanted by *me.* Yet you walked next to any fucking guy you knew *except* me. Even though I was *yours.*" The brilliant pain in his eyes nearly bowls me over with its intensity.

"I didn't want it to be them, I wanted it to be you!" I cry.

"It *was* me!" he shoots back. "But you wouldn't have it." He openly studies me, the muscle ticking in his jaw betraying his frustrations. "Even when you gave yourself to me, you still held back. You gave me your body, your time, but not you. Never you."

His gaze claws into me as if he can find me—the real me—inside here somewhere, and when he reaches out to take my hand in his hand, my emotions rage at the gentle squeeze he gives me. "I loved you, Pandora. I loved you so *fucking* hard."

Oh, how wrong I was to think you could hurt someone so much and ever find real closure. It just hurts more, and more, and more. "But that's over now," I whisper.

He swears and reaches out for me, but I edge back. "Don't. I'll never forgive myself if I cry right now," I warn.

"I cried for you, Pandora. Drunk and sober, I cried for you, and I'm not ashamed to say it."

"Don't! Stop, Kenna!" I spin around and blink rapidly, and thankfully, he doesn't touch me when he walks up to the window, stopping an inch to my right.

He sighs, dragging his hand through his hair as we both stare outside.

"Look, this is over in a week. Let's just try and be friends. I don't want to hate you, Mackenna. Hating you makes me miserable."

He turns me around to face him. His eyes are brilliant, and if my gaze weren't blurry, maybe I'd see the pain I can hear in his voice. "Whatever you want."

He leans forward and kisses my forehead.

The lump in my throat grows.

Framing my face with his big, wide hands, he kisses the tip of my nose, my chin, my forehead.

"Kenna . . . ," I whisper. "I think I'm ready to go home. This wasn't how I imagined it either."

He keeps kissing me.

My throat hurts. Like all my sins and mistakes are trapped in me, like everything else. Trapped like my love for him, and anything good I have to give. He rains kisses on my face, gently, as if he truly cares about me, bringing all the things that I'm feeling just under the surface of my skin to bloom in full view. For anyone and everyone to see.

Every touch feels multiplied in intensity. My breath's suddenly hitching. His voice in my ear says, "Are you planning my murder behind those eyelids?"

I open them. "No," I gasp. "I don't hate you anymore, I—"

"Then look into my eyes." His eyes keep holding mine as he lays me on the bed, my hair falling behind me. He flicks open the button of my jeans.

Our gazes remain locked.

My fingers anxiously work at his pants. What starts out slow begins moving faster. I hear the rasp of our zippers. The pound of my heart. Our breaths. My soft gasp when he shoves his long fingers into my panties and cups my sex. His groan when I shove my hand into his briefs and curl my fingers around his erection. I stroke him lightly, finding the tip already wet.

For *me*.

When he hands me over a condom, I stroke him lovingly while I roll it on his length. He sinks his free hand into my hair and secures the back of my head as he takes my lips with his, roughly, deeply, his tongue darting into my mouth as his finger enters me. A gasp leaves me. His mouth is not apologetic. It never is.

I squeeze his cock and rub the heel of my palm against his balls, wrapping my tongue around his. "Fuck me. Fuck me hard," I whisper.

And as he lifts me up and centers me on the bed, I curl my legs around his body, and then he pins my hands at my sides, lacing his fingers through mine.

"I said don't stop looking at me," he commands.

So I don't.

❤ ❤ ❤

I WAKE UP to feel him stroking my hair, and for a moment I'm too groggy to wonder what alternate reality this is. A reality where I get to feel a man's arms holding me close, like he desperately wants me there. His hands in my hair like he's obsessed with the feel of it. Maybe he wants to send an e-mail to the makers of my shampoo, commending them for leaving my hair with such a pleasant smell. Such silkiness.

I wake up feeling . . . the opposite of angry.

"Hey." He brushes his lips to mine, then catches my eyes open and he's smiling. He wiggles his brows to the cart of food in the living room. "Hungry?"

"Whaaa—? Where did that come from?"

"A button I found on this thing here called a phone. It read, Room Service."

"I didn't hear them knock."

"You slept like a log, and I was only too happy to be the one opening the door. I didn't want anyone getting an eyeful of that tush."

I look down at my nakedness.

And I gasp when I see my pussy.

"What happ— What the—?"

"You asked me to shave your sweet little pussy." He grins. "I could never deny you. You look edible, Pink. Now, you're really pink . . . all over."

"Ohmigod, give me something to cover up. I feel so bare. I can't believe what you do to my whoremones. I thought I'd dreamed it, you idiot!"

He tosses me my panties from the floor. "That sweet little pussy's extra red today because of how long I kissed it for." He grins as I slip into my panties. When he tosses me his T-shirt, I slide it on.

"At least it wasn't something permanent, like a tattoo," I say.

"You were ready for one that said, 'Kenna Kums on my Kunt.'"

"Pfft, you're such a boy." I dive into the cereal as he pours us both a coffee and grabs his guitar, strumming a little tune and writing down words. I watch him.

"I feel funny. Down there. Please don't shave anything else on me, okay?" I warn direly, adding sliced bananas to my cereal bowl.

He lifts his hand in mock innocence. "Babe, you begged me to. I liked your landing strip just fine. But you were being adventurous. Those drinks you had really got to your head. You kept telling me how much I bring out your adventurous side. Asking me how it'd feel to have me tongue you while every part of you was smooth and silky wet."

I groan, remembering in a haze what we did. How delicious it was. And fun. I remember laughing, squirming as he went. *Easy, now, I don't want to cut you, part your legs and stay still . . .*

Okay . . .

Panting. Panting and fighting the urge not to squirm.

Look down and watch me, let it get you wet. The second I soap this up and clean you up, my tongue's coming next . . .

"You're a dangerous man, Wolf," I chide, smiling when he just shoots me a smile and continues writing down some sort of song.

I love this. I love this moment so much. I feel comfortable, relaxed, the atmosphere full of fun memories of last night and naughtiness and lots of this man, playing with me like he plays with his guitar.

"Mackenna," I whisper.

He lifts his head.

It's in this moment, me watching him work, wearing his T-shirt, I feel that we're as intimate as we've ever been in our lives. It's the kind of intimacy I've never felt. Only with him. So long ago, that too feels like a dream all the time. "I had a good time last night," I finally admit.

His smile comes in a flash, and it is so adorable, he could be seventeen again. Seventeen and in love with me. Ready to take me away.

"Me too. Just like old times."

❤ ❤ ❤

THE NEW ORLEANS concert is incredible. Huge crowds, excellent sound, excellent performance. That night, rather than party with the band, Kenna and I go our own separate way onto Frenchmen Street. A thousand smells hit me as we walk down the crowded sidewalks. Bars line up, side by side. People are scattered throughout, drinking, making out, singing. The scent of sea salt, crawfish, beer, and sweat mingle to create a very distinct aroma. "Smells like sin," Mackenna tells me with a grin.

I think I manage to do the impossible—groan and smile at the same time. "You think about sex all the time."

He links his fingers with mine and tugs me toward one of the bars. "Want to bar hop?"

I think I'm smiling. Really and truly smiling. Like, ear-to-ear kind of smiling. I feel bubbles in my chest, the kind I haven't felt in a while.

Happiness.

"Yes!"

"All right, Pink. So take your pick. There's a jazz bar, a rock bar—"

"I've got a rockstar right here, so let's do the rock bar," I say.

We step into a different world. Rock music from the '80s blaring. Guitars on the wall. Images of rock gods everywhere.

But we don't last two minutes. Even with his aviators, people start doing double takes, and within forty-eight seconds, one screams, "It's Mackenna Jones from Crack Bikini!"

He groans in my ear but keeps it together and straightens, lifting up his palms to ward them off. "All right, I'm trying to chill out with my girl, guys."

"Don't pay attention to him, I'm not his girl. But we *are* trying to chill out," I say.

"Sing something for us!" one shouts.

"Not tonight. I'm resting my vocal cords."

"Sing something!"

A chorus begins as a group gathers around us. "Sing! Sing! Sing! SING!"

He rolls his eyes, laughing at them as he slides out of the booth. He shakes his head and placates them with his hands. "All right, all right. But if I go up there and sing, you leave me to cuddle up to Pandora over here."

When he jerks his chin in my direction, several dozen eyes stare at me and I mumble, "Thanks, asshole."

He laughs and leans over to whisper near my ear, "This is so they know how important you are to me."

"Important enough to dump after a fuck."

His smile doesn't falter as he meets my gaze. "Important enough that I write most of my songs about her."

He pushes through the crowd. He's taller than most people here. His skull looks so deliciously round today, and I sit in the booth and watch him take the stage. His magnetism takes over every room we're in. I swear, he was completely deluding himself thinking he wouldn't be recognized. And so was I.

But the people's faces? Their expressions? They look beyond thrilled—like this is the best day of their lives. How must it feel for him to have this effect on others? How must it feel to sing a song and make a difference in someone's life? To make them feel less lonely, feel . . . understood.

He taps the mic and laughs. "Testing, testing," he says. People roar, and the clown laughs again. He loves it, and despite myself, I'm grinning. God, he's completely beyond repair, isn't he?

He starts a song. Not one from Crack Bikini, one I've heard on the radio from Secondhand Serenade.

"You really Pandora?" A guy slides next to me and sets a drink before me, nodding to it. "On me."

"Nah, thanks, I'm good."

"Really. I'd like to buy you a drink." He's looking at me like he might have slipped something into the drink. You can never be too paranoid.

"I'm with him." I jab my thumb in the direction of Mackenna.

"Yeah, I heard. But you're not really *with* him, are you? Are you really Pandora?"

"Damn right she is."

Mackenna has completely dropped the song and headed over. He's looming over me and the guy. He plants a threatening hand on the table, then leans forward. "You're sitting in my spot, at my table, next to my girl, so as you can imagine, I have a bit of a problem with that."

"Hey, I just wanted a chat with her. Chillax, Gru."

"I don't even know what the fuck that means." Mackenna drops down next to me and shoots me a look of both amusement and disgust as the guy vanishes into the crowd. "Must you have to break hearts every second I leave you alone?"

"I don't have to, but it's fun," I lie.

"Not for me. One day you're going to lure a guy the size of a truck to you, and I'll have to fight dirty to get him away."

"I thought you liked dirty. You have a dirty mouth, a dirty mind, you love dirty sex—"

"Jesus." He pulls me to him and says, "Say 'dirty' one more time and I'm sucking the word right out of you."

"Dirty."

We kiss. The kiss is sloppy and wild and delicious, and it lasts a whole intense minute.

When we peel our lips apart, he grins and pushes the pink strand of my hair behind my face. "What's the deal with this pink on your hair?"

"Melanie. She thinks I'm bitter and suggested a little color might spruce up my mood."

"Did it help?"

"No, but she dared me, so I'm stuck with it for a while."

"I like it. It makes you girly."

"Is that supposed to mean I look like a man, otherwise?"

He grabs my hand and sets it on his erection. "Do you think I'd have feelings like these for a man?"

"Who knows what perversions you harbor."

"I'll be happy to experiment with you all you like."

My cheeks flare when I remember how I spread my legs and let him shave the small airstrip I usually have on my pussy. It turned him on, and it turned me on, and even remembering something so intimate makes me blush beet red.

"You're a world of contrasts, aren't you?" The words are spoken reverently as he eases his fingers into my hair. We're in our own little world. Rock music plays in the background. We may be in a booth, in the middle of a club, but right now, there's no one but us. "Pink hair on a set of black. Innocent bad girl. Sarcastic but sweet. Is it any wonder I could never forget you?"

My heart trips, and I turn my head away as I feel an awkward blush rise up my neck. "Kenna . . . don't."

He turns my head to his with the back of one knuckle, like we're a couple, and the gesture keeps making me feel weak at the knees. "It's the truth, Pandora," he repeats.

My body throbs in response, and I hate that he can hear the huskiness in my voice when I say, "Let's not confuse what we're doing here."

He laughs and leans back on the seat, studying me. "What *are* we doing here?"

I draw in a deep, steadying breath to calm myself. "Having fun. We're . . . getting each other out of our systems. Doing what we maybe would've done as teens if you hadn't left."

"I would've done much more to you, woman." He signals for a drink and sets the drink the other guy bought on a passing tray. "I can't fuck you fast or hard enough to make up for all the days I fucked you in my head, or had another woman in my bed."

I turn away, blushing beet red. "Kenna."

He turns me back to him. "It's the truth. There have been others—tens, hundreds, who even knows."

"Stop it." I'm getting angry and push him away.

"Don't," he says, gripping me close to him. "I'm trying to be honest with you."

"I don't want you to. It's too late for that."

"Why the fuck is it too late?"

"I don't want you to open up, because it makes me feel like I should too, and I can't." I stare at him. "I won't."

He looks at me, battling with something in his head.

Then he presses his lips to the crook of my neck. "You're so lovely," he whispers. "Even when you're not smiling, you're so fucking lovely, Pink," and the whisper is almost a song. I've never heard it before, but the feel of his breath as he murmurs into my skin sparks me up like nothing ever has. "Let me in. Tell me what to do so you can let me in—"

"You *lied* to me," I say.

"It wasn't a lie. I've never lied to you. I can lie about you—you taught me to lie about you when you wouldn't let anyone know I was yours—but I never lied *to* you, Pink."

"I didn't—"

He presses a finger to my lips, his expression pleading with me not to fight with him. "It's all right. I wasn't good enough then, but I'm good enough now," he says.

"Oh, really? Because you have fame and money?" I smirk.

"Because I'm a man, Pink, not a foolish little boy. Because I weathered shit, and I still grew and made something of myself. Because I'm here now, with you, and I won't be driven away. You cast me aside before, but I won't let you do that again. That's why I'm good enough now."

"You really mean that?" I ask, both puzzled and strangely warm in my chest area.

"Oh, I mean it."

Suddenly I feel it's important to clear up the fact that I did not cast him aside—at least, not willingly. "It wasn't you, Kenna.

My mother would never have understood," I explain, almost apologizing. Before I say anything more, I grab my glass and drain my cosmo.

Then sign for another.

❤ ❤ ❤

THREE HOURS LATER we're drunk. As we stumble into the room, Mackenna pulls my shirt up and my bra down, and suddenly his mouth surrounds the tip of my breast. I feel him jerk on his jeans, and his mouth only leaves my tits for the length of time it takes for him to get his shirt off.

"Fucking god, just look at you." He dips his finger into my jeans and runs his mouth along my throat. I love it so much, I impulsively drag my lips over his jaw, running my hands over that sexy buzz cut hair.

"You drunk? Hmm? You drunk?"

"You're drunk as fuck," I tell him.

"Yeah, but the kind of drunk that can fuck you like you want."

He goes and gets naked, then lights a cigarette.

He looks lickable.

The tattoo on his forearm peeks out as he takes a hit of the cigarette, the tip glowing as he does.

"What does that mean?"

He passes the cigarette over and I give it a hit, watching the smoke leave my lips.

"I tried quitting, you know," I say.

"Yeah, I can't quit for more than a few days. Especially touring. I get a fucking headache, and the only thing that quits is my good mood. Come here."

"Hmm. Most I've lasted was, well, there was this one year where I didn't smoke anything but e-cigarettes, but then I started up again. My only rule is to never smoke at home. Or in front of Mags."

"Nice." He's now referring to my body as he peels off my layers of clothing, and he looks at me as if he's branding the image of me naked into his mind.

My nipples are puckered as though begging for his mouth. My pussy feels damp and his eyes snag there. "So pink and shiny, this shaven little pussy."

He drags a finger over it, leading to my pink clit and lips.

"Fuck," he says, rubbing that finger over my lips. "I'm salivating here, babe. You're so beautiful." He lifts his gaze and watches my expression as he slides a finger over my sex again. I tremble.

"Stop saying 'babe,' Mackenna."

"Shh," he says, heading for the bathroom in all his naked glory, returning with a condom.

"We haven't even kissed and you're hard. You're always hard."

"You assume your perfect tits and that sweet pussy won't get me like this?" My eyes drop to his huge erection, and I lick my lips, knowing how much I want it. He takes my face in one hand, his eyes devouring me. "There's something innocent and alluring about you. Some innocence you don't hide. I want to feed myself into your mouth, baby, and I want to watch you feast on me."

He rolls a condom over his cock, and I groan in hunger and drop to my knees, his hands cupping the back of my head. "Come here," he coaxes, pulling my head toward his straining cock. "Come here and open your mouth."

"I want you, but not with a condom."

"It's flavored just for you, Pink."

I unroll it and his eyes darken dangerously. I smile drunkenly up at him, then I open my mouth around him, and the flick of my tongue seems to catapult his desire, because he groans and fists my hair as he starts pumping. "Oh, baby. Oh, sweetheart.

Ahh, Christ, Jesus, don't stop, Pink. Don't fucking stop until I'm dry. You like that cock? You wanted nothing between your perfect tongue and my fucking cock? Are you going to swallow me, Pink? Tell me how badly you want to fucking swallow me."

Quaking with need, I nod and work him slow. Curling my fingers around the base. Sucking the head. Savoring the drops gathering at the tip, and when he shoots off, he groans. When he's done I grin, because for this moment, I have him right where I want him.

Until he recovers.

And fast.

And when he slides down on the bed and tells me to sit on his face, he ends up having me right where *he* wants *me*.

EIGHTEEN

MEETING UP WITH FRIENDS

Pandora

My morning text two days later isn't actually from Melanie: it's from Brooke.

> **Brooke:** Are you in New Orleans? I just heard Crack Bikini's concert was the night before last.

> **Me:** Yes. We're leaving today for Jacksonville to stop for the night and then on to the next stop.

> **Brooke:** OMG we're leaving Miami today! Do you want to meet up?

"Kenna." I head into the shower and stop when I see him inside the stall, soaping up his beautiful body. I wait for him to turn the water off, and when he steps out, my breath catches.

"Whatcha doing there, Pink?"

"Looking at you," I say, not even shy about memorizing every wet, delicious inch of the eye candy that is Mackenna Jones.

"Anything you like?"

"Most of it, yes."

"Most of it?" He scowls. "Well, what *don't* you like?"

"That I don't know what that means." I motion at his tattoo, and he glances down at it with a scowl.

"I told you. It means I'm a jackass."

"And a cocky, self-confident man who thinks he's God would tattoo that on his arm? Pfft! Keep lying to me, Kenna."

I shake my head in chastisement, but he just smirks and says nothing—like he'd rather die than tell me. Then I sigh and explain, "One of my friends, her husband's a fighter and they tour all the time, and they just finished in Miami. She asked if we could meet up in Jacksonville."

"What kind of fighter?"

"I don't know. But the fights get dirty."

"What's his name?"

"Riptide."

"Whoa. Parents hate him?"

"I think they did, but no, that's not his name. His real name is Remington Tate."

"Seriously? Well, who's your friend?"

"Brooke."

"He was a boxer, no? Got kicked out when he went Tyson on some dudes at a bar or some shit? I like him." He grins.

"You like all men who make you feel like you're a saint next to them."

He grins. "So, you asking me to double-date with you and your friend?"

"Ugh. It's not a date. Forget it."

He laughs. "Where do we meet them?"

I stare at my phone. My stomach tangles because it feels so serious. A date. Double-dating. Me and Mackenna, Brooke and Remy. But I want to see Brooke. I haven't seen her in months, and she, Melanie, and Kyle are my only true friends.

Me: We're on! How about dinner?

Brooke: Double date? OH YES! Text me when you get in town and we'll have a reservation ready.

Me: It's not a date, so please don't say that in front of Mackenna.

Brooke: Holy shit, dinner with MJ from Crack Bikini. Remy doesn't believe me.

Me: Why?

Brooke: He listens to their shit all the time before he fights!

Me: Well Mackenna already confessed his man-crush on Remington going Tyson in the past so if Mackenna wants to date someone, he can date Remy.

Brooke: Sorry, my man's taken. :)

Me: You're such a possessive bitch now.

Brooke: He actually loves it! So we're on. See you tonight!

"We're on," I tell Mackenna. "But it's not a date."

We talk about them on our drive to Jacksonville. Having returned the bike, Mackenna is now driving a Porsche, and my seat is so sunken I can hardly see the road. It must have been too much to expect him to be monogamous with his car selection.

"And your other friend—Barbie?"

"Barbie lives with, and is marrying, the closest thing to sin that she could find."

"And this *sin* likes her?"

"Are you kidding me? He dotes on her. He'd break any one of the ten commandments for her—hell, I'm sure he already has."

"Wouldn't any guy do that for their girl? Do whatever it takes to make sure she's well and happy?"

I look at him in confusion. Because, *hello?* I used to be his girl. And when he walked away, he couldn't have been stupid enough to think that it made me "well and happy."

Unless he truly thought he wasn't good enough for you. . . .

The thought haunts me as he finds a parking spot a block away from the restaurant, and it isn't long before we spot Remy and Brooke, right outside. The first thing you see is, of course, him. He's large and eye-catching, with muscles that make his T-shirt cling to his shoulders and biceps, and his narrow hips encased in low-slung jeans. His hair is spiky and rumpled—like Brooke's just had her hands in it—and they're deep in conversation, him nodding with a smile, his finger rubbing her bottom lip while she talks.

"Hey!" I call.

They turn and Brooke squeaks, *"Pan!"*

Remington approaches Mackenna with a dimpled smile. "I'll be damned."

"I'll be next," Mackenna says right back, and they strike handshakes, pumping hard and smiling while Brooke and I hug.

"How *are* you?"

"No, how are *you?* Touring with Crack Bikini!"

"Yeah, this is Mackenna," I say, stepping back, gesturing. "Brooke, Mackenna. Mackenna, Brooke."

"It's so nice to meet you, Mackenna," Brooke says sweetly, but even as she shakes Mackenna's outstretched hand, she slips her free hand into Remington's, as if reassuring him that he's the one for her.

Remington looks down at her hand in his and smiles a secret smile. He doesn't strike me as a man who needs constant reassurance, but the way he squeezes her hand in some silent communication makes me feel warm inside.

We head into the steakhouse, and the restaurant is oddly vacant as we walk inside. "Remington's PA thought we'd have a better time if we rented out the place," Brooke explains.

"Hell, I'm already having a blast," Mackenna says, taking my hand in his.

It gives me tingles, and those tingles make me want to draw my hand away, but instead I find myself both scowling and laughing.

"I told you, this isn't a date," I whisper in his ear so only he can hear.

He turns his head and plants a quick, surprising kiss on my lips. One second his lips are on mine, shooting a gust of pleasure through my limbs, and the next they're gone. "And I heard you the first time," he says, smiling down at me.

He's observing me with that rather adorable wolfish curiosity he always watches me with, and since it unsettles me so, I decide to concentrate on Brooke and Remington instead.

A waiter leads us to a table at the back of the restaurant, and I notice all those protective gestures they have. He steers her by the neck, while she uses the hand closest to him to hook her index finger into the waistband of his jeans. He pulls the chair out for her to sit, whispering something in her ear that makes her grin. When she laughs, he bends over. I watch as he rubs his nose all along the shell of her ear and she smiles privately at herself and closes her eyes. Shutting off the world so she can focus on what her husband is doing.

He sits down, and Mackenna, apparently immune to the fact that these two people are quietly making love to each other, begins by asking, "So how'd you get into these Underground fights?"

I'm amazed at how courteous Remington is, because he seems
genuinely interested in Mackenna's questions, his thick arm outstretched, one hand firmly on the back of Brooke's chair. Her
hand is under the table, and I think it's on his thigh. I'm getting
all sorts of hot feelings inside me, and an even more noticeable
one that I always seem to feel when they are near. Longing. Because I ruined my chance at this.

That's when, as Remington briefly explains to Mackenna that
he'd fight wherever as long as he got to fight, I realize where Mackenna's arm is. He's in exactly the same position as Remington—
his arm stretched across the back of my chair, his hand resting just
behind my neck, as if he owns me.

Or, at least, thinks he does.

A tingle grows in my stomach, and I try unsuccessfully to
quell it. I've always loved those little gestures I see between Brooke
and her guy, but me? Oh, no. This is not for me. And definitely
not for me and Kenna.

Okay, maybe a little part of me wants something like this, but
not the rest of me.

I squirm, feeling uncomfortable. Then I slide my chair back a
tad, just to see if he drops his hand.

He doesn't.

In fact, he doesn't even turn to look at me.

I hear Remington ask Mackenna, "How'd you get your start
with the band?"

"Racer is so big," I tell Brooke at last, switching the conversation to talk about her son while desperately trying to ignore
Mackenna's arm close to my nape.

Brooke grins and starts telling me Racer's exact eating schedule, and how he's restless because he's just about ready to walk but
can still barely stand up for a couple of seconds.

When the waiter approaches, Brooke doesn't even pause, and I hear Remington order for her. She's still talking to me when I hear Mackenna order, and just as I flip open my menu to decide what I'm having, I realize he's also ordering for me. "She'll have the mandarin salad and the seared scallops."

Abruptly I leave Brooke midsentence and turn, rapping the side of his hard head. "Knock, knock?"

"Who's there?" he teases me.

"You just ordered for me without even asking me what I wanted."

He leans back with a smirk. "All right, Pandora. What was it you wanted?" He lifts one eyebrow, and god, the things I want to do to that smirk. Kiss it. Lick it. Bite it. All of it.

"The mandarin salad and the seared scallops," I finally admit, hating that he's making me smile back at him.

"And what did I order?"

That.

Smirk.

God!

All of a sudden I'm hungry, and it's just for that damn smirk of his. I've loved mandarins and sea scallops my whole life—since the days we used to steal away to the docks. And deep inside my brain, I keep hearing a silly little voice saying, *"He remembers."*

How can something so insignificant turn me to mush?

"I could have wanted something else," I argue, still smiling.

He cocks an eyebrow, still smirking at me. "But you don't. Trust me, I know what you want, Pink."

God help me, I want to kiss that smirk. To kiss him so hard, I'll be the one smirking back at him afterward. Instead, Brooke kicks me under the table and gives me the universal going-to-the-bathroom-to-discuss-the-guys sign.

Fine.

We excuse ourselves, and as soon as we're out of earshot, she's on me—anxious to know what's going on.

"What's been happening?!" Brooke asks as we storm into the bathroom.

In her short black dress and sky-high heels, she looks like a million bucks. I go stare into the mirror and look like . . . me. Like some angry little crow out to attack—pink streak and all. Brooke's face is lit up like from the inside. Like she knows she's worth something. To *someone*. Like she sleeps well at night because she's sleeping next to a blue-eyed man who looks at her like he's both coddling and fucking her in his mind. And that's hot.

"*Pan!*" Brooke says, with that radiance surrounding her and those gold eyes boring into me. "You need to tell me. I did not know you even *knew* this guy. Now he sits there, ordering for you, knowing things *I* didn't even know about you—"

"I used to know the guy. Now I've been hired to be in their stupid movie, and we're fucking." I wash my hands and try not to meet my own gaze in the mirror, but I sneak a quick peek and then force out the frown lines I'm wearing across my forehead.

"For real? You're fucking the Crack Bikini terrible threes?" Brooke asks, as disbelieving as me.

"The main one. But not for long."

"But you like him! Ohmigod!"

I scowl. "No, I don't!"

"Yes. You *do!*" she counters. "And he definitely likes you. I'm really digging the way he steals those long looks at you. Long looks, like his eyes are taking in all of your face, your temples, your eyes, your nose, your lips, your chin. Every time he looks at you it's like he takes in every inch of your face before he looks away. You make him smile too."

"He just does that to irritate me!" I cry, getting truly agitated by the excitement and fear Brooke's words are creating in me.

"No, he does not do it to irritate you. And how can you say that when you don't even notice when he does it?"

"He's a man-slut, Brooke. He looks at my mouth because he likes me doing stuff with it. I bet he's thinking dirty thoughts," I say. A memory of him feeding me his cock flashes through me, and I can't quite quell the bolt rushing through my body.

She laughs, then shrugs. "Maybe. Personally, I love it when Remington thinks dirty thoughts about me when we're with others. I can see it in his eyes. Sometimes I just brush my body against his to confirm my suspicions, and I love it when the evidence just slams into me and he growls."

I raise my eyebrows, then laugh. "Do you stop having sex with Remy when you have a baby?"

"Are you serious?"

"I'm just curious how . . . couples live when they have babies."

She grins, then her eyes gain a dreamy little sparkle in them as she admits, "We used to struggle when Racer didn't sleep all night. We needed to steal every one of our moments together. But Racer's such a good baby . . ." Her smile widens. "If anything, Remington is even more primal and possessive now. Just the thought of me being *his* makes him want me. *Badly.* Hell, if you sit down and say something about me and refer to me as his wife, you'll see what it does to him."

"Shit, I have to do that."

She grins happily. "Okay! But I get to pick on Mackenna too."

The guys are sitting down in their places—Mackenna drinking a beer, Remington plain water. I notice them watching us return. My body heats up through Mackenna's stare alone, but I don't want it to, so instead I watch Brooke grin at Remington, his gaze sliding appreciatively over her figure. She leans over and kisses the top of his spiky dark hair before sitting down.

"Melanie and I have really missed your wife, Remy," I promptly say as I sit.

The change is immediate as his blue eyes sparkle and one of his dimples appears, and I see him lower his hand from the back of the chair down to Brooke's neck. "What did she tell you to do?" he asks me in his rumbling voice, his eyes twinkling as he caresses her nape.

"What?" I ask him, distracted.

He grins and slides his hand deep into Brooke's hair, still looking at me, and I almost hear Brooke purr in her seat. "Did my wife tell you I like you calling her mine?"

"Yes!" Brooke laughs, but he moves really fast for such a big man, and he quiets her with a kiss. On the mouth.

For a full second, they're kissing. Not with tongue, but really locked—like Mackenna and I aren't even here. His hands splay on the back of her head, hers sliding up his neck.

"Is that what you wanted?" Remington then asks as he looks softly down at her.

The powerful way they stare at each other and the way he starts rubbing her lip with the pad of his thumb make me ache inside. A raw, hot sensation takes over me, and I blame it for making me ache all over when Mackenna takes my hand in his. I blame it for making me feel even blacker, hotter, more empty when Mackenna's fingers twine with mine, filling my chest with something I'm scared to feel again.

I should move away, but in reality, I want him closer. I need him nearer. Because I could have had that with him. We could have had a *family*. And as Remington chuckles as Brooke admits that she told me to tease him, and he starts teasing her about how she loves picking on him, Mackenna tips my head around to his in that proprietary, strangely sexy way he has.

Silver eyes capture mine.

"Nice to know you have a heart," he murmurs with tender eyes and an even more tender smile, and I can hardly stand that he noticed. "That doesn't make you weak, baby. It makes you human."

"I was not programmed to have feelings. It just wasn't coded into my hard drive," I lie, struggling to return to my grumpy, defensive self.

"So, how'd you two meet?" Brooke asks, and when I remember that I agreed to let her poke back at Mackenna, I want to groan, but instead I decide to answer for us. Just to make sure we remain in safe territory.

"In school. We used to go out in secret," I mumble.

"In secret, why?" This is from Brooke, and she's genuinely outraged.

"Mackenna's father went to jail," I say quietly, turning the spoon on my place setting, over and over.

"Oh no," says Brooke, her eyes wide, "and your mom—"

"She put him there," Mackenna finishes for her, his voice not betraying any emotion.

Silence.

Remington says, "Sorry, man."

He reaches for Brooke's hand, both of them now solely looking at Mackenna. "How old were you when that happened?"

"Seventeen. Doesn't matter anymore."

"Pan," Brooke whispers, her attention coming back to me in full force. "All this time you knew him and didn't even say. And he was singing about you!"

With a rumbling laugh, Mackenna reaches out to retrieve the

knife from my place setting with that adorable, kissable smirk that's driving me nuts. "Please don't even mention that. She has . . . *exceptions* to that song."

"Because it's a lie!"

He groans and rolls his eyes.

"So it was *you*, then," Brooke laughingly tells him. "The man we all wanted to hang for ruining her life."

"Don't, Brooke," I warn.

"She pine for me?" Mackenna asks, his voice growing thick—like it sometimes does when he asks about me. He seems superinterested, his predatory, wolfish gaze glimmering full force.

"Don't. No! Don't say anything, Brooke."

"No, she doesn't get sad," Brooke admits, with a curl of her lips. "She gets mad."

"Oh, she's mad at me, all right," Mackenna agrees.

I groan and bang my palm to my head, but in the end, we all burst out laughing.

❤ ❤ ❤

AFTER DINNER WE part ways, and Mackenna's eyes are somber as we head back to the parking lot. "Enjoy that?"

The daring lift of his brow surprises me. "Excuse me?"

"Enjoy that? Making me jealous?"

"What do you mean? Because I was watching Remington?" I stare at the sidewalk across the street. "All my friends have that and it makes me curious, but I don't want it. I don't need it. I want to be independent all my life," I lie.

He chuckles softly. "Your nose just grew about an inch."

"Fine. I may want it, but I don't think I'll get it . . . not that you'd understand."

"I understand. I want something normal too, you know."

I'm so surprised, I stop walking and whirl around to face him. "You want a wife? You have a freaking *harem*."

"So? I want a wife someday."

An elderly couple walks past us and I stare at their intertwined hands, weathered with age but still holding on to each other.

And they're not even talking, as if they know all they need to about each other.

Suddenly all the memories of walks with Mackenna, unable to hold hands because we'd be seen, hurtle through my mind, and a new thought teases me, begs me to find out if that's the reason he's now so determined to hold my hand. When he drives. When we were in the restaurant. Even after we fuck.

The question hammers at me, at all my precious walls, and I'm so torn, I'm powerless to resist him.

Especially now, when his eyes glimmer in the moonlight, his face patterned with all kinds of interesting shadows that make him look hotter, his lips softer, his lashes longer.

"I'm not a jealous guy," he says, studying me intently. "Fuck, maybe I am jealous. I'm insanely jealous. How come you smiled at him and not at me?"

"Because we're fuck buddies. You want to think only you can make me smile."

"I can make you smile. Hell, I can make you laugh like nobody's business."

I try to start walking, but he swings me around and takes my shoulders in his hands, whispering an order that sounds almost like a plea. "Mash up a song with me."

"What?"

He pulls me close to him and hums against the top of my head. "Come on," he urges, ducking to softly kiss the top of my ear. "Mash a song with me," he repeats.

"You make me do some stupid things," I groan.

"All part of my charm, Pink. Now come on," he presses, his voice lulling me into a relaxed mood. Plus, how to resist the twinkle in those wolfish eyes? I love those eyes, even though they haunt me, see me, build me, break me . . .

I clear my throat, readying myself to lose what little pride I have left, and I give it a try. " 'Like a virgin . . .' "

He laughs and adds in that low, unique baritone of his, " 'Take me over, take me out, give me something, to dream about . . .' "

" 'Like a virgin, feel so good inside.' "

" 'Tastes so good it makes a grown man cry . . . Sweet Cherry Pie!' "

I start laughing. We're so ridiculous, but Mackenna eases me back against a storefront window, adding some awesome lyrics from Miss Independent. " 'And she move like a boss . . . Do what a boss do . . .' "

" 'I don't believe a masterpiece, could ever match your face,' " I whisper from Kylie Minogue.

" 'When I see you, I run out of words to say . . .' "

God. It feels like he's singing to me. And . . . is that "Beautiful," by Akon?

I'm so affected and drawn into the moment—the sudden memory of when I lost him—I go for a slow one from the Fray. " 'Where were you when everything was falling apart . . . all my days, spent by the telephone . . .' "

He comes in with Guns N' Roses' "Sweet Child o' Mine." " 'I hate to look into those eyes and see an ounce of pain . . .' "

And I'm suddenly full-blown emotional with Rihanna's "Take a Bow." " 'How about a round of applause . . . standing ovation . . .' "

He drops his voice and strokes his silver ring across my lower lip, just like I watched Remy rub Brooke's. " 'And you can tell everybody, this is your song . . .' " Elton John.

" 'I'm falling apart, I'm barely breathing . . . ,' " I softly sing, from Lifehouse's "Broken."

And then him, his voice low and smooth, " 'Pretty, pretty please, if you ever, ever feel like you're nothing, you're fucking perfect to me.' "

Pink's perfect song in his manly voice makes me pause, and suddenly I can't think of anything because I both feel serenaded and accused, as though I just unknowingly pieced my feelings into random songs and random words, and blended them with his.

He's watching me, waiting for something to happen.

"This right here." Wearing a genuine smile, he looks up at the sky, then swings his finger between me and him. "There's nothing better. No better song. I could mash songs all day and be in heaven."

"You have horns, Kenna, you'll never set foot in heaven."

"All the more reason I need to find my own little version of heaven here on earth." He smirks, and looks at me in his sweet, wolfish way as we once again start walking toward the car.

"See, a song was made to be alone. A duet?" he says, thoughtful as our feet pound the sidewalk. "Every singer has a part. Everyone knows what they're saying. But a mashup, you take two songs created to stand alone, and you mash them. And although they're meant to be alone, together they're crazy and don't even make sense, but somehow, they do."

I start past him, down the block. "Whoa, what's wrong?" he says.

"I can't do this."

He stops me and pulls me around. "Yeah, you can, Pink. You *can* do this."

"Being with you again is destroying me!" I cry.

He stares at me and takes me by the shoulders. Anger and

frustration and love—yes, *love!*—rear up in me, but my voice is weak and forlorn.

"What is it that you want, Mackenna? What do you want from me?"

He clenches his jaw and looks at me with eyes that scream their torture. "I had your heart once, Pink, and it wasn't enough. I have your body now, but it's not enough." He holds my face in order to force my eyes to stay on his as he demands, "I want your mind, your dreams, your hopes, your fucking soul. I want it all."

I feel like I just lost a battle.

I feel . . . destroyed.

I kid myself that I hate him, but I don't hate him. What I feel for him is unchanging and unstoppable. Nothing about my feelings for him has changed—only the other feelings it gave me. It used to feel good, loving him. I felt whole, excited, happy to be alive. Then he left and I hated feeling that love. It ate at me, corroded me, haunted me. Now here I am, thinking I could find closure while sharing his bed. His kisses. Learning more about him, and what he's doing. Liking it too much.

I can't kid myself into blaming him for my mistakes. I can't kid myself into blaming him for me not being able to get over him.

My anger was my disguise. But now he's taken off my mask.

And I. Love. Him.

I still do. Always have, always will. I love this man—this rock god—as much as a drummer loves his beat. But it's clear to me that we can never be, even if the miraculous would happen and he could love me back, and be true only to me. Even then, it could never work.

Ever.

He has no idea, *no* idea. But I do.

"You can't have it all," I whisper, praying he doesn't hear the tremor in my voice. "You already took it. You took it, and now I have nothing left to give to anyone."

"Listen to me," he says with quiet command, forcing me to look up at him, into his face, carved with relentless determination. "The woman I see now is not nothing, she's everything. *Everything*. You broke me too, Pink. Us . . . us broke me."

He reaches into his jeans pocket, and I blink at the ring he holds out.

His promise ring.

Is this a promise ring?

What are you promising me?

Me.

My stomach plummets as I see the familiar yellow gold band, the tiny diamond in the center held up by six legs, as if begging for attention. "Don't," I whisper.

He clenches his jaw. "Pandora, I didn't leave you because I wanted to. I left you because I had to."

"No you didn't. You didn't have to!"

"I fucking did. And if you don't believe me, you can go ahead and ask your mother."

"What?" Tears blur my eyes. "What does she have to do with anything?"

"She never wanted us together, babe. I'm sure that's no news to you."

"That still doesn't mean you had to give her more power over us than she already had over me."

"She had power over my dad. Over his sentence." A stony look crosses his face, and his voice grows hard with rage. "She offered to cut his sentence if I left you alone. She told me I wasn't worth even a moment of your day wasted thinking of me. I promised her I'd be back for you. Hell, I told her I was going to be good for any woman's daughter, especially hers. All I was waiting for was for my dad to serve his sentence. I have been planning for years to come back to you, Pandora!"

"No! Mackenna, do you realize what you're saying?!"

"I'm telling you the truth."

"I need to talk to my mother," I suddenly say, my chest close to imploding from the pain delving into our past is causing. "I need to talk to my mother." I run to the corner and hold my hand up for a cab while Mackenna calls after me.

"What the fuck are you doing?"

When a cab screeches to a halt, I climb inside and close the door, my world spinning. "Drive! *Now.*"

The car screeches past him as he flings his arms up in the air, and I think I see him mouth, "What the fuck?" but I can't be sure.

I'm close to unraveling, and I tell myself that I will. That when I'm back home, I'll have a good long cry, even if it takes me months or years to heal. But I can't break now. Not when I still need to know the truth.

My mother has her faults. She's bitter, true. She's overprotective, but . . .

I can't fathom she would do this to us.

Break us apart.

Exploit her power.

Make me experience the same pain of betrayal she felt after the truth about my father's affair came out.

An indeterminate amount of time later, I find myself at Lionel's open door. I don't even react to Olivia, visible right on the bed behind him. "It's off. The contract. It's over. I'll give you the money back."

"What . . . ?" He glances back at Olivia, twists the lock so the door doesn't close on him, and steps out wearing just a hotel bathrobe. "What the fuck did he do?"

A wave of protectiveness washes over me. "It's not Mackenna. It's me, all right? So whatever deal you had with him . . . please, just honor it. I just need to go home now. You got some footage. Ask Noah, he caught us kissing in the plane. And fooling around in the car. He caught us . . . looking at each other too, I'm sure. And when we were locked in the closet, he probably caught the sounds of us kissing too. But please"—I'm begging him and I don't even care—"I can't be here anymore. I had an out from the contract saying if I didn't fulfill, every cent would be turned back. It will be. I'm out. I quit."

"You can't quit!"

This last comes from the low, angry, painfully familiar voice of Mackenna. I spin around and there he is, eyes glimmering with anger, ready in his battle stance. But he looks . . . confused. Like he doesn't know what's happening here. One minute we're mashing songs, the next I'm running. But can he blame me for running, when he ran too? All I know is that I need to be home. I need to stop this from spiraling. I need to talk to my *mother.*

"I need to go home," I tell him in the strongest voice I can manage, searching for even an ounce of pity in his face.

"Miss Stone," Leo says, but Kenna stops him.

"If that's what she wants, I'll fly home with her."

"Really?" I ask, wide-eyed.

"Yeah. Really."

An intense wave of relief and gratitude washes over me. And love. A painful, intense, overwhelming love that makes me wrap my arms around myself as my entire body trembles. "Thank you."

"Argh! Fuck this!" Leo explodes. "Jones, if you take her home, our deal is off. Do you hear me!" he yells as Mackenna heads to his room in the opposite direction from mine.

When he answers, Mackenna's voice is unwavering. "So be it."

NINETEEN

LET GO

Mackenna

"If you think I'm letting you ruin whatever deal you have with Leo, you're wrong, Mackenna. I'm flying out of here, and I'm doing it alone."

"Says who?" I contest, crossing my arms with a frown as I watch her pack. She's got her suitcase up on the bed, and boy, is that lady on a mission to pack, and pack quickly.

"Says me!" she cries, then stops to look up at me with the same eyes that kill me in my dreams, every single night. "Please. If you're worried—don't be. I'll be *fine*."

"Yeah, but I won't."

She laughs and looks up from her suitcase as I approach. Now she's blushing, and I like it. "Kenna."

"I'm serious, I won't. Be fine."

Because truth be told, while she's packing, I'm panicking. For real. I don't want her to go, and I sure as fuck am not inclined to let her fly without me.

"Promise me you'll stay here," she says, clutching some sort of undergarment in her fist as she shoots me a warning glare. "You have a concert and I have . . . to go. Promise."

I take the undergarment from her hand and fling it aside, squeezing both her hands in mine. "Pandora, I'm not letting her stop me from being with you again," I tell her gruffly.

"Mackenna, this has to be a misunderstanding . . ." She trails off, then she's up on her toes, taking my mouth, hard, leaving me winded. A hungry kiss. Like she's fucking desperate for more.

When she turns to keep packing, I stop her and force her to face me, because all this? It's eating me up. "She may deny it. Are you going to believe her over me?"

"She won't deny it," she whispers, dropping her gaze to my throat. "If it's true."

I drop my hands and a low, bitter laugh leaves me. Not lie about it? Yeah, right. That woman has been hell-bent on keeping us apart for years. It's always been me. Never good enough for her—and even then, like the masochist pussy I am, I still fucking wanted her. "It is true. I won't let her break us up, Pink," I angrily warn.

"We're not breaking up, we weren't even back together!" she counters.

"Then let's," I insist.

"What?" she gasps.

"You heard me. Let's officially get back together."

I dig out my mother's ring from the pocket of my jeans. I don't care she threw it back at my feet. The fact that she'd kept it all these years tells me what she won't tell me in words.

I saw her watching Brooke and Remington. I know she longs for that—craves it even—and I want to give it to her. Hell, I've been itching to get free of the crazy band hours, the fans, the paps, the cameras too. I want no one but this girl, but if I'm not good enough now, then fuck me, I'll *never* be good enough for her.

"We can't get back together," she whisper-gasps, then plucks at some imaginary lint on her black T-shirt. "It's not as if we can change anything, or pretend that we didn't . . . fuck up."

"True." I reach around her and lower her suitcase lid so she stops packing for a hot sec and focuses on me. "But see, I don't want to talk about the past right now, Pink. I want to talk about the future."

She's holding her breath.

"New York concert is in five days, right?" I press.

"Right."

"So go home. Do what you need to do. But come back to me." She stares at the ring I'm holding up, and I stare into those confused, dark coffee eyes. I've done this before, except six years ago, she was excited to see this ring.

Is this a promise ring?

What are you promising me?

Me.

But now she looks trapped. Sad. Lost. The tensing of her jaw indicates some deep frustration. My voice roughens with emotion because I don't want her to be lost, I want her to feel certain, of *me*. I want her to find whatever she's looking for, in *me*.

"I want you to come back, Pink," I whisper, my voice husky as I hold her startled eyes with my own. "Not because they're paying you to, but because you *want* to."

"Kenna, what are you doing?"

He tips my head back. "In my life, there have been three times when I've had to make important choices."

She can't breathe.

And neither can I.

It's been a long time since I've opened up like this to anyone. In fact, I can only remember opening up to one person like this in my life—and that person is standing right in front of me.

"The first time was when I left you. The second was when I joined the band. And the third," I stare deeply at her, "the third one is right here, right now."

"Kenna, this isn't your choice. Me going home is *my* choice."

"You're right, but then I also have a choice here. You see, I *choose*"—I emphasize the word—"not to live without you anymore."

She stares at me with those eyes that make my head spin, biting her lower lip in the way that makes my teeth ache.

There's pain in her eyes.

Hell, I feel pain inside me.

But I can feel, deep in my gut, that she feels for me the same way I do for her. She's just fighting it harder.

"I can't do it so easily. I won't leave my cousin, my friends, my life. I can't! You don't mean this." She's shaking her head frantically as if I've just proposed death instead of just the idea of being with me.

"You won't have to leave your cousin, baby . . . I'm leaving the band."

"What?" She's stunned now—her suitcase, her packing forgotten as her mouth gapes wide. "But the band is a part of you."

"So are you," I point out cockily, then I lower my voice. "In fact, you're the biggest, most important part of me."

She stares at me like what I've just said is pure, raw torture. Like it's hurting her, really hurting her. But I can't let her go this time. I can't walk away from her for the second time in my life. "Pink, I like writing my songs, and singing, but I want you more. I want to settle down . . . I want something normal. For once in my life, I want something *normal*."

"I'm the furthest thing from normal, Kenna," she chokes out with a bitter laugh.

"Well, you're what I want. I want to give you normal."

"Riding on a bike? In a Lamborghini? That's not normal either," she cries, and although her eyes are red and a little wet, she still fights to keep from letting those tears out.

Frustration starts knotting up my insides, and I grab her shoulders to give her a little shake. "Fuck, Pink. Are we going to fight about this? Huh?" I chuck her chin up. "All right, fine. I concede. You're not normal. I'm not normal. But I want to give us our kind of normal—which might be weird and fucked up, but it works for us."

"I . . ." She glances at me, then closes her eyes and whispers, "You're tempting me in the worst way."

I take her palm and set the ring inside, closing her fingers around the precious metal, the value of which means nothing compared to her, and then I stare into her face and wait. My heart's a wild beast pounding in my rib cage. She's stunning—all white skin with dark-painted lips, eyes like dark pools of night, glossy dark hair with its adorable pink streak. Her little breasts, her little ass, her long legs, and those long, pointy boots . . .

I like it all.

I want it all.

"But you still won't say yes?" I press.

Say.

Yes.

Baby, say YES.

She won't answer, so I drop my voice to its lowest tone—the one I use when singing ballads.

"Come because I ask you to, not because they pay you to. Come if you ever loved me. If you can *ever* love me. Come see me, Pink. Come hear me sing at Madison Square Garden."

Her eyes soften with emotion, an emotion I can feel pooling in my gut.

"I thought you didn't like knowing I was out there watching you sing."

"That might be because I'd never had something I *wanted* you to hear me sing before," I admit then brush a kiss, first to her forehead and then to the top of her ear. "If you do decide to come, let Lionel know. He'll seat you."

"I'm not sure it's a good idea," she hedges, but she's got her fist closed tight around my ring. "You think I'll show up, you'll sing to me, and we'll live happily ever after?"

"That's what I'm going for." I smile at her softly, torn between shaking her, begging her, and flat out ordering her to do as I say. "Fuck, Pink, just say you'll come."

"Say you'll let me go home on my own. Your band needs you."

I hesitate. She seems desperate to get rid of me right now. I'm not sure if she'll come. But if she doesn't . . .

Just go after her, dude.

"If I agree, you'll come?" I say, trying to get something of an agreement out of her.

"Yes," she says, looking at me and opening her palm as if she thinks I want the ring back. I close her fingers around it again.

"Keep this. It belonged to the first woman I loved, so it makes sense it should stay with the last."

"Kenna!" she cries, but before she can make a thousand and one excuses as to why she can't make it to my concert—excuses about why she still can't open up—I head out of there, hoping that ring never finds its way back to me.

Like it did once before.

TWENTY

PANDORA'S BOX

Pandora

Usually at this stage of a journey—sitting on a hard plastic chair at the gate, waiting for the call to board the flight—my palms are sweaty, my heart is racing, and my stomach churns like I'm about to puke. But this time my attention is elsewhere, my eyes focused entirely on the little diamond. . . .

I can't stop staring at the little diamond, in those sleek little legs, high up in the air and begging for attention. It's priceless to Mackenna, and I know that no diamond in the world means more to him than this one. No diamond in the world means more to me than this one—because it was his mother's. And he loved her with everything in him.

Like I love my mother too.

My mother . . .

I think of her as I grip the armrest and hold on tight as the plane takes off.

Even with my clonazepam, the adrenaline rushes around my body so fast that I can't sleep. The pill allows me to relax briefly, but this time around, that's about it. I'm still too hyper, my brain too wired, my heart too busy feeling . . . stuff.

My mother had the perfect setup for a pain-free marriage until we realized . . . she didn't. She's wanted what's best for me. She was there on January 22.

There when the pain started.

There when my water broke.

There when I had the baby.

And there . . . when they took the baby away from where I lay on the birthing bed, never more alone.

No matter how much my mom hurt at the thought of me getting pregnant, she couldn't bear to see me go through an abortion. She's . . . human. But if she kept me away from Mackenna . . .

"Oh, is that an engagement ring?" the woman in the seat next to me asks. She looks about my mother's age, except she's far warmer and chattier.

I smile at her, and before I even realize what I'm doing, I'm extending my hand like some idiot ready for the altar. "It's a . . . promise ring."

Oh god, why did I take it? He doesn't know what he's doing, giving it to me again. He doesn't know who I am anymore, who I became after him. That we had a girl. Could have been a family. And yet I'm so fixated on him that I slipped on the ring again, and I've been turning it around on my finger ever since. Looking at it, lifting it to my lips, closing my eyes and kissing it, because I missed it like I missed him. His eyes, his smiles . . . the way we were happy.

"Ahh, a promise ring," the woman says, sighing when I return my hand to my lap. "Love is a wonderful thing," she tells me, gripping my arm with a little squeeze and a secret smile.

I smile at her and say no more. God, I'm just so fucking dazed. Dazed, excited, hopeful, and as frightened as Magnolia is of the monsters in her closet. I'm frightened of the monsters in *mine*! I'm having real trouble coming to terms with this new, wonderfully scary situation where Mackenna and I may have a shot. We have a chance. God, even the word "we" is weird! He walked away, made me ache, but now he wants me back. And though I act like I won't be back—and question whether I can ever really be back with him—did he ever really lose me?

How can you stop belonging to someone who has ravaged you like he did me?

How can your first and only love sweep through you like a tornado and not leave his mark?

And now my body's acting ridiculous. My heart, my lungs— even my brain. I feel like I did when I was seventeen and ready to run away with him, the critters wiggling in my insides when I remember the heated kiss he gave me a mere few hours ago before I boarded the plane. *I'll see you in New York?* he asked, kissing me again as if he couldn't help himself.

I said yes, but was that the truth?

Or did I lie?

You're a fucking liar, Pandora. You can't have a future without telling him what you did, what happened after he left. You have to tell him. You blamed Kenna . . . but you see now it wasn't his fault . . . it was all you . . .

God, I wish our mistakes never had to see the light of day. Like little monsters, they could always remain in the closet. But if I let my monster out of the closet, it won't just haunt me; it will haunt us.

BACK IN SEATTLE, I hail a cab and head home, my brain turning over my options slowly, the clonazepam dulling my speed. Right in front of me is the opportunity for a new start. A second chance. Why not? Anyone with just a little bit of self-love, anyone who loved Mackenna even a third of the way I love him, would give herself the chance.

Why not? a part of me screams.

I *know* why not, but I don't want to hear it. In fact, I'm almost ready to pack again for a whole damn year. I have almost managed to convince myself we can pick up right where we left off, at a time when I was ready to head off into the sunset with him. I'm already thinking of how his eyes will light up like the moon his inner wolf howls at when he sees that I've returned. I can almost taste the desperation in his kiss when I plant a good one on him. Because that's the kind of kiss that I'm going to give him when I see him again. The kind that makes a man stop asking questions and think of nothing but the woman in his arms—the woman luckily being me—and we can pick up right where we left off. Him and me. In love, all over again.

I'm already excited, letting the dreamer in me be dazzled by the promise ring on my finger.

She's in her office with the door ajar, sitting behind a huge desk that almost seems built to keep a perennial wall between the world and her. "Pandora," she says, and gives a light smile. But there's no emotion. Her voice doesn't waver very much.

Do I speak like that?

I almost shudder at the thought and hug myself, and that's the very moment when her eyes—dark like mine—flick to the ring on my finger. Her expression is overwhelmed by a fear I've never seen on her face before, and for the first time in ages, I hear a crack in her voice.

"He told you, didn't he?" she suddenly whispers, lifting her eyes to mine. She looks terrified.

I'm too stunned to answer, too dulled by my favorite pill.

My mother clears her throat, but her eyes remain wide and almost rabid for information as she gestures to the promise ring on my finger. Even though she remains in her seat, her gaze searches my face for clues, and several things strike me in unison:

It's true.

"Why are you wearing that ring? I thought you were over that boy."

I'm still very confused, but the adrenaline in my body is mounting fast, clearing my brain by the second.

"Over who?" I ask with deliberate slowness, narrowing my eyes.

"Don't play silly. *Mackenna Jones.*"

"Yes. I was with him." I extend my hand so she can look at it, and while she looks I look at how valiantly she struggles to keep her expression composed.

"And he told you. Of course. Now that his father's out, why hide the truth?" Her eyes flick up to mine. Cautious. Curious. Still with evident dread.

"What is it that you think he told me?"

An intense sinking sensation thuds within me while I wait.

I remember her in flashes.

A flash of her warning me to stay away from him.

A flash of her telling me, *He'll hurt you. He wants revenge. He'll be just like your father, just watch. Stay away.*

Flashes of memories assail me, especially the one where I sat staring out of my bedroom window and she came to stand at my back after we came home from the park, and without even asking what was wrong, she whispered, "It's for the best."

"You told him to stay away from me," I suddenly whisper when she doesn't dare. I remember Mackenna's anger at me and the hurt in his eyes when he saw me again, and it all comes together like a puzzle.

A puzzle that wrecked me. Wrecked Kenna.

And was devised and designed by *my mother.*

"What did you do? How did you make him?" My pain is so raw, my voice is just a whisper.

I know. But I need to know everything, I need to hear it from her. My own family.

My mother rubs her temples and inhales deeply, and when I open my mouth to yell at her, she cuts me off. "His dad was in trouble. Big trouble. He was facing many, many years in jail, as you recall. So I offered to cut him a deal. To lower the sentence if he stayed away from you."

"You did that to him?" I whisper. "You did that to *me*?"

"He was no good for you, Pandora! He had nothing to offer you but heartache. I thought it was for the best, so when I noticed that ring on your finger, I realized he would take you away. I advised him to walk away unless he wanted his dad to spend the rest of his days in prison."

"And you made me think he didn't want me all these years!"

"He *thought* he wanted you, but you were both too young to know what was best for you. Do you think you could've been happy leading the life some silly rocker lives?"

"Six years, Mother. *Six!*" I cry.

She stares at me, everything about her motionless.

And *emotionless*.

"We have a daughter," I whisper.

My mother almost flinches. Almost.

"A daughter that we will *never* get to see."

My heart is breaking even as I say it out loud.

"Pandora," she says, reaching across her desk as if to take my hand. I leap back, and she stands and starts coming around. "You were alone. You couldn't do it. You gave that baby its best chance."

"*No. Her* best chance was with *me*—with me and her dad. But you made sure he walked away from me hating that I didn't have the guts to even tell him to his face that we were over."

I feel the tears building, but I don't want them to come out. Not in front of her. I would not let her take my tears along with everything else.

I clench my teeth and hold back the volatile emotions threatening to break out of me. But even though I won't lose it, I cling to that anger—my old friend, familiar to me. "Why do you hate me? Why take the only love I've ever had? *Why*, Mother?"

She scowls for a moment. "You think I don't love you because I don't say it? I've tried to prepare you for real life. He was the son of a convicted drug trafficker. Do you want that for your daughter? Would that make you happy?"

I will not cry in front of her. I will cry alone, in my room, but not in front of her!

"I didn't know you were pregnant when I waited for him outside your window. Did you think I didn't know he was stealing into your bedroom? *Please*, Pandora. The devil knows more from being old than it does from being a devil. I wanted to protect you. Men never change. Men grow up to be who they are taught to be, and he was not good enough for you."

"Men grow up to be who they're taught to be, huh? Just like you taught me to grow up bitter, untrusting, and hateful? He was different, Mother. He cared for me. All he wanted was to be good enough for me, but he never felt that he was, because I never had the guts to tell you we were dating. He thought he was no good for me, and you sure as hell convinced him of that."

She sighs drearily as she reaches out to squeeze my shoulders. "I can't undo what I did. I just hope you understand."

I shrug off her touch and step back. "I understand. I just wish that you'd taught me forgiveness, so that right now, Mother, I could not only understand but I could forgive you too. But you didn't, did you? You taught me to hate my dad. To hate Kenna for leaving, even though it was you who chased him away. I can never forgive myself for giving up my daughter. We all fucked up, Mother. And one of those fuckups was you not teaching me how to forgive. Because now . . . I don't know how."

"Pan?" I hear a little voice, followed by the creak of the door behind me.

My mother's expression softens when she looks at Magnolia. I can see—and have seen through the years—that she's also suffered guilt over giving up the baby. The way that she sometimes looks at Magnolia as if wondering about the granddaughter she'll never have by her side, the one she'll never see. She tries her best with Magnolia, as if that will absolve her. And so do I—as if that will absolve me.

"Hey, Mag," I say, swallowing back my sadness as I kneel and open my arms.

She hits me like a cannonball and squishes me tight while she gives me a sloppy kiss on the cheek. Then she pulls back and tells me, "I made a list, come see."

"Okay, let's go," I say, faking excitement.

"Pandora?" My mother's voice stops us at the door. She looks as miserable as ever. "I can't undo what I did," she repeats again in a whisper.

"Neither can I," I whisper back.

"Come!" Magnolia says, tugging and tugging.

"Pandora!" my mother calls again. I stop, close my eyes, and turn one last time. Something awful is gripping my stomach, and there's no way of stopping it. I feel my ring on the hand Magnolia is grabbing.

Come because you want to, not because they're paying you to.

"I'm sorry."

Two little words. Important words, but they won't give me back my guy, my baby, my choice, my past. "So am I," I say sadly, then I hug Magnolia to my legs and absorb her happy little energy before she drags me over to her room.

"What is this?" I ask when she hands over a paper marked with neat red letters.

"Things I want to do when I grow up," she says with a huge grin. "You said to make a list! It's a long one." She turns it over, and I see more letters.

Wear pink in my hair like Pandora.
Bake a cake with one hundred lollipop candles.
Go on a safari.
Have a pet giraffe (from the safari).

I read all her tiny little wishes, feeling her enthusiasm by my side, and I remember that once, I was just like her. Dreamy and hopeful and alive. "You know, I used to have one of these," I confess. "When I made lists."

"What did it say?"

"It said . . ." It hits me. Suddenly I *remember* what Mackenna and I did on our recent road trip, and I'm shocked.

You sneaky bastard, you remembered my stupid lists, didn't you?

"One of them said, 'Ride on the back of a motorcycle.' Another: 'Go on a road trip.' And I also wanted to kiss a rockstar . . ."

I can't go on. Impossible to. I stop and plant a smile on my face while my heart swells like helium has just been pumped into my chest.

"OOOH!!! Is it true? Is it true? Did you go on a road trip, Pan? Did you go on a road trip, and ride on a motorcycle, and kiss a rockstar?"

I nod, feeling dangerously emotional—but isn't that what Mackenna and Magnolia do? Bring out the gooey stuffing in me that nobody else can see? With infinite tenderness, I kiss her temple. "Yes, I did. I fell in love with him. And before he was even a real rockstar, he was my rockstar."

"You're my rockstar," she says, grinning.

"And you're my Magnificent."

TWENTY-ONE
ROCKSTAR IN WAITING

Mackenna

I'm in makeup. Sitting in a stupid chair, playing with a lighter while Clarissa, my makeup and hair artist, draws kohl under my eyes.

"Let's go with a streaked white-and-silver wig today, to match your eyes," she says. "It'll make the black leather jacket and pants pop more."

"Not wearing a wig today."

"Oh?"

"Yeah, don't feel like role-playing today." I ease the wig off my head and curl a hand around my skull. With my eyes kohl-darkened, the silver of my irises is brilliant in the mirror. My diamond earring glints. I feel like kicking ass, but I also feel like there's a girl out there in this world kicking my ass.

And I still don't know if she's coming.

She looked away when she said she would. A sure sign she's lying.

But fuck, I can't think about that now.

On the outside, she's a bluffer—she always has been. But I

know the girl within. I fucking know what she hides. A heart big as an ocean.

A heart that says, *Mackenna. Fucking. Jones.*

"So, Leo said you asked him to get in touch with her?" Lex asks from his seat, getting his makeup done as well.

"She's not answering her phone." I flick the lighter and watch the flame, then let it die before flicking it on again.

"Think she'll be here? Kind of boring without her now."

"She'll be here," I lie. At least I have to pretend she will be, because when I go out there tonight to sing my new song, it's her I want to be listening. *Please just come to my damn concert, Pink, and then we'll figure out what to do with you and me . . .*

I swear, this girl has done a number on me my whole life. When I was sure she loved me, she ditched me. When I was sure she wanted nothing to do with me, she comes to my concert and sends a bunch of tomatoes flying at me.

I sure as fuck don't know what to expect of her, but I know I'm not a seventeen-year-old without a future anymore. I'm Mackenna fucking Jones, and I'm going to damn well have her if I want her.

And I want her, all right.

I'm restless, tired, wired, but most of all, I'm craving the taste of her. The feel of her. I need to get her in my bed, where she protests less, and keep her dazed. Dazed from her orgasms. I need to strip her of her clothes and her bravado until she's trembling in my arms. Until she forgets to curse and tease me because she's so busy moaning for me to fuck her harder.

I can't deny she's the best sex I've ever had.

But it's not just because she's a fucking goddess, because she is. A dark Medusa, I'm under her spell, and all I want is to be in her. And I love being in her because I love her.

The way she smells.

The way she smiles like she doesn't want to but can't help it.

The way she kisses with all that angry passion inside her.

The way she goes to pudding in my arms, but as soon as we're done puts up her bitch act just to bring out my asshole, and force him to give her bitch another tumble . . .

She's been giving herself physically, but that's not enough for me anymore. I can grind against her, force her to take every inch of my dick. I can grasp her arms by the wrists, keep her pinned, and make her cunt devour me.

And still it won't be enough.

I think about it happening. How the scene will play out. What I'll do to her. What she'll do to me . . .

"Kenna," she'll moan. And she won't be any hotter than she is, because she can't be. Because she's perfect.

And still, I'll want to hear the words.

I won't be gentle with her, but I don't think she'll want me to be. I'll suck, lick, feel her twist with desire, the ripples of her body around mine.

She'll tremble as I suck her tit, trembling still as I spread her thighs apart. She'll thrash under me, rocking up to my body the way she does—greedy, hungry, like she'll fall apart if she doesn't get me in her. Like my dick is all that holds her together. Her nipples will grow red and puckered from my kisses, and I'll give them a rest and go to her mouth, until she's flushed and gasping too. Saying it.

Saying what I have been dying, for years, to hear.

I will watch her lips form the words.

Three. Only three.

Because I'll still want them.

Her lovely face, pure white in the dark. Those rounded shoulders, plump breasts, her perfect ass, and hot, wet, delicious pussy lips. All of that, mine for the taking as she says,

"I love you . . ."

And when that happens, I'll hold her in place. She'll toss her head as I hold her immobile, and there's no way she won't know who's taking who. Her nails will rake into my back as I dive into her heat, telling her again and again that I feel the same way. That she's the only one for me. Showing her with my hands, my lips, my body, she's the one for me.

"What are you doing if she comes?" Lex presses, snapping me back to the dressing room. I toss the lighter aside and rise to my feet as I slide my bare arms into my leather jacket.

"I'll be waiting."

"And if she doesn't?"

"Then I'll be hunting her down."

TWENTY-TWO

MY FRIEND MELANIE SAYS NOT TO WAIT FOR PRINCE CHARMING—HE COULD BE STUCK AT A CONCERT

Pandora

So I heed her advice.

The flight triples my anxiety, but I'm starting to become a pro at this. Once on board, I pop my clonazepam and apologize to the guy in the seat next to mine, saying, "If you need to use the toilet, just wiggle past me, 'cause I sleep like the dead," and he laughs and says, "No need."

Next thing I know I'm being shaken—rather violently—by the flight attendant, letting me know we've arrived in New York.

New York.

Madison Square Garden.

And Mackenna Fucking I-love-you-you-delicious-motherfucker Jones.

I hail a cab at the airport, lugging my roll-on suitcase behind me. I packed enough for a week, but I don't know what's going to happen. I don't really know anything except that he didn't walk away. That *he* came back for *me*.

The minutes stretch as we head toward the concert. I drum my fingers on my thighs, fidget with my fingers, my hair, peer restlessly out the windows. We've barely moved three feet in the last half hour.

"Oh my god, this traffic," I tell the cabdriver, my legs aching with some first-time impulse to run. Just run to him, get him back, talk to him. *Come clean at long last . . .*

"There's a concert happening . . . hard to get close."

"I'll walk from here," I tell the driver, slipping him a couple of bills and then, regretfully, hauling out my luggage and looking toward the entrance to Madison Square Garden.

The stage is set up and lit with warm light. I spot one of the roadies and rush forward. "I need to get in," I say, breathless. He instantly recognizes me—I can tell by the twinkle in his eye as he pulls open the rope and ushers me inside. "Head to the back. I'll take care of this for you," he says, gesturing at my suitcase.

"Thank you."

"Opening act's about to be done," he says.

That very instant, the wild music playing in the background shuts off, the lights shut down, and I shuffle to the lower side of the stage, holding my breath as I hear a violin playing in the dark. My flesh pebbles as a soft, haunting tune begins, and when the lights turn on, my eyes fixate on the exact figure they illuminate.

Gah, I love him so much my heart aches in my chest.

He's down on one knee, a headset with mic curled around his jawline, his head down, and as the rest of the orchestra begins to follow the tune of that haunting, slow violin, Mackenna starts singing.

Like a sleepwalker, I take a step closer to the stage, not close enough to be seen, for he's in the opposite corner, lost in his own world as he starts a slow and mournful verse.

You flick the candy cotton pink strand in your hair
And I pray to the gods that you'll be there
In my dreams, fantasies, and nightmares
I'm so scared I'll never see you again

His words start building with the music, now sounding hopeful.

And you can try hiding behind your anger
And I can try running away
But at night as I sleep, you come crashing in on me
And I'm scared, 'cos you're the only girl for me

And a big instrumental climax joins in as he sings, louder this time.

You're my girl
You're my girl
Pandora, you're my girl
I can't ignore ya
I've always adored ya
Pandora
I implore ya
You're the only girl for me
It's written, it's meant to be
You're my girl
You're my girl
Pandora, you're my girl

Sky high, thigh-high leather, in all kinds of weather
Tonight, now, then and forever
Come on over, my girl, sink your claws into me
I'm not scared, 'cos you're the one and it's meant to be
You're my girl
You're my girl
Pandora, you're my girl
I can't ignore ya
I've always adored ya
Pandora
I implore ya
You're the only girl for me
It's written, it's meant to be
You're my girl
You're my girl
Pandora, you're my girl

The rest sounds almost improvised, chaotic even, as the sound comes to an end.

I should never have dissed ya
Lied about how much I missed ya
I need your sexy fire in my life
No one else can hold a match
To the candle that's you, you're a catch
You make me mad
You drive me nuts
You fill my heart
And kick my guts
There's nowhere I'd rather be
My vampire queen

Yelling, touching, kissing, fucking
Pandora, you're my girl

When the song ends, there's a beautiful silence while thousands and thousands of lighters shine in the darkness, the last verse echoing throughout the stadium.

Emotions tighten my windpipe to the point where it's hard to breathe. This is why he wanted me here.

You think I'll show up, you'll sing to me, and we'll live happily ever after?

That's what I'm going for . . .

Happiness and love curl like partners in my tummy. I could be seventeen right now. I'm chronologically older and outwardly bitter, but inside, I'm still his girl.

The one who thought one day he'd come back to me.

The one who hoped that one day he'd realize it was a mistake to leave me.

I thought he didn't want me, but he does. And now I fear this will all go away when he realizes what I did . . .

My throat is raw with unsaid words, my body heavy and warm. For a long moment, I feel as if I'm floating and in a trance, and as I watch Mackenna scan the crowd for me, my reaction is instant.

I shove through to one of the roadies. Without a word, he lets me in, and I run as fast as I can, hearing Lex's shout up on-stage, "All right, people, you heard the man," the shout stirring the public into a roar. Breathing heavily, I stop at the side of the stage, and my guy—my guy—seems to be struggling to get back into himself. He just spilled his guts out in front of thousands of people, and I can see him still looking for me among the crowd.

I'm so frantic for him to see me. If I had a tomato, I'd send it crashing onto his face. His gorgeous, famous face I want to kiss.

I take a step forward onto the stage, when Lionel stops me. "He's the worst kind of mess. Can you explain to me what the fuck is going on?"

"Let me pass. Please. *Please.*"

"You going to kiss him?" he angrily demands.

"YES!"

A new song starts. A flicker of apprehension hits me when I see all the thousands of people out there, but it only fuels my determination.

Every light is shining on Mackenna as his vocals tear through the speakers. A dozen dancers start crowding him.

"Leo, *move over!*" I plead.

When Leo steps aside, I storm onto the stage. I don't care how much I didn't want to be here—now nothing will keep me from him. Not this stage, not Leo, not the lights or the fans or my mother or his father or *me.*

I feel the cameras follow my every step as I move forward, the lights from above suddenly shifting in my direction as I cross the stage. Mackenna's legs are spread apart, his muscles bulging and thick, his ass tight in leather. He's facing his fans, his vocals holding them in their grip when I press behind him. The moment my body makes contact with his, I feel his skin tighten as if he recognizes me. A hot knot builds in the middle of my throat. Tit's and Liv's hands trail sensually up his side, but when the girls see me, they pull their hands away and move to dance a few feet over.

I want to weep in gratitude when I realize they're finally no longer my enemies. How could they be? They're letting me take over.

I glide my fingers up the muscles of Mackenna's back, slowly, sinuously pressing my body to over six feet of pure, hard male. I feel the supple muscles tense beneath my fingertips, and I feel, rather than see, his sharp inhale of breath when I brush my hand up his front.

Do you recognize me, you fucking god? Do you?

Pressing my lips to his skin, I graze his shoulder with my teeth, nipping him playfully. Then I can't take it any longer and I swipe out my tongue, tasting him.

He curls one arm around my waist and tugs me around, not missing a beat as he continues singing. Circling him while making sure the most parts of my body connect with his, I step in front of him. Shamelessly I press my lips to his chest as I move with him.

That's right, it's me. And I'm going to rock your fucking world like you rock mine, Mackenna Jones.

I slowly move my body against his, pressing my tongue to his puckered brown nipple. Circling. Rubbing the hard little point. Letting him know, in front of all these people, that I want him.

I trail my hands over his muscles, thinking how perfect he is. I'm always so reserved and contained, but he's the one I want, the one I love, and I want him to know it. He pulls me hard against him and rocks me at his side, running his hand down my body. That wasn't scripted. None of it. The way he squeezes my ass. The way that, between those hot, rumbling lyrics, I feel the heady sensation of his lips against my neck. He's stealing touches every moment he can. In charge of things. Of his song. The dance. Me.

He swings me around to face away from him, then pulls me back to him and swoops me so my hair falls away and I'm arched with my head hanging back.

Silence falls.

Catching his breath, he lets me straighten and touches my

forehead slightly with his. Before he knows what hits him, I anxiously tug his microphone down to his chin and press my lips to his. His mouth—so familiar, so hot, so wanted—was waiting for mine. He kisses me harder than he's ever kissed me, until my lips and mouth—my every cell—are burning like fire. The lights flare, and there's a silence as we keep going, our heads slanting to one side, then the other, our kiss only stoking our desire.

Then I pull away and caress his jaw with all ten of my fingers, and whisper into his mouth, "You're mine. I claim you. I love you. You're mine."

The fans roar behind me. *Holy shit, I forgot all those people were there.* I face the ecstatic crowd, my lips lifting at the corners. When I turn back around and my wide eyes meet his wolf ones, I want to weep with the raw emotion I see there.

How do you tell the guy you love how much you love him and how badly you fucked up?

I wait a breath or two, until my quickened pulse has quieted. Then I slip a small note in his hand and whisper in his ear, "Meet me at this hotel. There's a key waiting. Please come."

I turn to leave, but he spins me around by my wrist, growling out one word: "Wait."

He plants a harder kiss on me, pushing his tongue in to connect with mine and triggering sparks across my nerve endings and bolts of lightning to my toes. Releasing me, he smacks my rump to send me on my way.

"Now that," he murmurs in the sexiest, roughest voice ever as he addresses his fans, "was Pandora."

My smile hurts my face as I hear a roar erupt from his fans. And I carry this smile as I retrieve my suitcase from the roadie and take a cab to the hotel.

❤ ❤ ❤

I'M SO NERVOUS. So excited. I think this is what cardiac patients must feel like when their hearts start acting "different."

I've never been so nervous or excited in my life.

Even when I stole from my bed to see him at night . . .

Rushed to the window to receive him . . .

Reliving, in my bed, my very first kiss with him . . .

After he saved me from the school bullies. After I held his hand outside court. The night I met him at the docks, where, before we even said hello, before a word was spoken, he pushed away from the column he'd been leaning against and I picked up my pace, and before we knew it I was in his arms and he was in mine, our lips locked and moving, hot and fast, our breath wild, our hands moving. "You came," he murmured, holding my face and kissing my temple, chin, cheek, nose.

"Always," I whispered back, clutching his jaw and loving how his hands felt big on my face, like he still had a couple of inches to grow into them.

I loved him like crazy then. But that level of crazy is nothing compared to now!

Melanie would be proud. Hell, Brooke would be proud. Even Magnolia would be proud.

I pace around the hotel room as I wait for him, then I go check my appearance in the mirror. Fuck. *Do I look stupid?* I put on some earrings and switch my boots for a pair of heels, and I paint my nails pink instead of the dark purple-black I usually wear. I exchange my leather jacket for a soft white silk top too. God, it's so obvious I want to please him. Because I like it when he calls me "Pink." I want to look girly and soft, but . . .

Okay, fine. Let it look obvious that I want him. He called me his vampire queen . . . and I want him to be my king. For him to take a chunk right out of my heart, bleed me out, and carry me to his bedchamber. Lair. Wherever he fucking wants!

I'm pacing around, rubbing my bare arms, when I hear the *click!* of the door. I swing around, feeling like some stupid eighteenth-century maiden, about to swoon.

Because he's swoony, swoon, swoon, right here, in my hotel room.

My rockstar.

A rush of emotion sweeps through me when he shuts the door and just stands there, looking at me with those greedy silver eyes that want to eat me up, inch by inch. Rivulets of sweat drip down his chest. He's wearing a pair of white jeans with a silver belt—looking very much the rockstar. His wrist is covered in thick cuffs, and the silver ring on his thumb glints in the light. A visceral tug jerks me on the inside as I think of how much I want to feel that silver ring brush against me. My chin, lips, my nipples, my sex. God, yeah—why stop at my lips when I can feel it trail deliciously everywhere?

"You came." The gruff tone makes my skin pebble.

He takes the first step toward me, but I raise my hand to stop him and blurt out, "Kenna, we can't have a future if you don't . . . if you don't really know who I am. What I did. When you left me."

He laughs softly and drags his hand over his delicious buzz cut in a way that drives me crazy. "I made a mistake too, Pandora," he tells me, his eyes shining with regret as he takes in the visual of me like I'm some sort of vision he can barely believe. He spreads his arms out. "Baby, we were young, and that's all right, we know better now. We won't hurt each other anymore. I had no future, nothing to offer you, I still shouldn't have walked away, no matter what you said . . ."

"You! You had *you* to offer me, Kenna."

He stares as I extend my hand to show him the ring he gave

me. I'm wearing it, proudly, on my finger. And don't I wish that I could be just as proud of my words.

"I know what my mother did," I painfully whisper. "I didn't then, but I do now."

He stares more, eyebrows pulling low over his eyes.

"Mackenna," I say, my voice turning huskier and darker, "*everything* you think you know about me, *everything* you could possibly feel, it could go away right now."

A flash of wild grief grips me as I pause for breath and he murmurs, "The way I feel isn't going anywhere. It's not changing. It's not ending. It's . . ."

"Kenna, I suck. I *suck*—"

"Whoa, baby." He stops me with an incredulous laugh. "Call me any names you want, but I'll be damned if I let you sit there and insult my girl like that—"

"I was pregnant, Kenna."

The words drop on him like a bomb.

I can't go on for a moment, a spurt of anxiety seizing me. I measure him for a moment—how still he is.

"When you left, I was pregnant," I force myself to finish.

The shock holds him immobile, while the pain quietly cracks me open. This is my box. The box of bad things Pandora should never open. Here it is, every last part tearing out of my soul so that the one person I want to love and accept me will know.

"What the fuck are you saying, Pandora?" His voice is distant already. It's one hundred percent disbelief.

Oh, the look on his handsome face. I will remember it every day to my death. The morphing of his eyes from silver to shocked gray. The lines of his perfect features freezing in disbelief.

It takes every ounce of courage in me to breathe out the rest. "We have a little girl."

He keeps standing an inch away, his chest not expanding at all, not even for air.

"She's a little younger than Magnolia. It was a closed adoption." I can barely look at him, watch his eyebrows slant, his lips thin, his jaw clamp. "I gave her up, Kenna," I choke out, the hardest five words I've ever had to utter in my life.

He hasn't breathed. Or moved. Nothing. I'm hugging myself just to keep my body from falling apart.

"It kills me not to know . . . ," I continue in this wretched whisper. "I don't know if she has your eyes or mine. I don't know if she's happy. If she belongs . . . or not. But I know I needed you with me. I needed you to take us away. I didn't want to be weak and give her up, but I couldn't do it. Mother said I couldn't do it. And I was frightened, and I felt betrayed, and so I gave her up . . . like I thought you'd given up on *me*."

I can't look at him. He's too still, too silent, curling his fingers into his palms at his sides, his knuckles white.

His lack of reply frightens me.

He will never, ever love you again, Pandora . . .

Never call you "baby" again, or "Pink," as if that's your name and despite your darkness, you own it . . .

"That's why I switched schools," I continue. I scrape my nails over my arms, up and down, up and down. "And met my new friends. Melanie and Brooke, and Kyle."

He's staring at me like I've just ripped his heart out, for real.

And I'm about to cry for the first time in six years.

"I was going to abort. I had nothing to offer her on my own." On some level I knew, somehow I knew, once I talked about this to someone, to him, it was going to burst out of me, and now it's like squeezing the toothpaste out of a tube—you cannot put it back. And like the toothpaste, my confession is oozing out of me nonstop. "But I was underage, and the clinic contacted my mother. That's how she found out that I was pregnant. And even if what my mother did to keep us apart was wrong . . . using your father against you . . . she's not evil. She'd just lost my father and she was consumed with worry over losing me too. She wanted me to have the baby. She said there were parents out there, better parents, who could give our baby a better chance. So I said yes, but . . ."

I clutch my stomach.

"But I didn't know I'd grow so attached to her in those nine months. She was a part of you and I loved her for it, but it hurt having her inside me too because you left Seattle without me." I glance away and then back at him, keeping my eyes in the vicinity of his throat, where I see his pulse pounding hard and violently.

"I signed a form to say that I wouldn't try to find her, but I know she's out there. We will never know if she's bullied or has friends, or if she knows who she is. Never know if she has a good mother, because no matter how good they might have looked on paper, what if she didn't get a good mother? She was probably better than *me*, but I still . . ." I lift my eyes to his, and I think the hurt, impotence, and pain in them mirror the way I feel. "I wonder if she fits. Maybe she's grumpy, like me, and people don't understand her. Or maybe she's restless, like you. Or she could be beautiful and musical and fun, like you."

Okay, I can't keep going, but when I stop all I hear is Mackenna's voice, cracking as he speaks.

"Pink," he says, then he clears his throat and shakes his head, falling silent for a long moment, dropping his head as he breathes, in and out, in and out. "Your mother came to me—"

"Kenna, I know," I admit, taking a step toward him. "I owe you an apology."

"No, Pink. I owe you six fucking years. *I* owe *you* being there for you and for *her*—"

"No, I waited too long to tell you, and then you were . . . gone. And you were famous. You were making your dreams come true, and I couldn't tell you anymore. If you didn't want me, I was sure you wouldn't want her."

"Baby, I would've come to you. I fucking loved you." He pulls me into his arms, and I feel how hard he's shaking, how much my news has rocked him. I tighten my arms around his waist and kiss his thick neck, and all I can do is kiss it again, and again, as he stands there holding me, his emotions barely contained in his taut, straining body. "We have a daughter," he whispers almost reverently in my ear.

"We lost a daughter," I whisper, hanging my head in shame.

He catches my chin and lifts my face to his.

"We *made* a daughter," he corrects.

There's a spike in my very throat, but I manage to speak through it. "Yes."

Clouds suddenly darken his eyes. "My girls *needed* me . . . but I wasn't there. I was hurting. A rebel, unwanted, writing a stupid song about how much I loathed your kiss." He rubs my lips with that silver ring that I crave so much, and my whole body shivers. "When really, your kiss was all I wanted. One more kiss from you. For these lips to tell me their owner loved me."

"We can't see her . . . can't talk to her. You have no idea how much I regret it."

"We will talk to her," he assures me with steely finality, his ring still skimming over my chin and my neck. "I'll find a way for us to talk to her."

Love flows through me. For years I haven't dared even hope . . . but now I can't help feel anything *but* hope. "You don't hate me?" I hesitate for a second but can't stop my hands from sliding up the back of his neck to his head.

He laughs bitterly, biting his lip uncertainly for a moment

before lifting his gaze to mine. "I've hated you, your mother, my father, being apart from you . . . I've hated all that I could for as long as I could, but I'm fresh out of hate, Pink." He's still biting his lip, his eyes a mix of regret and, above all, acceptance. "I love you," he whispers. "So we screwed up. We screwed up big. Holy shit, but I don't want to screw up again. Do you?"

"No, god, no."

"Then do you love me? And I mean for real, Pink, the non-stop kind."

This is the thousandth time he's asked me if I love him.

My heart quakes in my chest in response.

I close my eyes, gathering my courage.

"Come on, babe. Only three words." He brushes my ear with his lips, his voice urgent, almost pleading. "They're like magic. Say them, and good things start happening."

"I said them to you in front of thousands of people, you greedy man," I whisper-laugh, then, completely serious, "Kenna, I haven't said them to a man in my entire life, except to my dad, and look what he did to us."

"Holding back those words wouldn't have made it hurt any less." He strokes the pink strand of my hair between his thumb and index finger. "So, he made a mistake. Difference is, he didn't have a chance to fix it—but we do. Come on, Pink, say it, tell me. The next couple of decades, you will say those words to me, and that's a promise I'm making to you right now. Now, tell me that you love me."

"I fucking do!"

His laugh is deep, delicious. "You still won't say the 'L' word?" he asks. "After all we've been through? All these years apart, when we could've been together?"

The quivers in my heart are spreading down my limbs too.

Love.

It's just one word.

But when it's so real and true and you feel it in your heart, when it has hurt you and you're afraid to lose it again, it becomes more than just one word. It becomes everything. *Everything* this man is to me.

Quietly, suddenly, Mackenna ducks his head and slips his fingers into the straps of my top, then eases it off my shoulders. He kisses my bare skin, his lips both loving and tender, and the kiss crashes against my walls like a wrecking ball. When I make a soft whimper of pain, he lifts his head and his gaze is a whirlwind of contrasts, framed by desire and need.

"It's going to be all right, Pink, I promise," he whispers. "She'll know that we love her." Strong, gentle hands curl around the back of my head as he kisses my forehead. We stay there for a moment, quietly mourning, when soft, fevered kisses start raining down on my face—more feverish and wetter by the second, and when he lets go a low wolf's growl, I know that he needs me. He needs to be close. To feel our connection. To reestablish it. God, I need it too.

"Do you need me like I need you?" I ask him quietly, almost pleadingly. "Do you plan to gorge on every inch of me like I plan to gorge on every inch of you?"

His words are textured, his face intently serious. "Have I ever given you doubt that I won't?"

I shake my head and then, because I need him, because I want him, because I *love* him, I slowly peel off my top.

I need him now more than ever. I need to know he's here for me, and I need to show him I'm here for him. I need to feel his love like it's his forgiveness . . .

Something my mother never taught me, but Mackenna will. Because of the way he looks at me now—accepting me with all my darkness and all my pink as he lifts my hand and looks at the ring I'm wearing—I know he feels my acceptance like a brand as well.

I undress for him and then quietly ask him, "What do you want to do with me? I'm your prize tonight, so winner's choice." Then I stand there, naked except for a little smile.

"What did I win?" he asks cockily, opening his belt.

"Me."

"Is that so?"

He drops his pants to the floor, and he's so beautiful that my mouth waters at the sight of all his tanned skin. All of that for me, to devour like candy.

With a soft grin he reaches out and briefly brushes his knuckles across my nipples, always so damn pesky and puckered up like pencil erasers. And then he curls his fingers around my breast and leans over.

He sucks one, latching on to it with a wet sucking sound, like a baby would, then my other nipple receives the same treatment. And my pussy? He slowly starts fingering my pussy. More wet sucking sounds coming from the way my body wants to suck his finger in me. "You're so beautiful, so gorgeous. My perfect pink wicked little witch. I'm going to make love to you tonight. I'm starting over with you—starting now. Tonight. My plan is to lick my way up those long legs, right up to your pussy, then give a good long suck to your tits. You like?"

"Oh, please," I moan, undulating my body as I slide my hands up his muscular arms.

He grins—no, not grins. It's that sexier-than-thou smirk on his lips that makes me want to bite his dirty, sexy mouth off. I start nibbling, and the sound he makes drives me mad with lust.

"Kenna."

His hand covers one of my breasts, his breath on my face, his eyes holding mine as he kisses one of my temples. "Feels like the first time, doesn't it?"

I nod and exhale, but it's not him making me nervous.

It's me.

I want to say it. I want him to know it. I gulp back the words I want—*need*—to say, but he waits for them. Like he's waited for them in the past.

I'm ready. I'm so ready and frightened, but it doesn't matter, because he's the one, the *only* one, for me. My hands on his delicious, warm skin say it first. My lips brush his muscles, saying it next.

"Kenna . . ."

He groans. He seems to know. "Say it, Pandora. Say it like you mean it."

My chest rises and falls as he brushes his thumbs over the crests of my breasts so my nipples poke him. My panting breaths come faster and faster. "If I say it, promise to say it back immediately," I plead.

"I make no guarantees," he teases as he pinches and tweaks my nipples, and the movements cause my pussy to contract with wanton little ripples.

"Kenna," I groan, gripping the back of his head, pulling him to me. "I love you."

I kiss him, pulling his lips to mine, and suddenly I don't need him to say it.

I need for me to say it . . . and say it . . . and say it. Say it until he asks me to shut up.

I need to say it for all the times I didn't.

"I love you." I slide my hands around his shoulders, up to his head, angling my mouth to take his lips again. A shudder rocks his lean, powerful body. "I love you," I whisper, both seductively and tenderly, fingers stroking down his back, gripping his ass, then one hand comes around to stroke his erection.

He groans. God, I love when he groans. The huskiness in his voice. "Yeah, Pink, show me. Show me you want me. Tell me you want me. How you love wanting me."

"I love what you do to me, how I want you," I murmur, rasping my lips against the stubble of his jaw before I nibble his lips again.

I feel him stiffen when I stroke my fist up his length. "Argh, baby," he growls, sounding pained and yet instinctively rocking himself deeper into my hand. "You're a fucking little tease, aren't you?" He rams a hand between my legs and slides the middle finger between my pussy lips. "A sweet, hot, horny little tease who just wants to be fingered like this."

He eases his finger inside me, and whatever I was going to reply comes out as a moan. I part my thighs wider. "Oh, yes, Mackenna, please me. Please me like only you can."

His lips curl against my temple, and he presses into me again. "Talk dirty to me," he whispers. "Tell me what you're thinking. What you want."

"I'm thinking your cock is much thicker. And longer. And . . . better . . . than your finger. Though your finger is nice . . ."

"Nice?" He rubs it deeper inside me.

"Oh. Yes. Yes, like that . . . *please*."

His lips curl higher against my temple. He inserts a second finger inside me, and it feels just right—just *right*—as he nibbles my lower lip. "Do you like it when I do that?"

"I do," I gasp.

He groans. "Pandora?"

"Yeah?"

"I fucking love you, Pink." He watches my reaction with a sexy smile, then he brings that sexy mouth to mine. A mere brush sets me off. And then he covers my mouth with his as I feel it. Fireworks. Exploding in my body as his finger eases into me again and his tongue penetrates my mouth. Yes, please. So hungry.

He knows I'm coming, because he parts my lips with gentle pressure and sinuously slips his tongue inside, still rubbing his finger inside me.

I twist my head and whimper. "Ahh, Kenna . . . *Kenna!*"

His mouth smothers my sounds and he slides two fingers, three, into me, until I feel impaled, possessed, pinned, taken. His mouth is just as fierce over mine. I feel like he is gorging on my soul, and I want him to gorge it even more.

When the contractions cease, I lie panting on the bed. The moonlight illuminates me head to toe, nothing covering me anymore. I say nothing as I look at him, all glorious and manly; I only chew on my lower lip, anxious to be kissed again as his eyes rove up and down my body.

"What are you waiting for?" I gasp.

"What's the rush?" He smirks. "We have all night." His hand starts at my ankle, and then he drags it with painstaking slowness and expert precision up the side of my body, up my hips, curving up my waist, my rib cage, to cover one puckered breast.

"You're driving me crazy," I cry out.

He ignores my cry, still looking at me with a glint that tells me he likes driving me out of my mind. He lowers his face and kisses my nipple. Draws it into his mouth. I cry out softly and arch upward, crippled with pleasure.

"Oh, God, please . . . again." I hook my legs at the small of his back, twine my arms around his neck, and catch my breath.

He pulls back, then pushes inside. I'm trembling the second he's seated inside me, and he grabs my hair in his fist and starts pumping like mad.

"You're so tight."

"Ooooh!"

Cursing, he holds me down and starts thrusting, and I gasp at the intensity of our lovemaking, our breaths, our gasps, his growls, "Say it, gorgeous girl. Say it to me again." My sex feels greedy and sensitive as he drags in and out, my muscles clenching around him once again. Another orgasm is building. I bite my lip and toss my head, and when he pinches my nipples, I explode, feeling him tense and come so powerfully. I have never, ever seen him come like this before.

"I love you," I breathe, panting.

He groans out, "Love you too."

When we nearly pass out on the bed, I keep blinking and staring at the ceiling.

Fuck. I can't believe I said that. So easily it came this time. No more fears. No more insecurities. I am in love and I'm owning it like a badass!

"I love you," I repeat, rolling to my elbow and kissing his jaw. "I'm in love with you, dick-douche-jerk-fucking-face, I LOVE YOU!" I cry, and start laughing when he rolls over to squish me and yells, "Finally, the woman makes sense!"

I sigh and hug him to me. "Kenna . . . what are we going to do?"

He's holding me as I lie, luxuriating in bed, when he lifts my hand up to his mouth and he kisses the second most precious thing he's ever given me in my life. His mother's ring.

"We're getting married."

TWENTY-THREE
ENDS AND BEGINNINGS

Mackenna

Guess there's something bittersweet about a beginning, because it almost always requires an end. My beginning right now requires I end my stint with Crack Bikini.

Six years, almost.

Enough to learn, live, sing my fucking heart out. Hell, enough to realize I don't want to die a rockstar.

I want to die a family man . . . who used to sing.

I told Lionel I needed out way back. Told him I wanted to make music my own way. At my own pace. In my own time. I told him I want to have friends at the bar where I nightly perform, build some roots—somewhere.

No. Not somewhere.

I want to build some roots in Seattle with my girl.

She's my beginning, the beginning I've craved for six years—one I never knew I could have until I saw her again. But saying goodbye to Crack Bikini isn't without some pain.

The lyrics I'm recording aren't without some pain.

Pandora's tormented. She keeps asking if I'm sure I want to leave the band. She says, "You don't have to leave it for me."

"No, Pink, it's for me," I promise her.

The truth is it's for me, for my father. But mostly, for *us.*

We're at our headquarters. The place where the guys and I have recorded, nonstop, several songs. Pandora waits outside, chatting with Lionel, while I tape not the one song I promised Lionel but two.

Through the window, I see her. The smile on her face? Yeah, that shit's rare and precious. It's what gives me the strength to go on, get these tapes down, get it over with.

The guys will get two singles from me for the new album.

The rest will be instrumental; heavy on the guitars. The boys are excited about mashing those guitar-heavy orchestral songs with a variety of popular songs from different singers. It'll probably be the perfect music for dancing at any fucking bar.

"You sure about this, man?" Lex asks when I come out to say goodbye. We do a hand salute we used to do when we were younger, and I slap his back.

"Yeah, as sure as you are of keeping that ugly dragon up your arm."

"Kenna, dude, anytime you feel like stopping by to work on tracks, tour with us . . . ," Jax begins.

"I'll just stop by without warning, catch you two bastards unawares," I kid, doing our handshakes too.

Lionel has seen this coming, I know, since my father was released from prison and I mentioned wanting to be closer to him. Have some time to spend with the only family I got.

"Anything I can do to change your mind?" Lionel asks.

I reach out for Pandora, who's been standing a bit to the side, giving us some privacy. I grab her by the back of the neck and pull her close to me. "Won't ever be ready to leave my vixen again."

"Kenna, but your music . . ."

"My music will always be with me." I tip her head up, her

gaze somehow both dark and playful. "Am I finally going to hear that song you promised to write to me?"

She flushes beet red. "The first one doesn't fit anymore."

"Write me another one, then. Better yet, would you like to write one with me?"

TWENTY-FOUR

SPARKLING SHINY
NEW LIFE

Pandora

The moment has been testing me to the point that I'm blinking and staring at my nails, my feet. Mackenna Jones leaving Crack Bikini . . .

All this time, I've been watching him inside the recording studio, pouring his heart out into the two singles he wants to leave behind. The prickles in the back of my eyes won't cease. I tried texting with my friends, letting them know I'm coming back home and that . . .

. . . I'm moving in with Mackenna Jones.

Brooke and Melanie nearly burst my cell phone. While Mackenna recorded, the twins hovered by my side. I sensed they were both happy and sad, but mostly sad for themselves, happy for us.

"Always had a thing for you, that guy did," Lex promises.

Jax jabs a thumb toward his brother. "What he said."

My smile trembles a little. What can you say? Goodbyes are

a bitch, and this is the first time in my life I ever get to have one. No goodbye to Mackenna when he left. None to my father. None to my daughter. This is my first goodbye, and it's a doozy.

"So have I. And guys," I add, my voice cracking as I finally admit, "consider me your number-one fan from now on."

"Awww, she likes us, Jax!" Lex shucks before they both lunge at me. We're hugging, and when they start playfully squeezing my butt, Mackenna promptly comes out to pull them off me.

"Back off, dweebs."

That's when Lex turns to him. "You sure about this, man . . . ?"

And I know Mackenna well enough to know that, tough call or not, he's very sure about this.

EPILOGUE

Pandora

Seattle is wholly different when you change the lens through which you see it. One day, it's a place where you got your heart broken. A place that feels lonely even with thousands of people driving, walking past you. One day it is the rainiest, most depressing city in the world. And another day, it's the place where you want to live the rest of your life. Because it's the place where you have your little cousin, your friends, your job, and your boyfriend.

Your boyfriend.

Did I just sigh?

Me. Sighing.

Grinning.

Happy, hopeful, forgiving.

How can all this happen in a few months?

I know now, from life, that it takes only a second to break you. But with time, with effort, it takes a little longer, but you can make it. There's something about someone knowing your deepest, darkest secret and still loving you despite what you did that gives you hope. That makes you want to be better. Never disappoint yourself, and them, ever again.

There's also something about learning to forgive . . .

Both others, and yourself.

I feel different now. I feel it every morning when I wake. The sense of looking forward to your day. Life doesn't suck anymore. People don't suck—well, not everyone.

During our first week back in Seattle, Kenna and I found an apartment close to where we're opening a rock bar.

The idiot wants to call it Pink, and all my friends—Mel, Brooke, and Kyle—wholeheartedly approve. I'm decorating in my trademark silver and black, and, now that we're owners of a future establishment, I decorate by day while Mackenna heads to the studio he bought just three floors above.

He's recruited a couple of bands to play at Pink during the week. And, even better, as a special favor, Jax and Lex and Crack Bikini will be performing opening night.

They call all the time, those two goofballs. Trying to coax Kenna back to the band. He laughs and banters with them, says, "Hell no" and "Fuck off." He's currently working on a new album called *Bones*. I'm crazy about the songs. They're so bare, different from what he created during his time with Crack Bikini. Edgier. More raw.

At night, he takes me out, whether I protest that I'm tired or not. He's a prowler—another wolfish trait.

On the weekends, we invite Magnolia over. She loves it with us. Even my mother is trying to make amends, so even if she doesn't like having to let me take Mag some weekends, she lets us have our way. Her way of trying to make peace with Mackenna.

I still remember the first time they met—Mag and Kenna.

Mom dropped her off. We'd prearranged the visit, so we were expecting Magnolia. I rang her up from the lobby, and suddenly the door of the apartment swung open and there was Magnolia, her eyes bright with curiosity as she asked, "Pan, Pan, who is he?"

She curled around my legs like a cat, and I clutched her to me as Kenna set aside the guitar he was fiddling with and headed over with a smile I remember finding heart-meltingly adorable.

I noticed her study him.

And I noticed him study her.

"Aren't you going to let our guest inside, Pandora?" he asked me, intrigued.

"Who are you?" she asked in return, frowning.

"Who are *you*?" he shot back, lifting one eyebrow and reaching around me to shut the door behind us.

"I'm Magdalene," she said.

"Magnolia," I corrected, laughing.

He smiled down at her while she surveyed him.

"Magic Mike, say hello to my boyfriend, Mackenna," I said, giving her a little nudge forward.

"What does this mean?" she went on to ask of the tattoo on Kenna's forearm. "Why are you wearing bracelets? You like boys, don't you?"

"Mag!" I laughed, ushering her into the kitchen. "Come on, we're making homemade pizza."

Over the mozzarella sprinkling, Mackenna looked at me, as intent as ever. "She's—?"

"A little older than our . . . um, yes."

We shared a moment of sadness, then he came up behind me, took my hand, and set it over the five Chinese symbols on his forearm as he whispered in my ear, "It means 'I Live For You.'"

"What?"

He laughed and moved to help Magnolia add the pepperoni slices. "I'm not repeating it. I was drunk and had one thing on my mind and one thing only."

"Me?"

"Yup. That wasn't the best tattoo to help me forget you, was it?" he murmured.

"But you wore it proudly?"

"Only because it was the truth."

A month before the movie premiere, we hear that the movie trailer is becoming famous for showing me charging across the stage to kiss Mackenna, whispering with ferocity, "You're mine. I claim you. I love you. You're mine."

Surprisingly, this has gotten me an online fan club. So unexpected! I even interact with the fans sometimes. As long as Kenna's fans don't lynch me at the premiere, I'm good with anything. He's promised me, they won't touch me.

And I believe him, because, sadly, they'll probably be too busy trying to reach out over the red cords to touch *him.*

Anyway, just a week before the premiere, I find myself calling Melanie with my most excited voice yet. I'm so happy, my voice has a new tone even for me.

"We're getting *married.*"

"Squee! OMG! How? When? When did he ask, and how did he ask you?"

"Well, we'd already said we would, but he asked in an uncheesy way, or I'd have flung the ring back at him," I say, looking down at my ring, then up at my man, who's lying with his arms crossed behind his head, the bedsheets barely reaching his waist.

"If you're telling me Grey's proposal was cheesy when he told me flat out we were getting married, you are deranged—it was the best, most un-cheesy proposal I've heard."

"Kenna proposed in bed, while . . . *you know* . . . insert your most volcanic fantasies here . . ."

"Wow, that *is* un-cheesy. Not something to tell the kids, huh?"

"Just get over here!"

"Be there in a bit."

Then I call Brooke and Remy.

"You're getting married! *Remington!* Guess who's getting married?"

He briefly grabs the phone. "Congratulations, you two."

Soon Melanie appears, her intimidating boyfriend by her side. "Maleficent, getting married?!" She hugs me with her usual mix of glee and tenderness, and we rock in each other's arms while our men have no other choice but to introduce themselves.

"Greyson," I hear Melanie's fiancé say. "Congratulations, man."

"Mackenna," Kenna offers, slapping and shaking hands.

"God! Look at this ring, it's obscene! One *seriously* obscene ring, Kenna, you did good!" Melanie says in complete delight. "Greyson, have you seen anything so pretty?"

"Never," Greyson murmurs, but I notice he's looking at Melanie, not my ring.

Mackenna quickly pulls me over to one of the living room couches. Greyson and Melanie settle on the opposite one, and we have a great time swapping meeting stories and celebrating. Even Kyle stops by with his girlfriend to toast with us.

Later, the men start talking about their respective businesses and I find myself asking Melanie for good ideas for a wedding reception. She can't even believe it's actually *me* asking.

"Seriously, this is almost creepy, Pan!" she swears.

We laugh it off and so does Kyle's girlfriend, Terry, and soon, my grin starts to hurt on my face. All this time, I feel Kenna's hand moving on my bare arm and shoulder—a gentle reminder that he's by my side even though he's talking to the boys and I'm talking to the girls.

I keep stealing touches, squeezing his hand, rubbing his hard thigh—just so he knows I don't forget for a second who I'm with from now on.

That night, I slide into bed with my guy and start kissing him with all the passion I feel. I nibble on his jaw and slide my hands over his sexy buzz cut and press as close as I can get. I nibble on his lone diamond earring and then on the ear where my ring-diamond used to be. There, I whisper what I used to be so afraid of saying. I didn't say "I love you" for so many years, yet now I can't say it enough. I can't hear it enough. And Kenna shows no signs of asking me to shut up either. He rolls me beneath his body and takes control of the situation, with one sure, perfect move, getting up as close and deep as possible to me.

One day later, it's Sunday morning and we're listening to I Heart Radio, like we usually do when we wake up. Then it happens.

"So, now we get to hear the first single from Crack Bikini's new album. This is 'Lullaby.'" And suddenly we both grow quiet. And there, in his arms—where I feel loved and accepted, warm and safe, wanted and forgiven—I close my eyes and listen to his heartbeat with one ear, and his song with the other.

Young and in love
We thought we were invincible
If you're lonely or sad
Need to feel someone's there
Precious baby, let me sing you our lullaby
Let me sing you this lullaby
You may be five or six next year
You may be fifteen in a second
Growing up in a record

Lipstick, girlfriends, boyfriends, first times
It hurts we will never be a part of that
We couldn't give you what you needed
Couldn't keep you by our sides
But, baby girl, we can give you
All our love, right in this one lullaby
Your mom and I
Thought you'd have a better life
We were broken, young, and wild
Our sweet girl, you will never know why
But for this moment here's a lullaby
We'd turn back the clock
I'd man up and stop
Make sure you knew who you were
You were hers and mine
But time, that's something we never recover
Mistakes we make, promises we break
Things we can never get over
So here I stand
Hoping you can understand
It wasn't you; it was us
Nothing wrong with you
Our little baby girl
You were perfect; you still are
So here's your lullaby

" 'Lullaby,' " the voice on the radio crackles in. "Already topping the charts as the singer and his fiancée hold a worldwide search for all the girls born on January 22, five years ago . . ."

Tears trek silently down my cheeks while Mackenna quietly cups my face and lets them fall into his palms. "What will we do when we find her?" My voice breaking, I swallow. "We can't take her away from her real parents now. But we can't not try to be a part of her life in some way."

"We'll do whatever she wants," he promises me—and his eyes, they look as wolfish as ever.

ACKNOWLEDGMENTS

As always, this book would not be possible without a tremendous amount of help from an amazing number of wonderful people.

With immense gratitude to my supportive family, my husband, my children, my parents.

To all my author friends who both beta read and cheer, or pass on the Kleenex for the tears (you guys know who you are!), and who I cherish more than words can say.

To the very special Kelli, CeCe, Angie, Ryn, Kati D, and Dana, who helped me prep this baby and always have the best, most amazing feedback for me.

To my editor, Adam Wilson, my publisher, Jen Bergstrom, and their hardworking team at Gallery Books—thank you for supporting my work, getting it on those bookshelves, and working with me to make it the best possible.

To Amy, truly, you are a dream agent, and I am blessed to have you in my life.

And to you, reading this right now, thank you. You let my words touch you, and now I live to try and do just that.

Katy

ABOUT THE AUTHOR

Hey! I'm Katy Evans, and I love family, books, life, and love. I'm married with two children and three dogs and spend my time baking, walking, writing, reading, and taking care of my family. Thank you for spending your time with me and picking up my story. I hope you had an amazing time with it, like I did. If you'd like to leave a review and help readers find the REAL series, I'd appreciate it so much. If you'd like to know more about books in progress, look me up on the Internet. I'd love to hear from you!

Katy XO

Website: www.katyevans.net
Facebook: www.facebook.com/AuthorKatyEvans
Twitter: https://twitter.com/authorkatyevans
E-mail: authorkatyevans@gmail.com

To get a text reminder of Katy's newest releases, text REAL-SERIES to 313131.